IMPERFECT LOVE

Juniper Springs 4

MELISSA SCHROEDER

Edited by NOEL VARNER

Cover Art by SCOTT CARPENTER

Photography by WANDER AGUIAR

Model LUCAS LOYOLA

Harmless Publishing

To my fellow Swifties who love the music as much as I do. And especially to my favorite Swiftie, Audrey. Spending time with you as we listen to the music, watch reaction videos, and clown about all the fun details has been some of my favorite experiences as your mother.

Also by Melissa Schroeder

The Camos and Cupcakes World

- Camos and Cupcakes
- The Fillmore Siblings
- Juniper Springs

Melissa Schroeder's Instalove Collection

- Dominion Rockstar Romance
- Mafia Sisters
- Faking It
- The Fighting Sullivans
- Single Titles

The Camos and Cupcakes World

- Camos and Cupcakes
- The Fillmore Siblings
- Juniper Springs

The Santini World

- The Santinis
- Semper Fi Marines
- The Fitzpatricks

The Harmless World

- The Harmless Series
- A Little Harmless Military Romance
- Task Force Hawaii

Check out the rest of Mel's books by:

- Interest
- Series
- Entire Backlist

Contents

Chapter One

Avery

The clank of dishes and the murmurs of customers fill the silence as I sit in one of my favorite restaurants while my sister stares at me like I have lost my mind. This is nothing new for me. I have spent most of my life with my siblings looking at me this way.

I draw in a deep breath, enjoying some of my favorite scents. Brown sugar, cumin, and paprika with a bit of smoke. I love good barbecue, especially from my sister's man, Mason. The place is packed, but we always have a reserved table. It is one of my happy places.

"I'm still trying to figure out how you ended up renting a house from Estella Howard," Liv says as she digs into her salad, drawing my attention back to her.

She's older than me by a decade, and I have always envied her. She's a kick-ass mom and so organized she makes me feel like a sloth. I love sloths, but sometimes I wish I was more like Liv. What would it be like to have a quiet mind? I have never had one. There has always been something going on up in my brain. And yes, that sounds like a lot of fun, but lately, I can't seem to quieten it down up there. My brain continually works twenty-four hours a day, seven days a week.

It's been that way since my Grannie Pam died. In fact, the noise seems to be deafening at times. I just don't know what to do about it.

I notice Liv giving me a look that tells me she wants more from me, so I smile. "I mentioned that I was looking for a place to rent at the last meeting, and she said I could rent her house."

Liv could be a model with her height and her amazing hair. Oh, and she's built like one too. Slim with just enough curves. She sets down her fork and looks at me, worry apparent on her beautiful face.

But back to the look. It's another look all my siblings give me. Being the youngest of a family of five isn't easy. Sure, by the time I was born, my parents were tired, which made it easier to get away with things. For example, curfew was sort of a guideline and not so much of a rule. All my siblings were old enough to care for themselves, so I got much more attention. My brother and sisters have always been jealous of that, but now I get the *looks* from all of them. It's like they think I can't manage my own life.

Did any of them graduate from high school at sixteen or finish their MBA while building a thriving business? No. I did that. But they still treat me as if I can't handle my life.

Sure, I'm an acquired taste, but once people get to know me, they love me. Mostly.

"First, what meeting?"

I roll my eyes and make a face. When I would do that to my parents, they would laugh, and I would get away with changing the subject. Grannie Pam, that was another story altogether. She was the one person who didn't let me get away with everything.

I sigh and push aside the wave of sadness that hits me. I'm still trying to deal with her loss and can't break down in public. Again. I'm just thankful none of my family knew about my crying jags. The cashier at the HEB was uncomfortable when I did it last Tuesday in San Antonio.

"I was at the last LOL meeting." This is true, but it isn't the entire truth. Estella offered me the house in a different situation altogether. Still, we first met and hit it off at the LOL meetings. I love those old broads. And yes, they love that I call them that.

Liv blinks as I continue eating. The moment the brisket hits my tastebuds, I hum in appreciation. Even if my sister didn't love Mason, I would vote for this as the best barbecue restaurant in all of Texas, and that's saying a lot. Barbecue is as sacred as football in this state. It's just a plus that I get to eat here for free, and Mason cooks for me a lot at Liv's house. And the truth is, I came here often before they started dating.

"Why were you meeting with the old women?"

I shrug. "They wanted a lesson in social media, so I taught them about Instagram and TikTok algorithms."

"And they understood?"

I frown at the skepticism in her voice. People always discount senior citizens. Don't get me wrong. There were some challenges in the group, especially with Mrs. Finkle. She was so not getting TikTok in general—but who does? And often, the app changes as soon as you understand an algorithm. I teach people social media, and I don't always get it. But the attitude that once a person retires, he or she has nothing to offer the world is just bullshit. It pisses me off.

"Yes. You know there is an aeronautical engineer in the group? And a few teachers?" My sharp tone garners some attention from some of the tables nearby.

"Sorry. I didn't mean to offend you."

I nod as we eat in silence for a few moments. I don't have a quick temper, but it's hard to get back in a good mood when someone gets it going. I just hate that people throw away senior citizens, discount them, or act like once you hit sixty-five, your life is over. It isn't, especially these days.

"Are you doing okay, Avery?"

I glance up and see the concern in her gaze. This is different from the condescending worry. This is worse. It's her *Mama Worry*. She already has too much on her plate these days. She doesn't need me to be added to the meal of obligations. I'm here to support her, not the other way around. I'm single, with no kids, and have a lot of financial freedom. Sure, I don't feel like taking on new clients, and I might have gone dark for the most part on my social media, but it's not like I need the money.

"Yeah, I'm good."

"You know you can talk to me about it, right?"

I blink against the burning of unshed tears.

"Yeah."

As much as my family irritates me, I really appreciate their support. Grannie Pam moved in with us when Mom opened her dance studio. I was five, and Grannie Pam was my whole world. Losing her messed with my mojo, but I'm getting it back. Well, I would if I could get more than a couple hours of sleep, and to do that, I need to get my brain to shut down.

"Good. As long as you know, I will always have a box of Froot Loops in my pantry for you."

I smile, warmth filling me. I think Liv gets me the most out of all my siblings. I know I'm an odd duck in our family, which means a lot. "You're the best."

"I know. Sammy told me this morning."

I chuckle. My nephew is a pill. "I'm guessing it wasn't about gravy. He told me the other day that Mason made the best."

She rolls her eyes and chuckles. "No. Not my gravy. Although, I swear he could get it any day of the week. Both the kids can get Mason to do almost anything for them."

I listen to her talk about the latest schemes Sammy has dreamt up and how Callie seems to have learned to relax a little. I'm thrilled for her and the kids. They deserve it. Losing her husband, Sam, had been hard on all of them. Mason fits in nicely with them.

But now that they are settled, I feel unsettled. I felt that way before then, but I could use the distraction of helping Liv to deal with it. I know I will have more time to think about myself and my worries, and I don't want to do that. Not right now.

And so, in true Avery fashion, I push those thoughts aside and dig into my food. Later, I promise myself. I'll deal with all that crap later.

Chapter Two

Jon

"Do you want to tell me why you're heading to Juniper Springs?"

I glance at my mother and sigh. I don't want to admit I'm running away from a crazy woman. I didn't want to tell my mother in person, but she wanted to have brunch. Mom doesn't intrude too much in my life, so I give in to her when she asks.

"I just need to work on some stuff, and too many people know where I live."

She gives me a look that tells me she doesn't believe me. "But…Juniper? You always say you hate it."

I do. It's the epitome of everything I hate. Too many people and everyone thinks they know me. That's not the case. They know my father's side of the family. Kind of hard not to know the Howards. My grandmother is the wealthiest woman in the county, the queen bee of the entire town. My cousin has a massively successful home improvement show based there. But, if I can sneak into town late at night, I might be able to avoid most people. Thankfully, my grandmother has a house she keeps for me there. I have no idea why. After thirty years, I've learned not to question Estella Howard.

"True, but if no one knows I'm there, I can do some work."

She crosses her arms and looks at me. We don't look that much alike, except we share the same color of eyes. It's a distinctive blue, darker than most, with lots of gold.

"You actually think you won't set off the Juniper Springs Express by being in town?"

I hear the humor in her voice, and I'm glad for it. Her marriage to my father was brief and painful. Mom's been good about not trashing my piece of crap father. But she's happy now, thriving, in fact.

Today, she's practically glowing. There were some rough times for us in the early days. Getting divorced wasn't easy for her. My father didn't support her physically. We always had money, but she had her hands full with a kid who was too smart for his own good. I was always causing problems at home, most of them electrical and some of them dangerous. But she forged ahead and gave us a great life.

Once she left my father, she went back to school. She graduated with a Ph.D. in sociology and now teaches at the University of Dallas.

"Maybe, but I don't have to answer the door."

She laughs. "Oh, Jon, you are such a stupid man for being a genius."

Before I can respond, an older man steps up to the table. He's at least six feet tall and has curly blond hair cut short over his ears. The button-down shirt matches his green eyes and looks tailor-made for him. The dark Wranglers and cowboy boots complete the outfit.

"I hope I'm not intruding."

I open my mouth to say something, but my mother beats me. She turns at the man's voice, and then I see it. She lights up. Then everything falls into place. Now I understand the reason she dragged me out to brunch.

"Ted. Sorry, I haven't had a chance to tell Jon you were joining."

The man leans down and kisses my mother, then they both turn toward me.

"Jon, this is Ted Franklin. We've been dating for a few months."

He reaches across the table to shake my hand. For a brief second, I stare at it but, soon enough, pull myself out of my stupor to take his hand. I've met other men my mom dated. She was never serious about any of them. This feels different.

"Sorry to barge in, but I was getting antsy."

I nod. "I take it you're why we had to have brunch today?"

He sits down next to my mother. "Yeah, she thought it was important that we meet."

Before I can respond, the waitress steps up to the table.

After taking our orders, the waitress leaves. The silence that fills the air makes my hands sweat. I don't like this.

My mother clears her throat. "Ted and I have decided to move in together."

I blink. My mother has a social life and has had boyfriends, but she's never moved in with one of them.

"Uh, that's nice."

Okay, I could have handled that better. I don't do well in these situations. I need to plan and think things through. She knows that, so I don't understand why she's springing this on me in this manner.

"Do you think that's a good idea?"

"Jon." My mom is not happy with me. She's frowning, and while she still glows with happiness, I feel she's getting ready to metaphorically slap me upside the head.

"Sorry." I glance at Ted. "No offense, but I don't know you."

"No offense taken. She told me you were protective. And before you worry about any more offending behavior, I expect to be investigated."

"Ted, don't—"

He shushes my mom. "Hey, it's what I would do with my mom if I was in Jon's place."

"I'm a smart enough woman to pick a partner for myself." I hear that tone and know she's about to get huffy with Ted. Mom is all about empowerment. Being divorced in her mid-twenties really did a number on her and taught her to stand up for herself.

"Don't get huffy with me."

I blink. I've been so wrapped up in my own problems I haven't been paying attention to my mom, but this Ted apparently has.

"Excuse me, Mr. Franklin, can I take a pic with you?"

I glance at a man who looks like he's in his thirties.

"Sure, but let's go over there," he says, pointing at the restaurant's waterfall feature.

Once we're alone, my mother says, "You should have handled that better."

"No, you should have told me ahead of time. You know how I am about change."

Change is a massive problem for me, at least in my personal life. For as long as I can remember, I've needed longer to prepare for disruption. Mom knows this. In the past, she's helped me deal with it. She has the courtesy of looking contrite.

"Sorry. We've been dating for about nine months. He's been dying to meet you, but I wanted to be sure."

There's something in her voice that tells me this guy is important. "You love him."

"There's a reason we're moving in together."

"Sorry about that," Ted says as he joins us. "I know how you feel about having your picture taken."

I look at my mother, who shrugs. "You know I talk about you a lot."

"Your mom is so proud of you. She's always bragging about your company and everything you've accomplished."

"Is that a fact?"

He nods. "And before you ask, I already own shares in Lone Star Tech, so I'm not after that. I don't need it."

"You own shares in my company?"

He nods. "Before I met your mom. I didn't even make the connection until I saw your picture in her house."

"You knew what I looked like?"

That's odd. I avoid the camera, although my PR folks would like me to be more amenable to photos. I date a lot of models, so the paps tend to follow me around, but they are more about the women than me. I'm just the billionaire arm candy.

"Yeah. I don't invest my money without a good investigation into the company."

"Oh, and that involved my picture?"

My alert is going off like there's an F5 tornado bearing down on us.

"Yeah. I'm a little OCD when suggesting stocks to my clients."

"Clients?"

There's something about him that is familiar. I glance at the guy who asked for the picture and then back at Ted.

"Have I met you before? You seem familiar."

He shares a smile with my mother. "You were right."

"Ted is a retired Dallas Cowboy, Jon. He's a commentator now but runs an investment firm too."

I blink and work back through my mind. His voice was familiar like I'd heard him before. I sometimes run sports programs in the background because I'm not usually interested in them.

"Oh. That's why your voice is familiar. I don't watch a lot of football."

"But you know my voice?"

"Calculating statistics for a team's chances each year is a good way to clear my mind." I shrug. "I usually stick to baseball because there are more games, which adds more variables."

He nods. "That makes sense. Football doesn't have that many games, so comparing the number of games would be simple. Having a different pitcher would add another level of variables too. An NFL team usually has one quarterback."

"Yeah. But I sometimes run sports in the background when I'm coding."

"Ah."

Silence descends on us again, and I try to think of anything to say. I'm more than annoyed with my mother for springing this on me. She's the one who had me in therapy as a kid. She knows that situations like this aren't great.

"We were talking about Juniper. I have to be down next week anyway."

She cocks her head. "Why?"

"Grandmother's annual get-together." Estella has two parties a year. One for her birthday and the other one for a community party. Many people from Juniper come, and Estella does a silent auction for the charities she supports in the county. She also invites a lot of people from San Antonio and Austin.

"Oh, yes. I can't be there because Ted and I have a thing."

I frown. "When I tried that excuse, she said to figure it out."

"That was last year, and you were lying."

Ted snorts, and I cut him a look. "Hey, she also calls me on my BS, so I've been where you are."

I'm trying not to like Ted. I don't actively hate him, but I tend to spend time getting to know someone before I accept them. Still, there's something about how Ted talks about my mother that has me nodding.

"Welcome to my childhood. She was always calling me on my BS."

"That makes her a good mother."

I agree, so I nod.

"So, Juniper?" my mother interrupts, her cheeks pink.

"I already told you I have some work to do."

This is partially true. I have an offer on the table for the company. I haven't told anyone that it's under consideration. Trevor Smith is a friend, but this company was my baby, the first thing I ever built. And I did it on nothing but my brain. I had no help from my grandmother, although she tried to meddle.

It's just lately… I'm not feeling it. Don't get me wrong, I love my company. I am freaking proud of what we have built. While other tech companies have dealt with scandals, we've avoided them by not being assholes and having strict policies that help with diversity in the workplace. It's that simple.

Women and minorities have been hired and promoted at the same rate as white men, and we have a balanced executive office. If I hand it off to Trevor Smith and his family, that will continue. He revamped his family's company over the past five years similarly. That had to be more complex because that company has been around for over a century, and he has a board of old men. Old habits die hard.

"That's partially true, I'm sure. But does this have to do with Sienna?"

I roll my eyes. I would like to date a woman, and my mother not find out about it. Especially *that* woman.

Before I can answer my mother, the waitress arrives with our orders. Once we're alone again, my mother gives me a look, and I relent.

"She's gotten a little out of hand. I broke it off. She keeps telling the paps that we've made up."

"You should get out in front of that, Jon." My mother's

voice is very judgmental. It's not that she doesn't like me dating models, but she says I do it because they don't challenge me.

Again, Ted jumps in to rescue me. "That won't help."

"Why not?" my mother asks.

"You add fuel to the fire that way. Sometimes, it's best to let the story die away. One good thing about the twenty-four-hour news cycle is that something else always draws their attention away." He looks at me. "I completely understand. You don't even want to know some of the things they said about me and my kids."

I nod, and while I appreciate his support, there is no way I'm not going to still check him out.

"Don't worry, Mom. I'll slip into town, get some work done, then go to that party. With that done, I'll probably have to leave town, but it will give me two weeks of peace and quiet. Nothing ever happens in Juniper."

Chapter Three

Avery

I t's just after one in the morning, and I can't sleep. It's not that the house is new to me. I've been here three weeks, and I've never felt a connection to a place like I do to this one. The moment I walked in, I felt like I had arrived home.

It might be that I've been bouncing around for the last year. My lease had ended, and Grannie Pam suggested I see the world. So, I did. Or I did part of it. I've been stuck these last few months hopping between my parents and siblings with an occasional stay at a hotel. It has not been the greatest for my insomnia.

I sit up in bed and look around the massive master suite. The house is old, so a big bedroom like this wasn't as common back in the day. Estella and her husband lived here before they built the big house just outside the city limits, and since they were loaded, their house was top of the line for the time. I do know that Nancy, Estella's granddaughter, and her fiancé, Travis, did some renovations. Still, this room was this size from the get-go. I love the wood floors, the massive bay window with the seat perfect for cuddling up to read, and the garden.

I have spent more time outside than inside, which is odd for me. It resembles an English garden, with more gardens than lawn, massive pecan and live oak trees, and seasonally blooming flowers. There are mums blooming like crazy now, but there are other perennials and annuals. I would talk Estella into selling the house to me if I could afford it. Okay, I could afford it, but I would hate to deplete my savings. I love Juniper and being closer to Fritz and Liv, although I miss Cora and her menagerie. However, those kids are getting too old to hang out with their cool aunt.

I would be the cool aunt if you were wondering.

With my sister-in-law expecting and Liv and her two little ones, I can help. It's what I do to make up for being kind of a diva. Okay, a weird, quirky diva who wears PJs all day and eats cereal for most of her meals. It's the perfect food. Sure, there might be a tad too much sugar, but most of them have a ton of riboflavin.

Don't ask me why that's important, but they all seem to have it.

I'd hoped staying in an actual house and not a hotel for once would help me with my insomnia. It hasn't. I've had trouble sleeping since around the time I turned fifteen. I get bouts of it for a few weeks at a time, but then it goes away. This time, though, it's lingered.

I thought it had to do with the traveling. I can do my consulting from anywhere, so I can continue to work no matter where I am. I spent fall in New York City with my sister Gerry because everyone should experience walking in Central Park at least once while the leaves are golden. There was the trip to California for a convention where I took the time to see monk seals and wine country, then there was the girls' trip to Vegas with my sisters.

My inability to sleep worsened, so I decided to find a place and settle down. Unfortunately, it's only gotten worse.

"Meow." I look at Meredith. She's a stray calico I just adopted yesterday. Not sure how I'll travel with her, but I'll figure it out. I always do. She does not look happy with my late-night wandering.

"Sorry, sweetie. Mama needs to have a snack. You can go back to bed."

She gives me a look of disdain, then abandons me for the warm bed. I shake my head and turn toward the stairs for my after-midnight feeding.

As I round the corner, I hear a suspicious sound, something different than the usual creaks and groans of a house over a century old. I stand on the top stair, listening. Maybe I imagined it. I close my eyes because everyone knows that you can hear better with your eyes closed.

There. It sounds like something is at the door. What the freakity freak? I want to hide in my bed, but I creep down the stairs instead. Yes, I know, not smart, but I've been working on nine hours of sleep over the last three nights. The doorknob to the front door jiggles, then I hear a low masculine curse.

Oh, well, sorry to irritate my intruder.

"Probably changed the locks, so I'm forced to go see the old bat."

That sounds like someone who knows Estella. But why would anyone try to break into the house if they knew her? And who would go see her after trying to break in?

It's then that I remember my phone in my PJ bottoms pocket. I pull it out and dial 911. It takes two rings for someone to pick it up.

"Yeah?"

"Josh?" I whisper. "This is Avery O'Bryan. I'm staying in Estella's house on Preston Road."

"You mean Jon's house?"

"She said that she owned it."

"I'm sure she does, but everyone knows Jon stays there when he's in town."

Really? Does anyone else have an issue with getting help in a small town? Only I would have to talk to the town sheriff, who apparently is the 911 operator tonight, and discuss the ownership of the house that's being broken into.

"Did you just call to tell me you're staying there?" His voice is easygoing with a hint of humor.

"No, that's not why I called." I try to make my whisper as fierce as I can.

"Oh, then why did you call?"

I roll my eyes. Why do people always think I'm an idiot? I know I'm different, but I should be taken seriously. "Someone's trying to break in."

"Be right there."

He hangs up so fast it leaves me blinking. I peek around the corner and notice the handle wiggling again. There is also more muttering.

Dammit! The house is at least five minutes away from the police department. At least, I think so, trying to get my sleep-deprived mind to work. Things tend to get a little confusing when I'm deep in one of my bouts of insomnia.

I try to come up with something to protect myself. I'm

small, only a few inches over five feet, but I'm scrappy. My brother Fritz taught me how to defend myself, but one thing he told me was not to take on someone bigger unless I had to. He always told me to use anything to help. I remember a baseball bat in one of the rooms. I hurry to get it just in case.

When I return to the stairs, the front door opens.

Fear hits me first. It's a small town, and everyone knows everyone else, so the fact that the guy knows Estella means nothing. She's the wealthiest woman in the entire county. I hate being scared, and because of that, I know I'm not thinking straight with only about ten hours of sleep over the last few days.

My terror fades as rage rushes through me. How dare some dude do this? He has no right to scare me or intrude into my space. Before I can talk myself out of it, I launch myself down the stairs, screaming like a banshee.

The figure stops his forward progress, probably stunned by my screech. I trip over the last two steps in my rush to get down the stairs. All of a sudden, I'm flying through the air. He catches me with an oof but tumbles backward. We both crash back over the threshold onto the massive front porch. The baseball bat goes flying and lands on the porch with a loud thunk.

The first thing I notice is how good the intruder smells. Bergamot, tobacco, and something else I can't discern tickles my nose. I had no idea burglars smelled so delicious.

I pull myself up so I can look down at him. In the porch light, I can make out his features easily. Dark hair, blue eyes with eyelashes I would kill for. There's a dribble of blood on his fuller bottom lip. Damn, I must have hit his mouth. First confusion, then anger light his eyes, oh mama. His hands are on my waist, his fingers twitching the moment we make eye contact.

He is the most beautiful man I have ever seen, and I've worked with a couple of male models. Why am I even thinking that? Lack of sleep and the adrenaline coursing through my body must have scrambled my brain.

At that moment, Josh shows up, screeching to a halt behind the sedan the intruder apparently drove to break into the house. Once out of his car, Josh rushes to the front door, only to slow down when he sees who I am on top of.

"What the hell?" Josh says with a laugh. "When did you get back in town?"

The intruder looks up at Josh. "Is this a new thing? Did the LOLs set up someone to attack me when I got back into town?"

"No. The teenagers would have more of a reason to set that up." Josh's laugh barks out of him. "Avery O'Bryan, I would like you to meet Jon Howard."

My eyes widen as I look down at the man I just attacked. His eyes narrow as they study me. He's pissed, and for some reason, that's apparently a turn-on for me. My nipples pebble under his frowny stare.

"Jon Howard?"

He nods, his eyes flaming with irritation. Heat pools in my stomach and then rushes lower. Oh, God. I'm getting hot over someone being angry with me.

I have definitely lost my mind.

"Now, maybe you can tell me what the fuck you're doing squatting in my house?"

Chapter Four

Jon

My head is still throbbing as I sit at the kitchen table in *my* house. I have a cold compress on my lip as I glare at the woman who attacked me. Avery, according to Josh. She has yet to apologize.

"You can't really blame me."

She has said this five times in the last ten minutes and keeps getting increasingly belligerent. It's not making her any less attractive. For such a small woman, she packed a punch when she landed on top of me. Her chin-length dark hair is a riot of loose curls around a heart-shaped face. Dark brown eyes study me as if I've lost my mind. Like *I'm* the crazy one.

"Actually, I can."

She crosses her arms beneath her breasts. I try not to notice, but it's hard to ignore that motion. She's not wearing a bra, and I hate to admit it, but my attacker is stacked. When I finally tear my gaze away from her chest, her smirk tells me she saw where my attention was.

"I have a lease."

It takes me a second to get my brain to work. She's wearing an old shirt and sleep shorts. Most women would go get a robe or something. Not her. "You can't have a lease. This is my house."

"Is it?"

I try not to growl because she's got me there. Yes, I've always thought of this house as mine. My mother and I lived in the house after my parents split up. Then, when we moved away, it was always waiting for us when we arrived back in town. But now this woman lives in it, claiming my grandmother rented it to her. It's the first time that would have ever happened that I knew about. It's not like my grandmother needs the money.

Josh is on the phone with Estella in the other room, trying to sort out this mess. His low baritone is barely loud enough for me to hear, but there's a lot of laughing. That's not something I'm accustomed to hearing when someone is dealing with my grandmother. Usually, there's shrieking or crying. Apparently, no one alerted my grandmother someone was squatting in her house.

"Meow."

I look down at the cat. Yeah, I'm unsure if my grandmother would like the idea of a cat in her house.

"Meredith, get away from him. He's trying to make us homeless."

Jesus, this woman. She is insanely overdramatic. I put her age in her mid to late twenties. She barely comes up to my shoulder, so I tower over her. Also, she has the most amazing soft curves. Don't judge me. She had them pressed against me not too long ago.

For her part, the cat ignores Avery and jumps on the

table, then settles in front of me. She doesn't blink as she stares straight at me. It's unnerving.

"What's wrong with you?"

I open my mouth, but Avery gets up and grabs the cat. I realize she's not talking to me.

"Maybe she knows I'm a nice guy."

Avery gives me an eye roll worthy of a thirteen-year-old. "Meredith doesn't like men. You saw how she acted with Josh, and most females like *him*."

I try not to be annoyed with that comment. Why do all the women of Juniper Springs seem to be interested in him? But she is right. Meredith hissed at Josh and ran away.

"I still don't understand how you got into my house."

Another eye roll. "I signed a lease with your grandma. I just told you that. Did you hit your head? You should go to the hospital and check your brain."

I ignore her inquiry because I can tell by her tone she's being sarcastic. "Grandmother."

"No." She points to her chest. "Avery. Estella is your grandma. I think you should go to the hospital."

I can tell from her smirk she thinks she's funny. It also makes me want to kiss it off her.

With great effort, I shove that thought aside as I shift in my chair. This is not the time to activate the launch sequence because some pixie with sad eyes and a bee-stung mouth is making fun of me.

"No one calls Estella grandma."

Confusion moves over her delicate features. "Why not? She's your grandma."

"If you think anyone would get away with calling Estella grandma or grannie, then I know you don't know her at all."

She stares at me as she slips her fingers through the cat's fur. I watch as she moves her hand repeatedly, and another thread of need shivers through my system. I have never felt the dual emotions of irritation and arousal simultaneously. It's slightly unnerving.

"What do you have against your grandma?"

"I don't have anything against my *grandmother*."

She sighs. "You shouldn't take her for granted, Jon."

The comment is said in such a somber tone that it has me blinking. She's been anything but serious since she landed on top of me after letting loose a battle cry that had alarmed me. There's an air of sadness that clings to her right now, one that I am not comfortable with. Thankfully, Meredith hisses, breaking the odd moment.

Josh steps into the kitchen and shakes his head. "Hey, talked to your grandmother."

I smirk at Avery, who rolls her eyes. "What did she have to say?"

"She said to come to the house tonight, and you could sort it out in the morning."

"Ha!"

I tear my gaze away from the woman who stole my house and stare at Josh.

"She said what now?"

<hr>

MY HEAD IS STILL POUNDING as I go downstairs the next morning.

Am I in my house?

No. It's my grandmother's house, and this is precisely

what I was trying to avoid. I don't want to deal with her this morning, but I have no choice. According to Josh, Avery is renting the house from my grandmother, so I need her to kick that crazy woman out.

"Oh, there you are," my grandmother calls out from the dining room. "Finally."

I sigh and make my way into the massive room. Seated at the head of an empty table is Estella Howard, the matriarch of the Howard family and a holy terror to those who know her. They would never say that to her face, though.

"Grandmother."

"What would you like for breakfast? Pancakes?"

I nod, and she glances at one of the staff. They rush off to do her bidding. I don't take comfort in her knowing my favorite thing to eat for breakfast. Estella learns things about people, so she has control over them.

"Sit. There's coffee right there."

I stifle a sigh because she would get irritated. She finds sighing unseemly.

I take the seat next to her.

"So, I understand you met Avery?"

I pour myself some coffee from a silver carafe, of course. My grandmother still acts like she's landed aristocracy. "Yeah, you could say that."

Growing up, I didn't spend much time with my grandmother, but my mother insisted I come to Juniper for two weeks each summer and a few days after Christmas. I know Estella's differing moods of irritation. I sense her anger with my tone. Irritation is one of her few emotions.

"You must understand that Avery has been through a

bad time lately. She lives here because her sister and two young children moved here to work for your cousin."

"So, what you're telling me is that I can blame Nancy for all of this?"

She shakes her head. "Why would you blame Nancy?"

"It was a joke."

"Not a very good one."

Like she would know a good joke.

"Why are you letting her stay at my house?"

There's a long pause. "Oh, it's your house, is it?"

I want to scream out of frustration. This wouldn't bother an average person, but these conversations have always felt like interrogations. She might be in her seventies, but Estella Howard is sharp as a tack. They could probably hire her to work at CIA black sites, and they wouldn't even have to attempt any kind of torture. She would just stare at the offending person, and they would give up all their secrets. She'd always been like this.

"You know I stay there when I come into town."

She nods as Bessie, her cook, slips into the room and places a massive plate of blueberry pancakes in front of me. I glance up and smile. Bessie has been with my grandmother for over a decade, and she always knows exactly what I want.

"Thanks. How's your granddaughter?"

She smiles, her green eyes dancing. "Just fine. She's into dance now. And Jessica has another one on the way."

Jesus, Jessica is a year younger than I am. I can barely handle my own life, let alone two kids.

"Congrats."

She leaves us alone.

"Jessica was a year behind you, right?"

I frown as I pour maple syrup over my pancakes. "Yeah."

"And already has two children."

I glance up at my grandmother. There's something in her tone that makes me wary. It's not one I've heard before now. That's always suspicious. I don't feel at the top of my game, and that's the only way to deal with my grandmother.

"Yes. Do you have a point?"

"When was the last time you had a serious relationship?"

That question throws me for a loop. Seriously, my grandmother has only asked me about work. She might be an older boomer, but she definitely gets computers. I know she helped finance some of my education, not my father. I know she understands me when I talk about coding. Or at least, she pretends like she does.

"I just got out of one."

She makes a noise that sounds like a snort, but I must be wrong. My grandmother doesn't snort.

"That was not a serious relationship."

"You know about Sienna?"

What am I asking? Of course, she does. She keeps tabs on their entire insane family. The Howard family is vast and filled with reprobates and idiots. Her words, not mine. Apparently, the only family she accepts is Nancy and me.

"Yes. You were photographed here and there. Your mother told me."

My mother and grandmother have kept a relationship going through phone calls about me. While my father wanted nothing to do with me, my grandmother took a significant interest in what was going on in my life. Strike that. My father wanted nothing to do with me until I made my first million. When he reached out, I smacked back and told him to get bent. My grandmother never said anything, but I think she approved. She's been highly disappointed in all of her children.

"Yeah, well, she thought it was serious."

Sienna only lives in Dallas part of the time since modeling takes her all over the world, but I knew she was due back soon. We broke up about a month ago, but she seems to think we are still dating or that she can win me back. And that's why I had to skedaddle out of there.

"That's because you're a serious man. Most women will think that you want to settle down right away."

"Are you blaming me?"

She shakes her head. "No. But I'm telling you to loosen up a little, and this won't always happen."

I blink. My grandmother telling me to loosen up is like having a priest tell me to find a hooker.

"Excuse me?"

She shakes her head. "You were always a serious little thing. I thought that it was a good thing. Your father…" she sighs, which has me on high alert. She doesn't like sighing, remember? If she does it, it means there is something weird going on.

"What?"

She studies me. "You know I don't make excuses for my children, but they did not have an easy time of it. Then add in their father. He wasn't the best example of how to behave."

True. My grandfather was a bastard. He was horrible, having affairs and not even having the decency to hide them. I have always thought that dating in Juniper could get sketchy for me. There's a good chance that I'm related to half the town.

But my grandmother doesn't talk about my grandfather. It's like she would rather pretend he never existed.

"What does this have to do with me being serious?"

Another sigh. For a woman who would typically find sighing unseemly, she seems to be doing a lot of it. "I thought you would be the antithesis of your father. You had your mother's intelligence, so if I fostered your serious side, it would serve you well."

"It did."

"To a point. When was the last time you took a vacation?"

I frown. "What? I'm here."

"I mean a *real* vacation. Where you go to enjoy the local flavor. When was the last time you did that?"

"I went to Italy two months ago."

She gives me a look. "I saw the pictures. You were on your phone at the fashion show. You could have cared less. Did you take in any of the sights of Milan?"

"I…Grandmother, where is this going?"

"I want to make sure you don't waste your life. I want you to have fun."

I swallow, my mind racing with the possibilities for a reason for this chat. "Are you sick?"

She snorts and then starts laughing. "They wish."

"Who are they?"

"The Howard family. They think when I go, they will take over."

"So, what's going on if you aren't sick?"

She studies me for a long moment. Then, she says, "Things have happened in the last year or so that have me rethinking things."

In an instant, I realize what has her talking like this. Nancy and my grandmother always had a tumultuous relationship. Then Nancy was stalked by a former producer, and he almost killed her. I bet that's what this is all about.

"I thought you didn't believe in regrets."

"I have many regrets. How can I not when I married your grandfather? That was the biggest regret of my life, but it turned out well."

"What do you mean?"

She waves her hand. "After Nancy was in danger, we had some long chats. I realized I was hard on both of you, and she didn't understand why. It made me think that maybe you didn't either."

"I..." I'm at a loss for words, and it takes me a second to get my brain to function. "I never thought you were that hard on me."

"Are you being honest?"

"I am, but Nancy and I are different. She is also a girl."

"Women are tougher than men," she says. "Don't ever think differently, Jon."

"I know. Look at my mother."

"Yes, she was a surprise. A delightful one." She looks out the window. There's a butterfly garden right by the big window. I always wondered about it because my grandmother was never the butterfly type. But what do I know? Maybe she is.

Then she looks back at me. "You need to take time to enjoy life."

"I thought you didn't like people goofing off."

"Goofing off, as you call it, is not good if that's all you do. But taking time off every now and then is important."

I open my mouth and then snap it shut.

"So, you met Avery last night."

"We already covered that."

She sends me a withering glance, and I'm eight years old again, and I just fried her computer.

"What do you think of her?"

"Kind of hard to assess the woman other than she's very loud and acts before she thinks."

My grandmother chuckles. "I heard she tackled you."

"She came flying at me out of the dark."

"Don't be overly dramatic."

There is a tone in her voice that tells me she finds the whole thing amusing.

"Funny, I have a feeling Avery O'Bryan is a bit overly dramatic herself."

"I cannot argue that, but she's bright and has a good soul."

I frown. "What does that mean?"

Another withering look. "I'm having dinner tonight. Avery will be invited, along with Nancy and Travis. Six sharp."

"Yes, ma'am."

Then, using the cane, which I think is more of a prop, she levers herself out of the chair. Just before she leaves the dining room, she stops.

"It's good to have you here, Jon."

I blink. I don't think that she's ever said that to me. "Are you sure you're not sick?"

She nods and offers me a slight smile. "I'm more than fine. Don't be late tonight."

Then she leaves me to my thoughts, which of course, move on to the squatter who stole my house. My biggest problem is ignoring the heat that flares to life whenever I think of her. It probably has to do with the fact that I have felt every curve on her body.

I shake my head. I can't get distracted by Avery, or I'll never get my house back.

Chapter Five

Avery

My sister is staring at me like I have lost my mind. At least this is different from the condescending look she gave me yesterday. And yes, I'm accustomed to this look too. I like it better than the other one because this means I'm keeping everyone on their toes. It's sort of my superpower.

"Do you want to explain that again?"

I shrug and settle down in the chair in front of her desk. I'm in the *Flipping Texas* office. She works for Nancy and Travis. She runs their office and keeps it in order, which I find amazing. I could never be that person, especially since Travis apparently hates to do anything office related, like turn in his receipts for anything. Liv doesn't let him get away with it, though. I would just suggest we play hooky and worry about things later.

That's probably why she's looking at me like it's my fault.

"I said Jon Howard showed up last night and accused me of squatting in my house."

"That's *his* house."

"No, it's his grandmother's, and I'm renting it from her."

She takes a deep breath. I've seen her do this with my nephew. Most people would probably be embarrassed to be equated with an almost seven-year-old, but I see it as an accomplishment. I promised myself and Grannie Pam that I would live my life on my terms. Those terms seem to be juvenile and filled with Froot Loops. I'm okay with that.

"Why didn't you come back to my house last night?"

"Because I'm renting the house from Estella. And she sent word for Jon to stay with her, and we would sort this out tonight."

"Tonight?"

"Yeah, she's having me over for dinner. At the big house." I wiggle my eyebrows.

The people in the town have some kind of idea that Estella is uptight. Granted, she's a little conservative compared to me, but who isn't? There aren't a lot of people who live life like I do. Estella can be a little stiff but give her a massive glass of wine or a few shots of tequila, and she's so much fun.

Most people in small towns are always seen in one particular way. When you've lived decades in one town and are the wealthiest resident, people tend to think you are stuck up. There is no way to bust out of preconceived notions. And just between you and me, Estella is a huge Swiftie. We spend hours chatting about what each of her songs means and what she might be referencing.

We both hate John and Jake.

Liv's worried voice drags my thoughts away from Taylor

and Estella. That tone tells me she thinks I'm about to do something stupid. All of my siblings are great, but they will never see me as anything but the goofy youngest kid. The one who might or might not have blown up the chemistry lab in the high school back home. I look my sister straight in the eye so she understands that I'm not fooling around.

"Nope. Meredith wouldn't like it."

She's staring at me like I've lost my mind. Again.

"Who the hell is Meredith?"

"My cat. I have a feeling she and Houdini wouldn't get along."

"When did you get a cat?"

"A couple of days ago. You know I'm volunteering at the shelter, right?"

"No, I don't. When did you start volunteering there?"

"Last week. I'm mainly helping them with their social media. Adoptions are up about twenty percent thanks to their TikTok."

Her face softens. Liv likes to pretend that she's a hard ass, and she is in a lot of ways. She was widowed thanks to an IED when she was pregnant with Sammy. She had to raise her two kids on her own, and when it comes to kicking ass with schedules and making sure everything runs on time —like in this office—she's a queen. But she has a soft heart, and she knows I've always had this need to help. Not many of my other siblings seem to notice.

"Anyway, I have to go up there tonight for dinner. There will be a *discussion*."

I hope that Estella comes down on my side in this situation. I really like that house, creaks and all. And Meredith loves that backyard. The house has good bones, and Nancy and Travis made the most of those while updating it. Estella's granddaughter and her fiancé have the country's most popular home improvement show. As soon as I think of them, they walk through the door.

Nancy is a compact ball of energy with dark hair and the same shade of blue eyes her cousin has. She seems tiny, but her personality makes up for what she lacks in height. She's wearing a T-shirt with the logo of their show on it.

Her co-star and fiancé, Travis Spencer, is a big hunk of a man. He is well over six feet, has blondish-brown hair, and always has a ready smile. He reminds me of a big happy teddy bear. I mean, if the teddy bear is hot AF with muscles to spare.

"Hey, I heard you took out my cousin last night," Nancy says with a laugh.

"Where did you hear that?" Liv asks.

"It was on the Juniper Springs Express," I say.

Liv rolls her eyes. "That app."

Yeah, *that* app. Jon Howard, the intruder who smells like heaven with the most amazing blue eyes, invented it. I have a feeling that the townsfolk wouldn't leave him alone about creating it, so he did it to get them off his back. Don't get me wrong. I love this town, right down to the gay ducks, but they can be a bit much. It was set up to be like a community center on your phone. The LOLs have turned it into a gossip rag.

"I'm not the one he has to worry about. I saw a few comments from the teens on the JSE about making him pay."

Yeah, there has been a brewing vendetta against Jon. The teens hate they can't sneak around and do what they want in this town without one of the LOLs commenting on it.

Nancy laughs again and takes the seat next to mine. "That's true. We'll be there tonight, by the way."

"For dinner at the big house?"

"The big house? You make it sound like a prison," Nancy says.

I shrug. I think it is, at least for Estella, although she's started branching out a bit. She's become an LOL in the truest sense. I know it's important for older folks to have a community of peers. Until recently, Estella has been rattling around that massive mansion all by her lonesome. Okay, by her lonesome with a chauffeur, maids, and a cook. But still. A girl needs friends no matter what her age.

"Yeah, well, I hope she lets me stay in that house. I really love it."

"It was one of our first projects," Travis says.

"I thought I saw your hand in the back garden."

"It was my grandparents' first house," Nancy comments.

"Yeah, I think she told me that." She did. I think Estella has shared more about her life with me than with her grandchildren, which makes me sad.

She nods. "It wasn't a love match, but my grandmother loved that house."

"Well, I do too. I love the master bath. And the kitchen?" I roll my eyes. "I know Savannah will love it whenever she sees it." If my sister-in-law gets to see it.

Nope. I'm going to keep thinking positive, then it will happen.

I thought that way about Liv and her man Mason, and it

happened. I just wish it would have worked with Grannie Pam.

I shut that thought down as fast as I could. No crying. My family expects me to be happy and bubbly, and they are sure I have dealt with Grannie Pam's death. There's no reason to burden them with something I should be dealing with on my own.

And yes, I know I should lean on them if I need to, but I can handle this. I have Meredith and all the cereal a girl could want. I also have Taylor Swift songs.

"Well, I have some work to do, and I'm sure you do too," I say, rising out of the chair. I don't have any work right now by choice, but I haven't let my family know. I'm maintaining my clients, but I've put any new clients on hold. Other than the LOLs and the shelter.

"Okay. You know we can figure out a situation at my house, even with Meredith."

Of course, Liv says that. Old habits die hard. She's always trying to figure out how to do all the things, but she's working at letting some things go. And as someone who loves her to pieces, I can't let her take it on. She needs time with Mason, and the kids are getting to know him well.

"Don't worry. Estella is a fair person. Besides, Jon never stays that long, from what I hear."

"She's right on both accounts," Travis says. Nancy shoots him a look, and he shrugs. "You know it's true."

She rolls her eyes, and I see the resemblance to Jon now that she's frowning. How pretty would he be if he smiled?

Too pretty. I know to stay away from those guys. Heartbreak is not something I want to deal with right now, and Jon Howard is a heartbreak wrapped in some sexy cologne.

Also, he has something against me since I tackled him, split his lip, and stole his house—allegedly.

After leaving the office, I walk back to my house. One thing I love about Juniper is the ability to walk to most places. I grew up in a small town, which was more of a farming community. The downtown wasn't as great as Juniper—one of the reasons my old hometown is dying right now. Juniper's LOLs might be worried about the younger generation leaving town, but the tourist traffic is impressive.

It only takes about fifteen minutes to make it back to the house. People wave and smile at me as I walk past businesses and homes. It was never like this in my hometown. I was always the odd little O'Bryan girl. Yeah, I get that I'm weird, and I am okay with that. It took me a few years to understand that I'm not everyone's favorite. Still, I just never fit in with those folks. Even though I've known most of them all my life, I feel more at home in Juniper Springs. No one questions my eating habits or that I rattle on about nothing at all in particular.

As I step up on the porch, I cringe. Memories of my activities last night come flashing back to me. Travis is right. I did a number on Jon. But my brother Fritz was military and taught me how to defend myself, as did my cop brother-in-law. I have never had a problem punching a guy in the nuts. I am seriously proud of that, and it helped out more than once in my dating life. People, especially men, think I'm ditzy and that they can take advantage of me. Thanks to an ex with questionable behavior, I learned not to let men lie to my face or treat me as if I didn't matter.

I unlock the door and find Meredith sitting in the foyer.

Her little face is scrunched up, and her tail is dancing back and force. She's irritated, and I don't blame her.

"Sorry. Maybe I should start taking you with me when I'm not going out to eat."

Her nose twitches, then she stands and stalks away. So judgey. She's started to get territorial about me and this house. Just yesterday, she hissed at the neighbor behind us. Granted, he's weird AF, and that's saying a lot coming from me. There's something about him I don't trust, so maybe that's what Meredith picks up on.

He's renting the place but spends a lot of time in the backyard. I mean, I get it. Maybe he needs some nature time, but he's not the owner. He rented it through one of those vacation apps. And yes, I know this because everyone knows everything in Juniper. With that thought, I pull out my phone and bring up the Juniper Springs Express. I thought I might have to search for it, but we are the biggest news to hit. I start from the beginning of the thread.

Mrs. Petersen: I understand there was a ruckus on Preston Street.

Mrs. Fallon: Josh was called out. The old Howard house.

See. Nothing changes in small towns. I know they still own it, but from what I understand, Estella hasn't lived in it for decades.

Mrs. B: *Avery O'Bryan took out an intruder.*

Damn right, I did.

Five minutes later:

Mrs. B: *Oh, that's Jon Howard. She took out Jon. *gif laughing and crying**

Mrs. Fallon: *What do you mean?*

Mrs. B: *No intruder. Just Jon showing up.*

The conversation goes on for a while, all the way up until Jon finally leaves about thirty minutes after the incident. I roll my eyes. They really made quite a big deal out of it. When people woke up this morning and read the incident report, there was another rush of messages. Some are not so nice about Jon. Those teenagers are definitely after him. He'd better be careful.

I enter the living room and find Meredith standing by the sliding glass door.

"I guess we need to have our nature walk."

"Meow."

"Exactly."

I open the door, and Meredith prances out onto the patio. She moves over to the middle of the yard and into the sun. She likes to lay out there and soak up the heat. I putter around the garden, enjoying the mums now in full bloom. All the while, I feel as if someone is watching me. It irritates me, and I keep looking around, but there's no one there.

Just nerves, I tell myself, but I decide that I need to check out the name of the renter behind me. There is just something off about him. Of course, this could be because I've had no sleep and had an incident last night. If I'm going to make it to Estella's tonight, I should nap. With that thought, I head in, calling Meredith. A nap is definitely in order.

Chapter Six

Jon

I roll my shoulders and look at myself in the mirror. I can't believe my grandmother is making me go through this ridiculous meeting. That squatter needs to go, and my grandmother needs to understand that.

If she doesn't, hopefully, the background check I have my staff working on will turn something up. I just have a feeling Avery O'Bryan is after something. While my grandmother is probably one of the sharpest businesswomen in the world, she is getting older. Avery is cute enough that she might have weaseled her way into my grandmother's good graces.

Thinking about Avery has my entire body reacting. My pulse ticks up a beat, my cock twitches, and my palms grow sweaty.

My phone buzzes, breaking into my thoughts.

Trev: *Please tell me you're going to be in NYC soon.*

Trevor Smith is an old friend. I rebuilt an app for their hotel business—one of many of their companies. Still, he's grounded, mainly due to his time in the military. Now, he's the CEO of his family's business and is always on *TMZ* and other vulture sites.

Me: *Nope.*

Trev: *Way to support your best friend.*

Me: *I'm touched. I didn't think you had any friends.*

Trev: **gif-eddie-murphy-gumby-shame-on-you**

I smile. Don't get me wrong. We are an odd set of friends, I guess. We both grew up privileged. His much more than mine, but he's one of those dudes who feel comfortable being photographed and talked about. I would rather not deal with that at all.

When I don't respond, my phone vibrates with a call from him.

"What is it, Trev?"

"I was hoping you would be up to a weekend out."

As much as Trev seems to fit into the social life of Manhattan, he needs a break from it. I get it. He's in his thirties, runs a massive family business, and has constant paparazzi following him. The one outdoor activity I really like is fishing. Not sure why, but I love it, and so does Trev.

"You can go fishing by yourself. I'm busy getting my house back."

"Wait, what?"

I sigh. This is what comes from my orderly life being disrupted. First, that man my mother is moving in with, and then the lack of sleep last night. I do not like being here in my grandmother's house. And besides, that's *my* house. I want it back.

"My grandmother rented out my house here in Juniper."

"What the fuck are you doing there?"

Spoiler alert, Trev grew up in the best schools, including

prep schools and Harvard, but he was also in the military. His vocabulary is worse than mine.

"I had to get out of town. You know I can work anywhere."

"Why didn't you come here?"

Good question, although I'm pretty sure a lot of it has to do with the media. I want to avoid them. Hanging around Trevor Smith would do the exact opposite of that. No matter how careful he is, he always gets found out.

"I need to work, not go to a city so busy it hurts my head."

There's a long beat of silence. Trev runs his family's business because he's smart, not because it's a birthright. It's one of the reasons I think we became friends when I built an app for the hotel arm of their business. That and I didn't give a damn about his money. I'm pretty sure it's why he's probably closer to his old Army buddies than he is with the socialite set of Manhattan.

"What happened?"

"Sienna. She wanted more, and I said no. There might have been a little light stalking. So, I left town."

Yes, avoidance is my middle name when it comes to sticky personal situations. That's about all I learned from my father.

"Let's table that for another time. How did you lose your house in Juniper? I had no idea you owned property in that town you claim to hate."

"I don't own it. My grandmother does, but it's where I stay when I come to town. She rented it out to some idiot."

"There's more to this story."

I sigh. I really don't want to tell him what happened. It's

embarrassing that I was taken down by a woman who probably weighs 120 pounds soaking wet.

"I showed up last night, not realizing my grandmother had rented it out and got attacked."

"Attacked."

"Yes, the woman renting the house came flying down the stairs and tackled me."

Trev doesn't hesitate. He laughs out loud.

"Damn, Howard, I had no idea so much happened in that little town."

"Nothing happened. Josh showed up in time to explain who we both were—"

"Who's Josh?"

"The sheriff."

"You called the cops on her."

"No, she called the cops when she thought someone was breaking in."

"Okay, she must have been a bruiser to take you down."

I'm not built with muscles. More lean than bulky. One of my girlfriends had claimed I had a swimmer's body. But I'm over six feet and solid.

"No. She was kind of tiny and curvy." I close my eyes and try not to react to the memory, but it's useless. I shouldn't think of her that way, but I can't help it. All those curves pressing against me were more erotic than anything that's happened to me lately, and I have had sex in the last month. Even now, my entire body is tingling.

I don't tingle.

"What was that?"

I open my eyes. "What?"

"There was something in your voice."

A knock pulls me away from the conversation.

"I have no idea what you're talking about."

Another bark of a laugh. "Sure, Howard."

I open the door and find my cousin Nancy standing there. "What's up, buttercup?"

Most of my relatives on my father's side of the family irritate the living hell out of me. Nancy is the exception.

"Gotta go, loser," I say to Trev. Then I click off the phone, not waiting for an answer.

"Was that Sienna?"

I shake my head and give Nancy a hug.

"What are you doing here?"

"Grandma called me."

"When did you start calling her that?"

Estella Howard isn't a grannie or grandma type. Grandmother fits her regal bearing and her pain-in-the-ass ways.

"I do it when I want to mess with her. Just so you know, Avery is already downstairs having the best time with our grandmother."

Damn. I slip my phone into my pocket and start towards the door.

"Whoa, dude, don't worry. We'll get down there in a minute. I want to talk to you."

"What?"

"I want you to be nice to Avery."

"She stole my house."

She makes a rude noise that irritates the crap out of me. Nancy has always been more like a sister to me. We don't fit in with the other cousins, so we tend to gravitate to each other. "First of all, she didn't steal it."

"I beg to differ."

She rolls her eyes. "And who knew you were coming back into town? You have to give us a head's up."

"If I do that, everyone will know."

"Thanks to your jenky app, everyone already knows."

"I have never created a jenky app." Then it hits me what she said. Damn, if this has hit the paps, there's a good chance they'll be down here to ask me what's going on. "How does everyone already know?"

"The whole thing where you got your ass kicked by a woman who probably only comes up to your shoulder?"

"I didn't get my ass kicked."

"That's not what Mrs. B said."

"This was reported on the JSE?"

She rolls her eyes and turns to stalk down the hallway. Her ponytail swishes from side to side. "Seriously, Jon, everything gets reported on there."

"Nancy, hurry up!"

Great, Travis is here. It makes sense since they're engaged, but I thought I could keep myself from being embarrassed in front of another person I like. I don't like a lot of people.

"It's not fair that my fiancé can yell like that, and our grandmother just laughs," Nancy says with a scowl as she stalks off.

I follow her down the hallway to the stairs. This is the east wing of the family mansion. I get the privilege of staying on this side near my grandmother. And I do mean that. Other than Nancy and my mother, the rest of the family stays in the west wing. She might not say it to their faces, but my grandmother can cut a person down with just a room assignment.

The moment I step off the stairs, I realize that there's another voice in the group. An annoying voice. One that I'll never forget and might have dreamed about last night.

"How could I leave her there? She was lonely. Sorry, I didn't tell you I had a pet now."

She doesn't sound sorry. I wait for my grandmother to destroy her.

"That's fine. You told me you might get a cat or two."

Or two? What the actual fuck?

I step into what my grandmother calls the grand drawing room. I take in the scene. Nancy and Travis are cuddling on the couch, making me sick. Okay, not sick. I'm happy my cousin, the only cousin I can stand, found her true love. Or rather, Travis got his shit together and realized she was his soulmate. They work together every day on their home improvement show, so it's insane it took him that long.

My grandmother is sitting on her padded throne, something antique that is probably worth more than my car.

Then, there's my nemesis, sitting to my grandmother's right. I will say one thing for Avery O'Bryan. She cleans up good, as my mother would say.

Her dark hair is a riot of curls, out of control like the woman herself. She definitely didn't get dressed up for dinner. I would have never shown up to dinner with my grandmother in jeans and a Nerdvana shirt. And...no shoes. Her socks don't even match. One is pink with purple cats on them. The other is yellow with white polka dots. I inwardly twitch.

"Jon," my grandmother says, drawing my attention away from Avery.

"Grandmother," I say, walking over to her to kiss her on her cheek.

My grandmother is a force of nature. She rules the family with a steel grip, but she's tiny. In fact, she and Avery are about the same height.

"You were on the phone."

I slant a look at Nancy, who tries to look innocent, but she fails.

"Yes. My friend Trev."

Avery snorts as she strokes her cat. Yes, she brought her cat with her.

"Do you have something to add to the conversation, Avery?" my grandmother asks.

Ha. You do not talk under your breath or snort when Estella is around. She will cut you down.

I look at Avery, who is now smirking at me. She keeps stroking that cat like a Bond villain. And just like last night, it aggravates and arouses me simultaneously. This is not acceptable.

"No. Just thinking that Jon seems like the kind of guy who would have a friend named Trev."

I stuff down my initial response, which would have been *What the actual fuck would you know about Trev,* but I know better. My grandmother doesn't like outbursts.

"Okay."

Instead of getting irritated, her smirk turns into an outright grin. She knows I'm barely keeping it together. Before I can respond, Bessie comes in to announce dinner's ready.

We make our way into the dining room, like cast members of Downton Abbey. I take my grandmother by the arm and lead the way. Nancy and Travis follow us, and Avery…well, she brings up the rear with her cat, who is on a leash.

I kid you not.

The table is set for five, and I realize I will be sitting by Avery. I lead my grandmother to her chair at the head of the table. Nancy and Travis go to the right, sitting beside each other. Avery, for her part, is standing behind the chair to my grandmother's left.

"Do you want to sit next to your grandma?"

I blink because I didn't expect her to ask. I nod, and she smiles, pulling out the chair furthest to the left.

"Sit down, Howard. I'm so hungry I would eat an armadillo," Travis says.

I glance at my grandmother, waiting for her to tell Travis to watch how he speaks. Nothing, she just smiles.

I take my seat and realize I have entered the Bizzaro version of Juniper Springs, and it might be harder to get rid of Avery than I thought.

Chapter Seven

Avery

"Armadillos don't taste that good. Or so I hear," I say.

"They seem like they would be difficult to eat. With that hard shell and everything," Travis comments.

My nerves are strung out. I might talk a good game, but I'm worried Estella will kick me out of that house. Typically, I wouldn't feel an affinity for something like a house. I've just never been attached to a building. People? Yes. Listening to all of Taylor Swift's number five tracks on repeat when I need a good cry? Definitely. Buildings, not so much.

"According to my brother, if you're hungry enough, you will eat anything."

Travis opens his mouth to ask what, so I cut him off. Estella gets a kick out of the two of us, but she has her limits.

"I didn't ask. But you never know with him. He is a Fritz."

"What's a Fritz?" Jon asks.

I don't roll my eyes, but it's a close call. No, he doesn't know my brother, so he doesn't understand, but I'm agitated just being in the same room as Jon. Worse, Meredith, who hates all men on earth, seems smitten with him. Just like last night, she seems to be all in for Jon. She hisses at most men, including the very sexy and bulky—as in he could lift me up over his head with one hand bulky—Travis.

Oddly when Jon appears, she purrs. I need her to hate one man, the man trying to make me homeless, and she can't even do that.

"That's my brother."

He studies me with those deep blue eyes, and I would normally sigh. Jon Howard is not who I thought he would be. I'd heard the name but never took the time to look him up. I know I should in my business, but he doesn't exactly have a social media side to his business. I think he's more on the security side of things. And while he did create the JSE, I see what it was supposed to be. The structure is more like a message board for posting stuff like get-togethers, not reporting on teenagers sneaking around.

Back to the hunk of man sitting next to me. I usually don't go for handsome guys. Let me rephrase that. Conventionally pretty men are not my thing. I did that once, and it was a disaster, so I steer clear of them. Jon Howard is definitely pretty. Like, I am pretty sure he could be a male model or movie star or something.

His dark hair is more styled today, but I liked it when it was a mess last night. Then there's his mouth. So full, so kissable, and he hasn't shaved. I can just imagine those whiskers against my thighs.

Oh, no, not today. I can't fantasize about a man who is trying to have me evicted.

Those amazing eyes narrow as he studies me. "What?"

He's smart, and he's good at paying attention. I can't tell him I just imagined his head between my legs, so I do the one thing I'm good at: distract.

"Why are you so dressed up for dinner at your grand-ma's house?"

He glances around the table. I will say that I'm a bit underdressed compared to everyone else. Unless I'm told there's a dress code, I assume I just need to be clothed— including a bra. I'm wearing my newest shirt, and Estella takes pride in Nerdvana. She's probably never been there, but she likes a woman-owned business from her town doing so well. Plus, I've eaten here a few times, and Estella never seems to care what I wear.

"It's the way it's always been."

There's a tone in his voice I haven't heard in the short interaction I've had with him. This sounds more like a repeated rule. Something drummed into him.

"I really don't care as long as you're comfortable."

His head whips around to look at his grandma. I don't get it. I mean, I sort of do because Estella seems kind of scary. She has to be. The Howard family is a bunch of idiots, except those at this table. I did not come up with that notion on my own. I've heard Estella say it more than once. Not outright, but just the way she talks about everyone else.

Estella comes from a generation when women didn't have a lot of power. It's not great now, but she can still remember not being able to open a charge account without a male signature. Look it up. Insane, I know. Her husband was a douche canoe, from what everyone in town says. If she hadn't taken over when she did, the entire Howard family would probably be bankrupt. While I'll happily argue that there are too many billionaires running around, I know that Estella invests in this town.

Before Jon can respond to his grandmother's comment, Bessie enters with our salads. This is so fancy compared to the way I grew up. Five kids, several pets, a grandmother, and my parents didn't sit around being waited on. Life was loud, messy, and I loved it.

"What are you thinking, Avery?"

I glance down the table to Estella. She seems to relax around me. She's stiffer tonight than she usually is with me, and I would worry that it's because she's about to kick me out of my house. I have learned that she always acts differently when it's just us two. I don't know why. Maybe it's because I don't expect anything from her.

"I'm thinking how different this is from how the O'Bryans eat."

Nancy laughs. "Yeah, I bet. I have no idea how your parents handled five kids."

"You have four siblings?"

The horror I hear in Jon's voice makes me giggle. "Yes. Three sisters and a brother stuck in the middle."

"That sounds like a lot of work," he says.

I lean closer and try my best not to sniff at him. He still smells like heaven. "My folks say they raised four kids, but once I came along, I ran everything."

Maybe that's why they always think I can handle anything that comes my way.

"You did leave at sixteen," Estella says.

I glance over at our hostess. "You make it sound like I ran away."

"You just moved out?"

There is something in Jon's voice that I can't figure out, but then, I have a feeling I never will. This man is as sexy as they come, but he acts like he has no idea. Also, he's too uptight.

I lean closer and realize my error the moment I do. His scent hits me just like last night, and I feel dizzy. Or maybe my blood sugar is low.

"I went away to college. Graduated early."

He's looking at me with horror again.

"It's not *that* bad."

"No, what I think you're seeing is Jon realizing he isn't the only person who graduated from high school early," Nancy says.

I glance at her, then back at Jon. "Yeah? What age?"

"Same."

"And you thought you were a prodigy?"

"Stop teasing Jon, Avery," Estella says, but she's smiling.

"Sorry." I shrug. "I skipped a couple of grades. It helps to have three sisters who are all good at different things."

"How does that help you graduate early?" Jon asks.

"When I needed help with a certain subject, I would ask for help from a sibling. They are all very individual in their talents."

"That makes no sense."

Ugh, why does he have to be so persnickety? As soon as I think it, I snort. Jon would not like being known as persnickety. I would bet he would like people to think of him as stoic. His types always do. Of course, it does nothing to dispel his beauty. I mean, how does a person walk around being that gorgeous? It's annoying.

"Why are you looking at me like that?"

I blink and realize I let my thoughts show on my face.

"No reason," I say and turn to my salad. Thankfully, Estella asks a question that distracts Jon's attention from me.

"Your mother said she's moving in with Ted Franklin."

"The football player?" Travis asks.

Jon sighs. "Yes. She ambushed me with the information when we had brunch."

That wording is interesting. "You don't like him?"

"I don't know him. Surprisingly, she had him show up to brunch." He looks at his grandmother. "How did you find out?"

"She told me when I called her to tell her what happened last night."

"You called her to tell her you let someone move into my house?"

"No, Jonathon. I called to tell her you were taken down by a small woman. She found it very amusing."

Nancy snorts. "She thought it was hilarious."

"Wait, has everyone talked to my mother?"

"I haven't," Travis says.

He glares at me, his blue eyes sparking with irritation. My nipples get hard from just that look. What the hell, nipples? I cross my arms over my breasts so he doesn't see.

"I don't even know your mamma."

For a long moment, he stares at me, his gaze dropping down to my mouth, then quickly back up. Oh, no. My entire body lights up like the lights on the Riverwalk in San Antonio. I shift in my seat and almost groan. My panties are damp, and my lady parts are begging for attention from Jon.

Months of my libido being dormant seem to have ended. *What the hell, libido?*

"Jon, I talk to your mother regularly. I want to know why you didn't know she had a man in her life?"

Jon's head whips around, and I laugh.

"She's got you there."

"Shut up."

"Jonathon Michael Howard, you will *not* speak to my guest like that."

"It's okay, Estella. You know how some men have issues with being questioned."

She nods as she looks at me with a small smile. Our friendship started over nibbles at midnight at the Mystic Diner. We share one affliction, insomnia. I went there to keep from waking up my sister and her kids. Estella went because she loves milkshakes and didn't want anyone to know.

Jon looks between us and opens his mouth, but Bessie walks in with our entrées. Platters of catfish and bowls of roasted potatoes and coleslaw are left on the table.

Once we're alone, we all get our food.

"Are we going to talk about my house?" Jon asks.

Another snort from Nancy, and I glance over. She winks.

"Let's finish eating, then we can talk."

He sighs but says nothing else.

We dig into our food, and the talk turns to the JSE and other things, Nancy and Travis' wedding plans being one. It sounds like a lot of work. I like weddings, don't get me wrong. I love cake, and I love pretty things. It's just that a gathering with a bunch of people makes my skin crawl.

I haven't always been like that. But in the last few months, it's gotten harder to deal with tons of people at once. I can handle it sometimes, and it does seem easier these last few days with Meredith.

"Is there a reason your cat seems to have adopted me?"

I look over at Jon and shrug. "She usually hates men. I mean, she hissed at Travis, and he's hot."

"Thanks," Travis says happily. I smile at him. He's a good guy, and many people think he's stupid because he's pretty. Well, not like Jon. Jon looks like a movie star, kind of pretty. He's scowling at me right now, and I just want to ruffle his hair so his curls pop out again like they were last night.

"Hey, Jon," Travis says.

He pulls his gaze away from me, and I can take a deep breath finally. The only problem is that I pull in some of his scent again, then try my best not to get dizzy.

"Yeah?"

"Do you think you can introduce me to Ted?"

I shake my head. I worked with Nancy and Travis to teach them better social media skills. Travis is single-minded. When he sets his sights on something, he rarely deviates from that purpose. I always seem to have five million things moving through my brain, like right now. I know I should concentrate on my defense, but I can't. Instead, I'm wondering what kind of woman Jon dates. I bet it's a model type. She's probably almost six feet tall and wears heels.

I hate heels.

"Aren't you a celebrity?" Jon's voice has turned cold.

"Yeah, but he's…a legend."

If this was any other day, I would laugh out loud. The reverence I hear in Travis' voice is insane. I never understood why people were excited about football players or professional athletes. But this is Texas, and football is a religion here.

I take pity on Jon and probably on Travis when I change the subject.

"Estella, I think Jon would feel better if we discussed the house."

She nods, and I feel the vibration beside me increase. Why am I so tuned into this guy? Maybe it's the fact that I see him as an adversary. A hot, persnickety adversary.

"Of course, Avery," Estella says with a smile. "I always like to get right down to business."

Jon mumbles something, but I can't make it out.

"I think the only solution is that you share the house."

I blink and take my concentration away from Jon.

"Say what now?" I ask.

"Jon needs a place to stay, even though he won't tell me why, and you need a place to stay."

"But I paid rent for the month."

She nods. "I understand. So, I will half your rent for the rest of the year."

"What? Grandmother—"

She holds up her hand, cutting off Jon. "I signed a lease, Jon. I do not break contracts I've agreed to without cause. I know you say it's your house, but you haven't stayed overnight there for months, and I thought you were too busy with work. Avery hasn't given me any cause."

"What about the cat?"

"Avery said she was thinking about getting one and asked me before she moved in. She did not break the contract."

Living with Jon? I don't know if I like that. But…being able to stay here through the end of the year would be nice. Juniper Springs does a great fall and winter holiday season.

"Fine."

Jon's head whips around so fast I'm amazed he doesn't give himself whiplash. "What?"

"It's half rent for the rest of the year. I can't beat that."

Truth is, I could afford to buy the house. I have quite a bit of money socked away from my business dealings. Teaching people social media, especially celebrities, pays very well. I tried to buy the house, but Estella refused, so I'll take this.

"And you're okay with living with a strange man?"

The horror in his voice has me smiling. I lean closer. "Jon, are you strange?"

His gaze dips down to my mouth for the briefest moment, then bounces back up to my eyes. There is untamed heat there, burning within the depths of blue. Then, he blinks and pulls back from me.

"You don't know me."

I draw in a deep breath, trying to settle my hormones down. "I know that Estella and Nancy love you, and they respect you. Plus, there's a lock on my door, and I know how to defend myself."

One eyebrow quirks, and I bite back a sigh. God, what is wrong with me? I'm getting hot under my collar for some fussy geek.

"Is that a fact?"

"It is," Estella comments. "She had her brother teach the LOLs self-defense last month."

Another head-whipping action. How does he not bruise his brain? Just witnessing it makes me dizzy.

"You've had self-defense classes?"

Estella nods. "He had some good advice, just in case. I gather that he taught all his sisters. He said Avery was particularly vicious."

He wasn't lying, but I've never had to use it.

"So, see, I can handle you."

He looks at me with horror.

"What? Listen, you can stay here with your grand-mother, but I'm going to stay at the house. Your choice."

And with that pronouncement, I dig into my dinner, hoping that I haven't made the biggest mistake of my life.

Chapter Eight

Jon

The following day finds me at the grocery store. I grab a buggy and head off to the produce section. For such a small town, Juniper has a decent grocery store. Granted, it's the only one, but it seems to keep up with the times even without competition. Being a massive tourist destination might have something to do with it.

I stifle a yawn as I pick out some fruits and veggies. My grandmother warned me that Avery doesn't have much in the way of food at the house. What I don't get is how much she seems to know about this woman she met less than two months ago? It's odd. That's the only word I can come up with to describe their relationship.

"Jon Howard. How are you doing?"

I glance over my shoulder to find Mrs. Petersen smiling at me. A shiver of dread shoots up my spine as I try to keep my composure. She's practically the head of the LOLs and doesn't mind being a busybody. It's like she wears it as a badge of honor.

"Mrs. Petersen. How are you doing?"

I try my best not to use what my mother calls my 'leave me alone' tone. From the look on Mrs. Petersen's face, I think I might have failed. And if you think she's angry, you would be wrong. Nope, she looks like Sylvester, who finally caught his Tweety Bird.

"I'm doing fine. The real question is, how are you doing? I heard there was a commotion over at your grandmother's rental."

I grind my teeth together before unlocking my jaw to answer. "I'm fine. Just a misunderstanding about my house. Everything is cleared up."

"Oh?" she asks, genuinely surprised.

"Yes. My grandmother had us over to dinner and cleared everything up."

I know I'm repeating myself. And, yes, I'm lying a little bit. A lot. But Mrs. Petersen doesn't need to know about the living arrangements. I figure I can get rid of Avery pretty fast. Living with me is no walk in the park. I hate noise, and I keep what most people think of as atrocious hours. Even my mother, who gets up at about six in the morning daily, thinks I'm insane.

I have a feeling that the squatter will be out of my house in no time.

"I know your grandmother is happy to have you back in town." Confusion must show on my face because Mrs. Petersen smiles. "She talks about you all the time. She's so proud of you and Nancy. Well, I have to get some things for the LOL meeting this afternoon. You have a great day, Jon."

I nod and then shake my head. My grandmother might say she's proud of Nancy and me, but the truth is we don't embarrass her like our cousins do.

Knowing that if I don't get a move on, I'll be accosted by another LOL. I should have known they would be here at the crack of dawn. I turn down the pasta aisle and find Josh. He seems to be figuring out what kind of pasta to get.

"Hey, Josh."

"Howard," he says with a smile. "How's the head?"

"Eh. Not too bad. Isn't it kind of early for you?"

"I just got off work. I have the night shift this week."

"Right."

"Did you and Avery figure things out?"

"Yeah. Have you had any problems with her before now?"

"Well, not really. She's well-liked by most of Juniper, although she just officially moved here when she moved into your grandmother's rental.

"That's *my* house," I say with too much gusto.

"Uh, okay. *Anyway*, she stayed with her sister for a bit after moving to town."

"Her sister?"

"Liv works for your cousin and Travis. She's a single mother, so I figured she was helping her out with the kids."

"Avery? In charge of kids?"

Josh's mouth curved. "If you were a kid, can you think of anyone you'd want to hang with? I mean, kids probably get away with all kinds of shit."

A strange quiver hits my stomach at Josh's smile. He has always been known to date just about any woman in town or those visiting, or he did at one point. He has a good reputation with them, and I know the LOLs think he's the bee's knees. That was Mrs. Vincent's term, not mine, and she used it on the JSE. But I don't understand why I would be bothered by Josh's interest in Avery.

"You okay, Howard?"

I blow out a breath. "Yeah. Not enough sleep."

"Ah. I can understand that. Well, I'm going to throw together my dinner, then go to bed."

"Dinner?"

"It's the end of the night for me. I do better with eating meals like I normally would, so dinner at the end of the day. Let me know if there is anything you need."

"Thanks," I say, watching him saunter down the aisle, stopping to talk to another LOL. Jesus, they're coming out of the woodwork. I decide to get everything I need as fast as I can to avoid them at all costs.

By the time I arrive at my house, it's after eight. I grab my suitcase out of the backseat, along with a bag of groceries, then hurry up to the door. Why hurry? I've already had too many interactions with people this morning. I want to avoid dealing with them anymore—especially with any LOLs.

With the altercation the other night, we're now the subject of gossip. After discovering it had been reported on the JSE, I checked the postings. The truth is I tend to ignore the JSE. I could care less about what is going on. But after reading over the posts, I feel a little out of sorts. There are all kinds of ideas about what happened. One insane theory was that Avery, Josh, and I were involved in a love triangle, and it came to blows the other night. I mean, why would anyone think Avery would be interested in Josh? I know from the comments the LOLs believe he would be perfect for her, but they couldn't be more wrong.

I take the last step up onto the porch and pause. What the hell is going on in my mind? Why am I so aggravated by the fact that Avery might be interested in Josh? I like him. He was one of the few jocks who didn't give me a hard time. And from what I understand, he's a great sheriff. Still, the idea that he and Avery could be dating has my stomach churning. I shove that feeling aside and move to get in the house. I am standing out here exposed to any and all LOL entanglements.

I step into the house and shut the door. I expect it to be loud because that's Avery. She's loud and out of control, and everything I don't like. But it's silent. In fact, if I hadn't seen her car in the driveway, I would have thought she wasn't there.

"Meow."

I stop in my tracks and look at the cat on the stairs. She's definitely seen better days, with her ear partially missing.

What was that cat's name? Why is it important? It's not. I don't care about some random feline my unwanted house-mate owns.

"Meow."

I'm just standing here looking at her, feeling judged. It's stupid, I know, but I'm frozen in place. I shake my head to clear it and head to the kitchen, leaving my suitcase by the front door.

The moment I step into the kitchen, memories of my childhood come rushing back. Mom and I stayed here a lot when I was growing up. The floor is an off-white ceramic tile I remember, but most everything else has been replaced. Nancy and Travis gave it a facelift a few years ago, but they didn't change the bones of it—as Nancy says.

On the right is a U-shaped situation with a marble counter, farmhouse sink, and gas range. There's a breakfast bar with four stools. On the other end, there is a window seat and a table. It's one of the things I love about this kitchen. The garden boasts not only beautiful flowers but also herbs. I always thought it would be nice to plant some peppers and tomatoes.

Opening the fridge, I shake my head. My grandmother was right. Avery doesn't keep a lot of food on hand. There's a jug of milk, half and half, and two half-empty bottles of wine: one white and one red. I stash my perishables and open the pantry, a small cupboard next to the fridge. I blink. There are cooking things like flour and sugar, but I think those have been there for a while. I find about ten boxes of different kinds of cereal that have one thing in common: sugar.

"Jesus, is this all she's eating?" No wonder Avery's so argumentative and weird. She seems to be surviving on milk, sugar, and wine.

"Meow."

I jump and look behind me. The cat's sitting three feet behind me, watching my every move, her tail swishing back and forth. There is a look of irritation on her face.

"Sneaky little fucker, aren't you?"

"Meow."

"Get a grip, Meredith. I'm here for the long haul." Then I realize I remembered her name. "Meredith! That's your name, right?"

"Meow."

"Did she name you after Taylor Swift's cat?"

"Meow."

I open my mouth to respond, then realize what I'm doing. I'm having a conversation with a cat and expecting answers. See, this is what Juniper does to me. It makes me crazy, and I do idiotic things.

Rolling my eyes, I return to putting my groceries in the pantry. I have been here less than ten minutes, and I'm waiting for answers from a cat. I don't talk to animals. Hell, I don't like talking to humans.

That's what comes from spending time with a crazy person. The scary thing is that I haven't had that much time with Avery, but maybe it has to do with how she disrupted my life. I need to be on schedule. My OCD is more about ensuring I'm on time for everything and that I don't have any surprises.

My stomach grumbles, telling me that I need to eat. I should have stayed a little later for breakfast at my grandmother's house, but I wanted to get here and settled early. This is a battle, and I need to make sure that Avery O'Bryan understands I won't give up this house.

I pull out the eggs and cheese and make an egg white omelet. As I'm heating up the pan on the stove, I hear a loud thump on the floor, then a muffled exclamation which sounds very dirty. My mouth quirks up on one side.

Time to get up, princess.

I look over to comment to Meredith but realize she's gone. I frown but ignore the feeling of abandonment—irrational because I just met the stupid cat—and get to work on my breakfast.

I hear the flurry of steps across the second floor, then down the stairs. The door to the kitchen slams open.

"What the fuck?"

I glance over my shoulder and try my best not to react. The woman is walking around with an oversized t-shirt with the logo for Camos and Cupcakes across it. It hits her mid-thigh. I'm pretty sure she's wearing shorts under it. But maybe not.

It shouldn't be sexy, but I can already feel my body reacting to her legs' bare, smooth skin. I've seen thousands of women's legs, which have not affected me like this. I mean, they're legs, for God's sake.

I need sleep.

"Hey, Howard, wake up!"

I shake my head but still feel the tell-tale signs of arousal as it courses through my body. A typical reaction to shapely, bare legs on a woman I can't stand. And she is short, but those legs seem longer than any of the models I've dated. Not one of them has been under five eight.

"What are you doing?"

"I'm making my breakfast."

She looks at her phone.

"It's eight in the morning.

"Uh, yeah."

"Is this a habit with you?"

"Breakfast?"

She rolls her eyes. "No, being up at the crack of dawn."

"It's after eight in the morning. That's hardly the crack of dawn."

I turn around to start to work on my omelet. I need her to go away and put on some clothes. My hands shake, and I close my eyes and count down from ten.

"What the hell is that?"

I barely control the yelp that scratches my throat,

fighting to get out. Scowling, I open my eyes and continue to work on my breakfast.

"It's an omelet."

"Egg white?"

"Yes."

"Ick."

I make a huge mistake by turning to look down at her. Her hair is a mess, and she has creases in her skin that I assume are from her pillowcase. Her eyes are barely opened, and her lips seem fuller than they were yesterday. She's kind of a hot mess and really cute.

Nope. Not today, Satan.

I will not think those thoughts. She's my enemy. Besides, I don't go for cute. Cute, sexy women are a problem. They make me think I might want more, and she is not my type. Not personality-wise, at least.

"You don't like something healthy? Color me surprised."

She snorts. Her cat jumps on the counter to watch the exchange.

"How do you know I don't like to eat healthy?"

"You have no fruits or vegetables in the house, and your cereal choices are questionable."

She rolls her eyes and walks over to the coffee pot. I focus on the back of her head and not her legs. If I don't, I will lose all focus and start drooling. What is it about this woman that has my head spinning? She isn't my usual type at all, especially in behavior. She could care less what I think of her and has no problem letting me know. I hate to admit it, but I think I've gotten lazy. Since being named one of the most innovative tech people under thirty, I have gotten a lot of attention. Supermodels like to be seen with tech millionaire/billionaire types. Dating might have been a hassle, but I didn't even have to try hard to find dates.

Is that why she intrigues me?

She fills up the coffee pot and makes a bunch of noise, humming while she does it. I focus back on her and realize it isn't the coffee pot my grandmother usually has here, so I assume it's Avery's.

"I hope you like your coffee strong."

My eyebrows shoot up. "You're going to let me drink your coffee?"

"As long as that's not a euphemism for sex, then yes."

After that announcement, she scurries out of the kitchen. I blink and look at Meredith.

"Did that just happen?"

She licks her paw, jumps down from the counter, and stalks off after her mistress.

I have interacted with this impossible woman for less than five minutes, and I'm already discombobulated. This isn't going to be easy, and I remind myself of that. Avery O'Bryan isn't stupid. She graduated early from high school and college. Hell, she has an MBA. I learned that much about her. There are a ton of papers she's written and not just crap posted online. She's had articles published in some magazines, including academic-leaning magazines and journals. She has a reputation in the business. Sure, I think her business is silly. And no, I will not admit that out loud. As a man who has developed apps, I am not about to admit to the world that I find much of it frivolous. Granted, most of our work now is security for the tech world, but the company still makes a lot of money off apps.

Don't get me wrong. There's nothing wrong with fun,

but for someone who makes a living at it the way she does… it's weird. Maybe I'm grasping. She does help people build their businesses through their social media platforms. Travis and Nancy have taken lessons from her, and she's helped many nonprofits. She posts a lot of that stuff on her own page about that but not much about herself. In fact, it's as if she doesn't want anyone to know anything personal about her.

The women I date post their entire lives online, although I've told all of them they should be more careful about that. Avery—a woman who seems like the type that would post personal details—doesn't. It makes her a puzzle, and I love figuring out puzzles.

I draw in a deep breath and push out those thoughts. Getting tangled up even more with Avery O'Bryan would be a mistake, and I need to keep my head screwed on tight.

Otherwise, I could lose access to my house for the rest of the year.

Chapter Nine

Jon

I brush my teeth and pull on a pair of PJ bottoms, then settle on my bed, trying to get my feelings under control. I've always had a problem with being overwhelmed. Too many thoughts crowd my brain, and every nerve in my body seems to be on fire. I've dealt with it for years, but it gets worse when I go through bouts of insomnia.

It won't get any better with Mr. Egg White Omelet down there.

Just thinking about him standing there in a pair of jeans, hugging that amazing butt of his, and the black t-shirt that stretched out across a surprisingly massive chest. It isn't like Ed, one of my brother's best friends, but very few men are built like my favorite baker.

Jon is so lanky. I guess I expected him not to…what? Not to have muscles? And finding him in the kitchen cooking breakfast—even if it is gross egg whites—was…my body is vibrating with excitement still. My hands are shaking.

What the hell is wrong with me?

I fall back on my bed, closing my eyes.

"Meow."

I open one eye to find Meredith staring down at me.

"I was sleeping just fine until you woke me up."

"Meow."

"Exactly."

I know that I can handle this. It's not like I haven't been attracted to a man I needed to avoid before now. That's a lie. A. Big. Fat. Lie.

Me: *SOS*

Liv: *Who is this? What have you done with Avery?*

Me: *Liv! I know you have my number saved.*

Liv: *Yes, but the real Avery is never up at eight in the morning.*

Me: *That was before my roommate showed up bright and early this morning.*

Cora: *Hold on, I have to tell Bitsy Reynolds to get bent.*

I roll my eyes. Cora and Bitsy have a rivalry that goes back to high school.

Gerri: *Just got off. Did you say that you have a roommate?*

Liv: *When did you get a roommate?*

Me: *Estella said I could stay in the house if I shared it with Jon while he's here.*

Liv: *Why don't you move back here with me?*

Because I don't want to. I love my sisters, but they all act like I don't have my life together. I mean, yeah, I haven't had a good night of sleep in days—okay, weeks—but I've always been like that. My ADHD goes crazy at night, and I can't shut it down.

Me: *I like this house. Plus, I work at night.*

Lie, but they don't need to know that I'm barely working right now.

Cora: *So, who is this Jon, and do I need to send Mike down there to talk with him?*

Cora's husband is a Department of Public Safety Officer. I roll my eyes. Maybe I should have just texted our brother Fritz. Amazingly, he is not overbearing like my sisters.

Me: *No.*

Liv: *I talked to Nancy. She said Jon's got his issues, but he's a good guy.*

Me: *What issues?*

Cora: *And do they involve a well in his basement where he lowers the lotion for his captives to use?*

I can't help the smile. Cora has always been the smart ass of the family. I mean, we all are, but she's like the queen.

Liv: *No. He's a computer expert who has issues with people.*

Cora: *Like killing them?*

Before I can type out a response, my phone rings. It's Liv.

"What? We were texting."

"It's hard to have a conversation with Cora after she has a run-in with Bitsy. She gets really sassy."

"Yeah." I snort. "But it's always fun taking her out drinking after those run-ins."

She ignores my comment. "So, tell me, what was the SOS for?"

I sigh. "You know I don't like people in my space."

"Not true. Every time I visited you in college, you had a ton of people around."

I hate my family.

"People I liked."

"So, you don't like him. Come and stay with me. Or stay with Mason."

Liv's boyfriend lives next door to her.

"Yeah, that would so be something Mason would like."

I hear a murmur, and I smile. "Got company this morning?"

She sighs. "He just returned from taking the kids to school. He was here to make them breakfast. And stop trying to change the subject."

"I…I have a problem."

"What's that?"

I close my eyes. I should have texted this because it's embarrassing to admit to my sister out loud.

"I might find him attractive."

"Well, yeah."

"What's that supposed to mean?"

"I looked him up on the Internet. I've seen pictures of him." Another murmur from Mason. "No, love, you are the only man for me."

"So, you see my problem. He has to leave."

"You can control yourself."

"You say I have no self-control."

"You don't when it comes to cereal or chocolate or coffee. But you've always been a bit reserved in your relationships. At least since you dated Chet. Just ignore Jon until he goes away. Nancy says he never sticks around here for long, so I assume he'll be gone soon."

"You're right." I release a breath I had no idea I had been holding onto. "Besides, I have a lot to do."

"Yeah?"

"I'm working at the senior center, and then there's that dude renting the house out back."

"What guy?"

"He's renting the house behind mine, and he gives me the creeps."

"Wait, maybe you need to talk to Josh."

"Naw. I'm sure everyone would tell me I was imagining it."

That's what they tell me most of the time when I think someone is watching me. I've always had an active imagination, and with my interest in Murder, Death, Kill shows, it just goes crazy.

"Have you talked to him?"

"No."

"But you think he's a creep?"

"Yeah. Don't worry about it. I have Meredith to protect me."

"She's a cat. What is she going to do?"

"Her ancestors were tigers. She is fierce."

Said fierce cat rolls over on her back for a belly rub.

"Okay. Just promise me if you have any other worries about the neighbor that you go to Josh."

"Why?"

"Because he's the sheriff."

"No. I mean, why are you saying that?"

"As goofy as you are, little sister, you read people very well."

"Okay. But I haven't talked to the guy."

"Still."

"I said okay." I sigh. "I need coffee and don't want Mr. Egg White to drink it all."

"Egg white?"

"That's what I'm calling Jon."

"Good idea. Keep calling him that so he doesn't know you want to jump his bones."

I gasp. "I never said I wanted to jump his bones."

"Didn't have to. I can hear it in your voice."

My phone hasn't stopped vibrating against my cheek, telling me our sisters are texting.

"Kiss Mason for me."

"I will. Lunch?"

"Nope. I told you I'm going to the senior center."

"Okay. Come for dinner."

"Too much to do." And to be honest, my sister isn't the best cook.

"Mason's cooking."

"Why didn't you say that first? You know I can't pass up that."

"Brat. Love you."

"Back atcha."

When I hang up the phone, I scroll through the long conversation Cora and Gerri had and their realization that Liv and I were probably chatting. Just to get me back, Gerri sends me a pic of bagels. God, New York has excellent bagels. I miss them.

My stomach grumbles, and I frown. I had dinner last night but ate it early since I went to Estella's. I tend to eat dinner later. Okay, sometimes I have a late midnight snack of three bowls of cereal.

I look around for Meredith but don't see her in my room. She's probably downstairs somewhere. Hopefully, she will be terrorizing Jon. She's a great judge of character. She hisses over the fence at the weird guy renting the house behind us.

With everything that has happened in the last forty-eight hours, I completely forgot about Creepy Dude. That's what I'm calling him. With soft steps, I wander over to my back window and peek between the blinds. He's standing there, staring into my backyard.

He looks normal, or most people would say that. He's probably a little older than I am, with a bald head and eyes too small for his face. He has to be over six feet and weighs over three hundred pounds.

Then, all of a sudden, he looks up at my window.

"Eek!" I step back. There was no way he could see me. Right? I mean, I peeked through the blinds.

"Are you all right?"

I jump about five feet. My heart is hammering against my chest, and my head is spinning. When I turn, I find Jon standing in my doorway.

"What?" I ask, my voice harsh in the quiet room.

"I heard you scream. Meredith freaked out."

I look down at my cat daughter standing at my feet. Bending down, I scoop her up, then hold her close to my chest. She purrs, the vibrations filtering over my body, calming my nerves.

"I'm fine. The shifty neighbor behind us might have seen me scoping him out."

"Shifty neighbor? Mr. Tolbert?"

"No, Mr. Tolbert moved to Dallas to live with his son. He rents the house out now, and there's a weirdo back there looking into our backyard."

"So, he was sneaking a peek at his neighbor out in the

open? I mean, at least he's not spying between the blinds."

I frown at him. Ugh, Jon's the worst. Most people don't call me out on my shit. "Fine. Don't take me seriously about this dude. There is something off about him."

"Come on, your coffee is done, and it tastes amazing."

I blink at the change of subject. "What are you up to?"

"Nothing. I just…never mind. I'm going down to have my breakfast."

Then he disappears so fast that I blink. What the freak?

I look down at Meredith, who I'm holding like a baby, swaying her. "I guess coffee sounds good. Now, we have to go to dinner tonight. Do you want to stay here?"

She purrs.

"I know, but they have a big dumb dog. Don't get me wrong. I love Houdini, but he might want to eat you."

Another meow.

"Okay. We'll take your carrier just in case."

I make my way downstairs on jittery legs. It might be the lack of sleep or the fact that I'm apparently being stalked by my backyard neighbor, but I know better. As I step into the kitchen, I see Jon sitting at the table reading over his tablet. He's…okay, he's attractive. He's got one of those square jaws, and Lordy, his forearms are to die for.

He must feel me looking at him because he glances up at me. Suddenly, I'm sixteen and a freshman in college, and I'm scared that everyone will laugh at me.

"Are you sure you're okay?"

I nod but don't say anything else as I head over to get my coffee. Grabbing my favorite cup, I fill it and then doctor it up with enough sugar and milk to make me happy.

"That's a lot of sugar."

Of course. He has to say stuff about my coffee. I turn around and lean against the counter. "Do you have any other comments you would like to make? Any judgments on my behavior?"

Another glance and my knees feel weak. Those eyes are piercing. Jesus, this guy.

"No. If you aren't sleeping well, that might be one reason." He nods towards the sugar container.

"Or maybe it might be that someone tried to break into my house."

"I wasn't told someone decided to steal my house."

"Not your house."

"Or I would have ensured Josh was here to drag you out."

I roll my eyes and sit in the chair opposite him, setting my phone on the table. It continues to buzz, but I ignore it. Meredith rubs against my legs, so I lean and take her in my arms again. She sits on my lap, looking at Jon, but he keeps glancing at my phone.

"Aren't you going to check those?"

"Those?"

"The texts."

"How do you know they are texts?"

"I can see the screen."

"Rude."

"You're the one who laid it face up."

He's right, but instead of giving him that, I just keep petting Meredith.

"Really? You're just going to let that keep going on and on?"

I shrug. I know it's my sisters, and I can read through

them later. Important issues get phone calls. The fact that's bothering him—it's just icing on the cake I would like to have for breakfast. I wonder if the diner has cake ready for the day.

His eye starts to twitch, and I smile. I hope it's the one that Fritz calls my villain smile. He says when I smile like that, people should know they are fucked.

"You know you don't scare me with that smile."

"Hmm," is all I say to that.

"How can you just let the texts keep coming and not answer them?"

I shrug. "I learned how to put the brakes on being connected to my phone all the time. It's a hazard in my industry."

This comment catches his attention, and his eyes focus on me once more. God, I am going to have dreams about those eyes.

"You have an industry?"

"Yes."

"You call teaching people how to post on social media an industry?"

Disdain drips from every word. "You create apps for a living."

"I've created a few, but my primary focus is security. People spend too much time on social media."

"I agree with you to an extent. That's why I have no problem ignoring texts. But I do have a question for you."

"Shoot."

"Don't you find it hypocritical to develop apps and have such hatred for social media?"

"First, I don't have hatred for social media. I just think that time away from apps is a good thing."

I agree, but I refuse to let him know that I do. Truth is, I teach my folks that social media might be essential to build their brand, but you can't make it your entire life. Stepping away from time to time is necessary.

"Don't you date models? They basically spend their entire lives online these days."

His mouth straightens into a thin line. Oh, I hit a nerve.

"I didn't say that I…wait, we were arguing about your job."

"Were we?"

And just like last night, he gets that grumpy look. And oh, fuck me, it's hot. Maybe Liv wasn't wrong about me wanting to jump his bones. Ugh. Smoldering is no good. I can't have him sit in a t-shirt and jeans—old, conform to his ass kind of jeans—and look at me like that. I will do something foolish.

"I have to get ready."

I put Meredith down, grab my coffee, and rush out of the room. I can't be having thoughts about Jon Howard. I mean, okay, thoughts are okay. I have thoughts about Travis Fillmore, but I would never jump his bones. First, I don't poach. Second, he doesn't even know I exist past being a friend. Third, Nancy is scary AF.

I get to the top of the stairs a little out of breath because I practically ran up them and decide to go out for breakfast. I'm volunteering at the senior center today. Hopefully, they will distract me from this insane need to lick Jon's chest.

Dammit, now that I had that thought, it's all I can think about.

"I'm fucked."

"Meow," Meredith says from my bed. I glance over at her.

"Exactly."

Chapter Ten

Avery

Meredith and I arrive at the Senior Center just after eleven that morning. It has been a morning. First, Jon showing up early. Then my skeevy neighbor thought I was peeking through the blinds at him. Afterward, coffee with Jon left me a little discombobulated.

It has to be why I stubbed my toe, which caused me to cuss up a storm. I thought I heard Jon laughing, but I might have been imagining it. Also, I fell when trying to put my pants on. I mean, I've done it before, but I'm embarrassed that Jon heard that, along with a few more cuss words that would make Fritz happy.

I draw in a deep breath and open the front door to the center. The ladies are gathered, sitting at one of the tables, drinking coffee and gossiping.

I saw all the posts on the JSE about Jon showing up at my house. The comments about how he's living with me have been…cheeky would be the best word I could use for that. Of course, Mrs. James had a few choice comments about us living in sin, which gave me all kinds of ideas. All of them involved a naked Jon and my tongue.

I bet Jon hasn't read them, so he has no idea there's gossip about him. I can't wait until he sees it. If it bothers him, he might return to the big house. That would make everything better.

Even as I think about it, I push away the melancholy. I don't even like the man. How could I? He probably gets up at the same time Fritz and Liv do. Fritz was in the Army for years, and Liv is a former military wife. Getting up early is in their blood. I know. They're sick puppies.

Me...I like being up all night. I need to get a nap in today, or tonight could be rough. I stifle a yawn.

"Avery, dear, are you going to join us?" Mrs. Petersen calls out.

If there is a queen bee in this group, then Mrs. Petersen is it. She keeps everyone in order, ensuring they show up for all the civic duties they need to volunteer for.

I place the little pillow Meredith claimed as hers on the floor and leave her to her late morning nap. I think I should have been a cat. All the treats, people clean up after you, and you nap all day. That sounds like a life I could really get into.

I walk over, smiling. My siblings have always found my affinity for hanging out with the LOLs weird. I don't see how I wouldn't want to. My grandmother moved in to help raise me when Mom opened her dance studio. We were the best of friends, always getting into trouble together. Grannie Pam always said it was because we understood each other. We were both Aquariuses, which meant we saw the world differently than everyone else.

"Good morning, ladies. Are we working on TikTok this morning?"

"In a minute. Why don't you get some coffee and have a seat?"

I smile and do as Mrs. Petersen suggests. As I return, the door opens, and Estella steps into the center. I blink, surprised by her appearance. She is an insomniac like me and usually attends all-night events. She rarely shows up to the day events unless they are something special.

"Hey, Estella," I call out and grab another cup to get her some coffee.

I make my way to the table, setting the cup in front of Estella, then settle into the chair next to her.

"Thank you, Avery," she says.

"No problem."

"I am saying that all of that album is about Taylor."

That comes from Mrs. Denton. I turn to her. "What are y'all talking about?"

"Freddy here had never listened to Harry's album Fine Line."

"Oh. Yeah, it's about Taylor."

I should know. I've been a Swiftie from the moment I heard her sing. I wasn't even a teenager when her first album came out, but I've loved her since I listened to the songs on *Debut,* as all true Swifties call her first album. I've stuck with her through everything, even the #Taylorisover crap. I knew she would bounce back. Music is her first love, not the celebrity.

"Are you sure?" Freddy, AKA Mrs. Fredericks, asks.

"Yeah. I mean, one of the songs is Golden. Like *Falling,*

she had that scene in *Cardigan* with the piano and all the water."

"That is such a sad song."

"It's just like 1989 is about him."

"Really?"

I nod. "Mostly."

"You know so much about Taylor Swift." This comes from Mrs. Petersen.

I glance over at her. "I do. Been a fan since the first time I heard her."

The next few minutes are spent discussing which albums the ladies like the most. I find it weird that Mrs. James, who said I was living in sin, is a Lady Gaga fan. I would think she wouldn't be so judgmental.

"I take it my grandson is settling in this morning."

Estella doesn't ask a question. She makes a pronounce-ment. Like she ordered it, and it should happen. That's Estella for you. And the entire room goes silent, and I can almost feel all the LOLs leaning forward.

"I guess. He showed up at that crack of dawn, made some disgusting breakfast, then went to work in the office."

Of course, I leave out all the yearning I did. The only way I would admit to it is to annoy him.

"Oh. I hope he didn't get in the way."

I shake my head. "I'm not really…no. I like to work on my laptop in the den."

She nods knowingly. It's weird how much we seem to understand each other. We're an odd pair of friends—I guess that's what I would call us. She doesn't seem to invite other people to her house for family dinners. I liked them better when Jon wasn't there.

Still, she seems to understand my anxiety issues. I hide them from just about everyone, including my family. Whenever I act weird or say something outlandish, it's a way to divert their attention from whatever freak-out I am having. If I act quirky, they roll their eyes and go on their way. The one thing I couldn't take was the pity most of them would feel for me if they realized that many of my quirks were cover.

I shove that thought aside and focus on the ladies. People might think the LOLs are just old biddies with nothing better to do than gossip about what's happening in town. But they are so much more than that.

They organized a knit-in to send blankets to kids in Ukraine, they handle just about all the food drives in town, and they have worked on adding more diversity to the city council. These ladies have it going on.

"So, what do you think about Jon?" This comes from Mrs. Reynolds. She and her husband had a veterinarian practice for years. Their daughter and son run it now.

I shrug. I don't want to let on how I feel about Jon. If I start ranting about him, they will think I'm attracted to him. I *am* drawn to him, but what woman wouldn't be? He's hot in a totally nerdy way. I bet he even has vests.

"Avery, dear, you are okay with him living there, right?" Estella asks.

"Oh, yeah. I don't actually worry about him. I'm more worried about the guy behind us."

"Tsk, tsk," Mrs. Petersen says. "I don't know what that man's problem is. I smiled and waved at him, and he frowned at me and went on his way."

"You know how some of these people are when they

rent houses in small towns," Mrs. Reynolds says. "They say they like small towns and want the peace and friendly faces, but when you try to talk to them, they think you're going to mug them."

I smile at that. Mrs. Reynolds is just an inch or two over five feet and probably weighs less than a hundred pounds. Given his height and weight, Creepy Dude would be a lot to tackle.

All of them nod, and I see they are gearing up for a lengthy discussion on why small towns are fantastic, so I cut them off.

"Why don't we get started on your ideas for the LOL TikTok? Does everyone have a theme they want to explore?"

It's the one thing I told them to have ready when we started today.

They all nod, and we start to work. The time flies by as it always does with these ladies. Interestingly enough, Estella has TikTok on her phone but doesn't want to post. She tried to keep tabs on her new friends, although she didn't say that. Also, I know she wants to watch Nancy and Travis' videos.

By the time we start to pack up, it's been over two hours. Everyone heads off, but Estella hangs back.

"I wanted to make sure that you really are okay with Jon living with you."

I would love to tell her no, I am not okay with him there. But I know what she's asking. She wants to see if I feel safe. And while I am uncomfortable with my own attraction, I don't feel he would hurt me.

"Yes."

"Avery," she says, in that voice that I bet gets people

worried she will fire them. I don't work for her, and it takes a lot to scare me.

"Seriously, Estella. He doesn't give me creepy vibes, and you know I'm good at picking out a bad guy."

"Thanks to Chet."

Yep, one night, I talked to her about Chet. When you're eighteen and never really dated—and a nerd about to graduate after only three years in college—a hot guy paying attention to you makes you lose your mind. Or at least it did to me. I wasn't equipped to have one of the football players pay attention to me. By the time I figured out what a horrible person he was, I was damaged. Not physically, but emotionally. Now I know how to pick up on the cues I missed all those years ago.

"Yes, but learning how to handle men was an important task, and I did it in record time."

We have that in common. Only Estella was married to her asshole. In those days, divorce wasn't very common, and she would have been left with nothing, and he would have taken her children away from her.

"Good. You know how I feel about the rest of my grandchildren, but Nancy and Jon have always been good eggs."

I nod as she glances over at Meredith.

"Is she settling in okay?"

"Yep. She still hates Josh, though."

She hissed at him when he walked by today. We were sitting on the bench in front of the diner. I couldn't go inside with Meredith, so I ordered food, and they brought it to me. Josh stopped to ask me how I was doing, and Meredith sounded like she wanted to kill him.

"That's odd. I thought all females liked him."

"Well, not every girl likes boys."

She nods in that world-weary way. I get that there is even more beneath the surface of Estella that I will probably never know.

"I promise that Jon is annoying but not scary."

"Annoying?"

"First of all, he keeps saying I stole his house."

"Jon always thought that was his house."

The tone of her voice is different. I can't put my finger on what it is about, but there's something about that house and Jon. And dammit, I love a good mystery.

"Second of all, he eats egg whites for breakfast."

"It's healthy."

"I know. And yes, I know I have horrible eating habits compared to everyone over twenty. Still, I don't like being judged about it."

She nods again. "Understandable."

"Did you need anything else? I need to get over to my sister's for dinner. Mason is cooking."

"No, dear, you go on. I'll lock up."

Little known fact. Estella owns this building. Most people in town don't realize she donated it because she did it under an affiliate corporation. I bet Mrs. Petersen figured it out, especially when it seemed to be a place to gather right after all the LOLs complained about not having a building for their meetings.

I look over at Meredith. "Ready to go?"

She slowly rises as if she is one of the LOLs, then wanders over to me, first stopping to rub up against Estella.

Pleasure washes over the older woman's expression as she leans down to pet Meredith.

"You should get a cat."

"That's exactly what I need. I already live in a big house by myself. Let's add some cats to have people call me the crazy old cat lady."

I want to argue with her because pets can be good for lonely people, but Estella would never agree with me that she's lonely.

"Well, I'll bring Meredith over later this week."

"Yes. Come for lunch. It's going to be warmer in a day or two. We can eat on the terrace."

Yeah, I grew up with a back porch, not a terrace, but Estella is from another world.

"That sounds like fun."

After waiting for Estella to lock up, I head off to my car and decide to go to my sister's place early. A little nap is in order, in my opinion.

Chapter Eleven

Jon

At about eleven, Avery leaves. Blessed peace fills the house. Granted, I thought she would leave the cat, but she took Meredith with her, leash and all. She even hauled a little pillow with her. I shake my head and work on setting up a base of operations in the office.

I step in and smile. After my dad left my mom, we would come back into town, and my grandmother always had this house available for us, which became my favorite room.

Running down each side, there are floor-to-ceiling book-shelves packed with books from my childhood and teen years. A massive window looks out into the backyard and the birdbath. I would sit here for hours, working on my computer and watching the birds. I know my grandmother planted perennials that drew in butterflies and hummingbirds.

But the masterpiece of the room is a massive desk in front of the window. It's dark wood and ornate, which goes against things I usually like in an office. My tastes run more to sleek and modern, but I love this desk. So many memories rush forward. I actually came up with the idea of the JSE and designed it at this desk.

I put my laptop on the top of the desk and plug it in. I'm settled in for some work when my phone rings. It's Nancy. I would generally ignore her, but since I'm in town and she's not filming, there is no telling what she would do. More than likely, she would just show up.

"Why are you calling?"

"I love you too." Then she makes obscene kissy sounds on the phone.

"Ugh, stop that." Even as I say it, I smile. The only good memories I have of Juniper growing up were with Nancy. I have always suspected my grandmother ensured my mother had sole custody if Mom agreed to bring me to Juniper. I spent a lot of time with Nancy since we're close in age.

"You love me. Admit it."

"No."

She just laughs. We have a massive family, but Nancy and I can only stand each other. We bonded over the absurdity of our fathers and the fact that we think most of our cousins and half-siblings are idiots.

"I have Liv, who wants to talk to you."

"Liv?" It sounds oddly familiar. I'm trying to remember if I know anyone by that name.

"Your new roommate's sister."

Ugh. That's it. I rarely forget details. It's one of the things I pride myself on, but since meeting Avery, I can't seem to keep anything straight.

"I don't have a roommate."

"Sure, buddy."

Then the phone gets jostled around.

"Hello, Jon?" A soft yet firm voice says over the phone.

"Yes?"

"I'm sorry for using your cousin, but I wanted to invite you to dinner tonight."

I frown. "Is there a reason?"

She chuckles. "Yeah. Dinner. Plus, I'll be honest with you. I need to know you're a good guy. Nancy and Mason say you are, but you're living with my baby sister. I just…"

I might not have a big family, but I have Nancy and would feel the same way. Inwardly, I sigh. This means I need to go to dinner with her family, which will definitely not be a great experience. I don't do well with them. And by them, I mean people.

"Okay."

"Oh, great. Mason will be glad to have a balanced number. He says he's always outnumbered by the women."

"Glad to be of service."

Instead of getting upset with my sarcasm, she just laughs. "You have no idea. We'll be eating around six if that's okay with you."

"No problem." But even as I say it, my nerves stretch tight. I don't do well with people in general. This is definitely not going to go well at all.

"I'll have Nancy text my address."

"That will be fine."

"Oh, do you have any food allergies?"

No one has ever asked me that, but she is a mom. It probably comes with the territory.

"Nope. Just to penicillin."

"I'll tell Mason not to make any of that. Thanks, Jon."

Then the phone gets handed back to Nancy.

"You are going to dinner two nights in a row with people!"

Nancy says it in that way I know she thinks she's funny. She is such an ass.

"I blame you for this."

"You can blame that *model* for it. I'm assuming that's why you're here."

She never addresses the women I date by their names. It's not out of jealousy. She says it's because they are all too stupid for me. And I can't argue with her on that. None of them have been exceptionally bright. She also says they should have more respect for themselves.

I can tell she's walking away from Liv, probably to go to her office.

"Partially."

"Partially? I heard a rumor that she was stalking you."

"Where did you hear that?"

"Your mama. I talked to her this morning."

The women in my family are conspiring against me. Although I don't know what they're working towards, but something is coming. I can feel it. It's an itch beneath my skin, warning me that something is afoot.

And now I'm thinking like Sherlock Holmes. This situation is really driving me crazy.

"Why would she call you?"

"Because I'm amazing."

"Nancy."

There is no mistaking the warning in my voice.

"She's worried about you. She said that brunch mess was her fault and worried you were mad at her."

"I'm not."

"Okay." Her tone tells me she doesn't believe me.

"How worried should I be about dinner tonight?"

"Hmm, not too much. I mean, Liv is a sweetie, and you know Mason. He's a good guy. As long as Fritz isn't there, you should be fine."

"Fritz?"

"Her brother."

"Oh, right."

"Although, I will say he's not overly protective of the sisters. Liv says that Fritz thinks they are grown-ass women and can take care of themselves."

"Yeah. I can't imagine having that many siblings."

"Right? I mean, it sounds like a nightmare. So loud."

I smile. We both have half or step-siblings, but we never claimed them, and the feeling from them is mutual. They are as devoid of a moral compass like our fathers. The two of us are closer to each other than we are to any of them.

"So, you have no idea how long you'll be in town?"

I shake my head, then remember she can't see me. "No. I don't have much on deck." And I need to make a decision about my company.

"Okay. You know you'll have to come over and have dinner with us. And by having dinner, I mean we'll order in and pretend that I made it."

"Yeah, I would appreciate the ordering of the food. You are not a good cook."

"Look who's talking. You should ask your new roomie to bake."

"I don't have…wait, she knows how to cook?"

"Why would you think she can't?"

"She has about five different types of cereal."

"Her brother is one of the Camos and Cupcakes dudes. She apparently can make a mean cupcake. And I know how much you love those."

Okay, that is my one significant weakness. I do love a good cupcake. I've heard about the three former Army buddies who opened a bakery in San Antonio. There's a rumor they may even open one in Juniper Springs.

"Well, there is no evidence in the kitchen of any baking."

She tsks. "Poor Jon."

"Get bent."

She laughs, and I smile. She might irritate me, but we have always been more like siblings than cousins. I have always been thankful I had my mother, but Nancy's parents are both horrible. She spent her summers with our grandmother, and since I spent a lot of time down here during those summers, we were close. We're opposites in many ways but we understand each other's issues.

"Well, I need to get to work."

"Liar."

I can't fight the chuckle. See, my cousin knows me.

"Okay. I'm going to cyber-stalk this dude moving in with my mom."

There's a beat of silence.

"He has an excellent reputation, Jon."

"I know, but you…" I sigh. "I don't want her hurt again."

"Okay. Just don't get any PIs or anything. If that got out, it would be worse than that model telling everyone you're moving in together."

I stand up. "What?"

"Oh, I thought that's why you were in Juniper."

"No. I'm not moving in with her. We never even slept over at each other's places."

We spent a few nights together, but we used hotels when she was in Europe. I have avoided having women at my place since I dated Gia, the Italian supermodel. She started leaving things at my apartment after the first night. When I broke it off with her, she had a suitcase full of clothes and jewelry there.

"Oh well, she didn't give an interview, but I saw it on *TMZ* this morning."

Which means my mother will see it before long. Dammit.

"Let me go so I can get my people to issue a statement."

"You could ignore it."

"I would if it was just me, but this could affect stockholders and their bottom line."

"You should just sell that company and travel or something."

I have been thinking about doing that. I've had offers through the years and ignored them all. That's until Trevor approached me. I know he would treat my employees well. I just don't know what I would do with myself.

"Earth to Jon."

"Sorry," I mumble. "I need to get out in front of this or try to at this point."

"And call your mom."

"I will after lunch. She's teaching this morning."

After getting off the phone with Nancy, I make a quick call to my PR department to make sure they know how to handle the statement about Sienna. It's annoying to deal with this sort of thing. My grandmother is probably right. I should stop dating those kinds of women. I'm not about to settle down with a woman who would rather be in front of the camera for most of the day.

I grab another cup of coffee and start my research. It isn't hard to find information about Ted. He's a former Cowboy, so there's info about him everywhere. What I need is more than the fact that he was married before. He apparently leads a very private life except for his charity work. I don't want to hire a private eye, but I have a security team for things like this, so I contact them to give them Ted's name for research.

After hanging up with them, I think about my next move. I have a terrible feeling about Avery. She seems like someone who would stay here just out of spite. Yes, I have someone already looking into her. My grandmother is sharp and can handle herself, but I never take anything for granted. Estella is worth billions. For some reason, Avery's made a connection with her. It's odd, to say the least. Avery isn't even thirty, but she's hanging out with my grandmother. Estella has never been anyone's idea of a good time, especially a millennial.

My phone rings, and I see my mother's name. I could let it go to voicemail, but I have learned not to do that. She's not overbearing, but she knows when I'm trying to avoid her.

"You rang."

"Your grandmother says you have a roommate," my mother asks. I roll my eyes. I don't know what Estella is up to, but she has other motives for making me live with Avery.

As cold-hearted as she is, I thought my grandmother would kick Avery out.

"I have a housemate."

"A woman."

"A thief."

"She's a criminal?" I hear the amusement in my mother's voice.

"Not officially, but she stole my house."

There is a long pause. "Jon, are you okay?"

Why does everyone keep asking me that? "Yes."

"You aren't getting stressed out, are you?"

"No."

"Jonathan Howard."

"Okay, a little. She's…she doesn't believe in schedules."

"Oh."

"The only food she keeps on hand is fifty types of cereal."

"Hmm."

"And, well, she has kind of a filthy mouth."

Jesus, when Avery cusses, I can't control the way my body reacts. I try not to let my mother know how I feel about that. It's not like she used profanity in front of me, but I could hear her cussing while she was upstairs getting ready. It's not anything I have ever been into before. Never really thought about it, to tell you the truth. But for some reason, hearing Avery mutter *fuck me*… set all my nerves on edge. And not in a bad way.

"Nothing you aren't used to. I know what some of your programmers are like."

I shake my head. Sometimes I want to tell my mother I have done more with my life than just computer stuff. It's in the past, but there's always been this little part of me that wanted to share my work with the CIA.

"Is there a reason you called?"

"You're my baby boy."

"A fact that both of us have known for a while. I don't see the reason for calling all of a sudden."

She continues on as if I didn't make a smart-ass remark.

"And after getting off the phone with Estella, I thought maybe I should call you. She's worried about you."

I snort.

"Jonathon."

"You've used my full name twice in one phone call. I guess I must be in trouble." She doesn't laugh like I expect her to.

"Mom, I'm fine. I promise. I'm worried about this woman because she seems to have gotten her clutches into Estella. That isn't normal."

"Yes, it is an odd relationship, but according to Estella, she was raised by her grandmother. Seems like Avery might be comfortable with your grandmother."

"Still. Have you known Estella to ever do anything out of the kindness of her heart?"

"Yes."

I blink. "You have?"

"We had the life we did, thanks to Estella. She isn't a warm and fuzzy kind of person, but she did take care of us. Let's be honest. She could have fought for custody in court. She didn't, and I'll always be grateful for that."

I sigh. I know she's right. "Okay. But, like I said, I want to keep an eye on this woman. She's odd, to say the least. She brought a damned cat to dinner last night."

My mother laughs. "That must have been a hoot."

"Yeah. I don't think I've ever seen anything so weird in Grandmother's house." I smile, thinking about it.

"Listen, I just wanted to let you know what's happening in the real world. *TMZ* is reporting—"

"Nancy called. I have the PR folks on it."

"Well, then, I'll let you go. I have a department meeting in a few minutes. Talk to you soon."

"Love you."

"Love you, too."

Once we hang up, I decide to get to work. I came here for a reason, to get away for some peace and quiet to work.

Chapter Twelve

Avery

I stare in disbelief at my sister. It's not often any of my sisters can pull one over on me, but Liv has done it with little to no fanfare.

"You did what now?"

"I invited Jon over for dinner."

I frown at her. "Why didn't you tell me this before I came over here tonight?"

"I didn't think you would object to it."

That's a damn dirty lie, and she knows it. Liv is horrible at lying, and right now, she's looking everywhere in the dining room to avoid making eye contact with me.

"You thought wrong."

"He's probably on his way over."

"Yeah, he is. Why would you do this to me?"

"We needed another dude," Sammy, my nephew, says,

I glance down at him, then drop to his level. "What? I thought I was your partner in crime, buddy."

"You are. But Mason says this is a girl house, and having another dude around will even things out."

I look up at my sister, who's smothering a laugh. And just for that, I'm thankful. Until she hooked up with Mason, Liv took too much on and was way too serious. Now she laughs more easily, and she seems lighter somehow. That's what happens when you find your soul mate.

My heart sighs. It was so sweet watching her fall for Mason, and now, he makes her happy.

"I think I need to chat with Mason," I say just as there's a knock at the door. Houdini starts barking and running toward the front door. Meredith—who has been following the insane golden retriever around like he's her best friend—trots along with him. It's like she's forgotten she's a cat.

"Oops, too late. Go let your guest in."

"He's not my guest."

"Then your roommate."

"Housemate. We aren't sharing a room."

She smiles. "If you say so."

But before I can respond, I hear Sammy talking to someone. Yep, that boy loves to greet anyone at the front door.

"Are there any adults here?"

"That's debatable," I say as I enter the hallway. My breath catches because, well, it just does whenever I see this man. How does he look so handsome and romantic when I know he has the personality of a dead mouse? He should look like a ghoul, but instead, he's temptation dressed in jeans.

"Jon, this is Sammy, my nephew. Sammy, your mother has told you not to open the door to strangers."

"Yeah, but I know what Mr. Howard looks like. He's all over the JSE."

"I am?" Jon asks.

"He is?" I ask at the same time.

I hadn't had time to partake in the newest posts, mainly because I wanted to avoid anyone posting about me.

"Yep. Why did you beat him up, Avery?"

I choke on the laugh bubbling up in my throat. Jon hides his irritation well, but I can see his mouth twitch downward. There's something kind of adorable that he's standing there looking awkward AF. I don't know why I take pity on him, but I do.

"I didn't beat him up. I fell on top of him."

Sammy turns his head. "But why did you do that?"

"It's a long story," I say, trying to get Sammy to move off the subject. "Do you know who Jon is?"

"Yeah, a dead man."

"What?" Jon asks.

"There are all kinds of things posted on the JSE about how they all hate him."

I sigh. "Those are the teenagers because they got caught and reported on the JSE." I look up at Jon. "You might want to watch your back. They are furious about the way the LOLs use the app."

"Good to know."

"Is this a meeting of the minds?"

I turn and find Liv standing there, a glass of wine in her hand. First, that annoys me because I don't have one, and I definitely need some wine. Second, I know that Mason put it in her hand and urged her out of the kitchen.

"No. Sammy was just keeping Jon up to date on the JSE."

She frowns. "How do you know what's going on there?"

"On your phone."

Then he turns and marches off to the kitchen.

"I have to get better about using a stronger passcode."

I shake my head. "He's lying. He uses your iPad. Just an FYI."

She sighs, and I marvel that she's not having a meltdown. Before meeting Mason, she would have fretted over not being a good enough mom.

"You must be Jon Howard. It's so nice to meet you. Nancy has all kinds of wonderful things to say about you."

I move out of the way so Jon can step into the house. His shoulder brushes against me. Just that one little touch sends heat radiating through my body. It's then that I notice the bottle of wine in his hand.

"Nancy said this is one of your favorites from Russo Winery. I wasn't sure what we were having tonight, so I figured that was the best bet."

He's all smooth and smiley for Liv, and it irritates me.

"Thank you for this. Mason's out back. Everything else is done. He said he needed to know how you liked your steak."

"I like mine bloody," I say, following behind them.

"Mason knows what you like," Liv says with a laugh. "There's a glass of wine for you in the kitchen."

"Hot damn."

I veer for the kitchen and see the glass of wine sitting there, and, thankfully, my sister knows I drink my wine like Taylor. The ice cubes clink against the glass as I pick it up to take a massive sip.

"So, that's Jon," my sister says as she walks into the kitchen.

I turn and face her. "You've seen pics of him."

"Yeah, but he's kind of a hottie in person."

I frown. "I told you he was hot."

"Yeah, but you didn't say there was a sizzle between the two of you.

I snort. "There's no sizzle."

She gives me a look over her glass as she finishes off her wine.

"Hey, you should be careful how much you drink there, Livvie."

She tilts her head. "Why are you being weird?"

"I'm not being weird."

"You are. You never worry about how much I drink."

There's that little tickle in my stomach. It's hard to explain, but something is off. I don't know what it is, but it is not Jon Howard.

"I'm just worried about your alcohol consumption." I lean closer. "Given your age."

She snorts as she pours herself another glass. "You're so funny, little one."

Ugh, I hate that. When I was younger, they all called me that. I was a tiny baby, and the rest of my siblings are at least three inches or more taller than I am.

"Is Mr. Howard here?" my niece asks as she enters the room. Her hair is done, and she's changed into a dress.

"Yes. He's out back with Mason. What's up with the wardrobe change, kiddo?"

Callie shakes her head. "No reason." But her pink cheeks tell a different story. I let it go because I know Jon has caused a bit of a ruckus in town. Part of the reason is because of the teens. He's probably going to get his car egged at some point. The other part is that he is a wealthy man who is also hot.

My phone buzzes in my pocket, and I realize Liv has been texting with our sisters.

Liv: *I think Avery has a crush on her new roomie.*

I look up at her with menace in my eyes. She smiles, sipping from the glass in her right hand and looking at her phone.

Cora: *Oh, do tell. I'm at some boring meeting.*

Liv: *You shouldn't have run for city council if you don't like meetings.*

Liv: *And on the Avery front, Jon is here for dinner, and she's blushing.*

Me: *Liv has been drinking. Ignore her.*

Cora: *Girl, I looked him up. Jump on that.*

Liv: *I say yes. *pic of Jon**

"When did you take that?"

She says nothing but continues to smile and sip her wine.

I roll my eyes.

Me: *Not interested.*

Gerri: *Sorry. I was busy saving someone's life.*

Cora: *Oh, look at Gerri, being a surgeon. *gif of golf clap**

Gerri: *Rude.*

Cora: *It's my defining characteristic.*

Liv: *Back to Avery and Jon sitting in a tree.*

How am I the youngest one in this mess of a family? I mean, I'm pretty immature, so you have to understand that if I am calling my siblings immature, it's bad.

Fritz: *Why am I on this text? I'm in Puerto Rico.*

My brother and his wife travel for work. She's the host of a travel show that features cuisine.

Me: *Can I come see you?*

Fritz: *No, we're flying back tomorrow.*

Fritz: *Who the hell is Jon, and why are you living with him?*

I sigh and give my sister another nasty look. Before I can answer, I hear the back door open, and Mason walks in. My sister's boyfriend is smiling, but that's Mason. He's almost a decade younger than my sister and perfect for her. Jon follows him in, with Sammy behind and talking off Jon's ear.

"Then, you have to ensure they're ripe enough to be picked."

I expect Jon to roll his eyes, but he doesn't.

"How do you decide they're ready to be picked?"

Sammy goes on a long diatribe about testing tomatoes and how you can tell if they are ripe enough to pick off the vine.

"Interesting," Jon says.

"Jon, this steak is yours," Mason says. I look at the steak.

"Let me guess, you like it well done."

"Of course."

I make a gagging noise.

"*Avery.*"

Oh, look at Liv wanting to behave like an adult.

Callie comes in smiling, and then she freezes when she sees Jon.

"Uh."

"Callie, this is the man trying to make me homeless. Jon, this is my niece, Callie."

He smiles at her. My niece turns an embarrassing shade

of red. I can understand it. When Jon smiles, his eyes lighten, and suddenly, he doesn't look like the man I hate.

"Nice to meet you, Callie."

"Uh…hi."

Then she scurries over to my sister's side. She has been a little chatterbox about Jon. In fact, she practically interviewed me about him. And now she's half in love with him just because he smiled, and he has his sleeves rolled up, and, let me tell you, those forearms are impressive. I could probably take a picture and get thousands of likes within five minutes.

"Avery?"

I glance up at Liv, who is smiling at me. It's my turn to get embarrassed, but hopefully, I've covered it up.

"Right," I say, waving a hand. "Let's eat."

And maybe, by the time we're done, I'll have this man out of my system.

Chapter Thirteen

Jon

Dinner isn't as painful as I thought it would be. It's loud, but I have a feeling that has a lot to do with having children around.

The steak is tasty, despite the nasty looks Avery keeps giving it. On the other hand, hers is bloody, and she has no problem with the blood all over her plate.

"So, how long are you going to stay in town?" Mason asks me. I look up from Avery's plate.

"Not sure. I'm working on something, and I need peace and quiet."

"Good luck with that," Liv remarks. "Avery is the loudest of all of us."

"Not true. That's Cora."

Liv chuckles. "True. But then, with four kids, she has to be loud."

I feel a nudge on my foot and look at Avery across the table. She frowns at me.

"What?"

I shake my head and look under the table. Crouched

under the table are Houdini and Meredith, looking up at me as if I am their favorite person in the world.

"Oh my God," Liv says. "You two get out of there."

They slink off, casting sad looks back at the table.

"Odd that they get along."

Avery shrugs. "Sometimes, things don't turn out like you think they will."

"So, when you came up with JSE, did you think it would become what it is?"

That question is from Liv's daughter. She's the spitting image of her mother. Every time I look at her, she blushes. I really don't know what that's about. I have no experience with preteen girls, even as a preteen boy.

"No. Not at all."

"I can tell it was supposed to be a message board, right?"

I pull my attention away from Callie and look at her aunt. "Yeah. I didn't think they would figure out a way to make it into some kind of gossip site."

She snorts. "That's because you don't know the LOLs that well. They have several members who have mathematical backgrounds."

"Knowing math doesn't really help with changing things around."

"Uh, you know that Margaret Collins retired here, right?"

My eyes widen at the name. She was one of the biggest names at NASA for years, helping develop the space shuttle.

"I take it from your expression, you didn't know."

"Who is Margaret Collins?" Sammy asks.

"She helped put astronauts in space, dude."

The little boy's eyes sparkle with interest. "I want to meet her."

"I can arrange that."

I look at Avery as she pulls out her phone and sends off a text.

"You know her number?" I ask.

She nods as Callie says, "She's an honorary LOL."

Now, it's Avery's turn to blush, and I can't look away. It brings out the freckles that dance over the bridge of her nose. I shouldn't notice things like that, but I can't help it. It's one of those quirky things about her I can't stop thinking about.

"I heard you were dating someone, Jon," Liv says.

I look over at her, and while she seems sweet, I recognize that expression. I've seen it on my mother's face more than once. This is full Mama Bear Mode.

"I was. Not seriously."

"What was her name…Nancy told me, but I can't remember."

"Sienna."

"You dated a crayon?" My nemesis asks.

I look at her. "Rude coming from someone named after labels."

Instead of getting mad at me, she smiles as she sips from her glass of wine. She has ice in it, which is weird, but I know that's how Taylor Swift drinks her wine. There are so many clues that she is a Swiftie. The cat's name, the wine… they could be coincidences, but something tells me she spends a lot of her time online watching TikToks about Taylor's songs.

Don't get me wrong. I love Taylor, but I don't post videos.

"Have you had any problems?" Mason asks me, drawing my attention away from Avery.

I glance at him. We're about the same age but haven't interacted much.

"Problems? You mean other than some woman stealing my house?"

Avery gasps. "I did *not* steal your house."

Mason barely blinks an eye at Avery's theatrical behavior. I feel most people in her orbit grow accustomed to it.

"No, I mean with the teenagers."

"Why does everyone keep asking me about that?"

"Because they're ticked off about that app," Mason explains.

"What does that have to do with Mr. Howard?" Callie asks. I glance at the girl, who blushes again.

"He invented the app," Avery says. "There is a bullseye on his back."

"Why do you say that?"

"Dude, those LOLs use it to tattle on people. The kids in this town can't sneak around without it being reported on the JSE."

"Why would they sneak around?"

She laughs, then she sobers. "Are you serious?"

"Yes. I know this is a small town, but there are tourists."

She shrugs. "I dunno. I just know they sneak out."

"And I assume you were one of the teenagers who snuck out of their house."

She shrugs again, but her sister answers for her.

"I'm sure she did a little, but Avery was in college at sixteen, so she didn't need to sneak around."

I knew that. I had a full workup on her. Even if she hadn't stolen my house, she is in my grandmother's orbit. I don't let anyone get close to family members I like without knowing who they are. Thanks to my connections in the government, it isn't that complicated.

Avery has an impressive background. Graduated at sixteen with a BS by the time she was nineteen and an MBA by the time she was twenty-one. It's difficult to understand how this woman is the same person I read about. Granted, it probably takes a different kind of person to teach people how to handle social media. From what Nancy says, Avery has the patience of a saint when it comes to work. Travis is just not that tech-savvy, and Nancy had washed her hands of him on that front until Avery came along.

"So, you don't know how long you'll be in town?" Liv asks, pulling my attention away from Avery. There is something in her tone that has my hackles rising.

"I have no idea. I need to finish a new project, and Juniper is quiet."

"What he means is the crayon girl can't find him here, although I wouldn't be so sure of that." Avery is probably not wrong there, but I feel Sienna would break out in hives if she stepped foot in this town.

"Why would you say that?"

She rolls her eyes. "She stalks all her exes."

"How did you hear about that?"

Another eye roll. "There are all kinds of stories about it. I'm amazed you didn't check out her background."

"She's legendary for it," Callie says. She blushes the moment I look at her. That's getting disturbing.

"Legendary?"

"What do you know about Sienna?" her mother asks.

Callie shrugs. "There are always stories about her stalking people. I don't think she's dangerous, but it's like she doesn't understand why guys wouldn't want to date her."

Being with the woman had been exhausting. She expected more than I was willing to give. First, she wanted me to fly to every show she walked in. I don't have time for that. Second, she was trying to move in the week we started dating. Our relationship fizzled within three weeks, but she was gone constantly, and it took me forever to pin her down to break up with her.

"She's stunning," Liv says.

"Pretty doesn't mean squat," Avery says. "You know how I feel about that."

That earns her a sharp glance from her sister, but Avery shakes her head. There's a story there, and, dammit, now I'm intrigued. Avery's life is on social media, at least to a point. But what I find thoroughly interesting is how much is not there. Her social media focuses on her clients and has a lot of postings with inspirational sayings. She's a person who teaches people how to put their life online, but hers is extremely limited.

I agree with the less is more mentality about social media. Again, yes, that makes me a weird person to develop apps, but that's not all I do.

"You don't seem to be online that much."

She looks at me. I lose my train of thought. I can't remember the last time that happened, but those eyes get me every time she looks at me. They are dark brown, but there are flecks of gold in the depths of them.

"I'm on there enough."

"Avery says you should be careful what you put online." This comes from Callie. "She said there are idiots on the internet, and it's best to avoid idiots at all costs."

I glance between Callie and Avery and realize my roomie might be normal.

"I just say less is more. You don't have to share everything you're doing."

"But you teach people to do that."

Her gaze swings back to me, and I am there again. I can't think. I can't do anything.

"No. I teach people with small and big businesses to use social media to reach customers and fans."

"She helps Quinn Hawthorne," Callie says proudly.

"He's one of many," Avery says.

"Including my cousin."

"Well, mainly Travis. He can be a little manic in his posting, which wasn't helping their brand."

"What about Savannah's brother? The one who has a crush on you?" Callie asks.

Avery's face flushes pink, bringing out her freckles. "He does not have a crush on me. He's just flirty. He flirts with every woman."

"She's lying," Liv says with a laugh. "Austin does have a crush on her. And for the life of me, I can't understand why she doesn't go out with him."

"He's our brother's brother-in-law. You know how my relationships go. It will fizzle out, and then there will be awkward meetups every time the family gets together. No, thank you. I'm already awkward enough."

That is actually…rational. And not something I would ever think about Avery, but apparently, she thinks things through in certain situations. Then it hits me that she actually thought about this Austin guy. As in, should she go out with him, and that has me scowling.

"What makes you think it wouldn't work out?" Liv asks.

I suddenly don't like Avery's sister much.

"He's pretty, but he's not the kind of guy I'm interested in." Her gaze slides to mine, and I can't think. My body can't keep a solid thought in my brain. "She's just trying to embarrass me in front of you."

"I'm not, Avery. I don't know why you won't go out with him."

I want to tell Liv to shut the fuck up about this Austin dude, but then it hits me. "Are you talking about Austin Martinez?"

She nods. "His sister Savannah married our brother. We can't understand why, but she did."

I frown. "Is there something wrong with her?"

"Not her, with our brother."

Liv laughs, and I tear my gaze away from Avery. Her sister is shaking her head.

"Don't listen to her. We all love Fritz. We just give him a hard time."

"I can't imagine how horrible his life was for him growing up," Mason says. "So many girls in the house."

"Oh, please. I'm sure Everly has some horror stories about your behavior." Liv is still smiling at him when she says it.

Mason snorts. "You've met my sister. She's the one who terrorized us."

"I can see that," I say. "Just don't tell Everly I said it."

"May Houdini and I be excused?" Sammy says. I glance at the dog. He does not look like he wants to leave the table for fear of missing out on scrapes.

"Yes."

Sammy takes his plate to the kitchen and hurries off. Houdini gives one last glance at the table, then turns to run after Sammy. The pull of going out back in the fading light and playing with a boy is apparently too much to resist.

I feel something against my legs and look down. Meredith is rubbing her head against my leg.

"I'm surprised she isn't sticking her claws into you," Mason says. "That cat hates me."

Avery shakes her head. "She does not.

"Why don't y'all go out back and keep an eye on Sammy?" Liv says. "Avery and I will clean up."

"Oh, babe, I can do it," Mason says.

Liv smiles at him, and the two of them share a moment he has seen between couples. It's like there's nothing in the whole world but the two of them. And for the first time in my life, I envy it.

"No. You know the rules. You cook. I clean. Go keep an eye on those two out back. You know they can get into just about anything."

He leans over and kisses her, and Avery makes gagging noises.

I look over at her, but she's smiling, and there is love in her eyes. For all of Avery's faults, she really does love her sister.

"I can help clean."

"You're our guest."

"I'm your guest," Avery says.

"You don't count."

"Oh, nice. I'm going to let Mom know about this behavior."

Again, there's no heat in the words.

"Come on, Jon. Let's get out of the line of sisterly fire," Mason says.

Callie rises from the table, but Liv stops her. "You have homework, Callie. Go get it done, and then you can go outside."

I can tell she wants to argue with her mother, but she does her bidding with a frown.

Mason leans over and gives Liv another kiss, and I follow him out the door. The sun is setting, and the air turning a bit cooler. This is South Texas, so the nights in October can still be warm to most people.

Sammy has a stick, and he and Houdini are walking along the back fence. They seem to be having an earnest discussion about something. Mason chuckles.

"Boys and dogs."

I nod.

"So, I'm sure you know I dragged you out here because Liv wants me to talk to you."

I blink, my mind immediately searching for what Liv would want from me. "About what?"

"Avery."

I frown.

"Listen, I get it. You're a good guy. We didn't hang out because, let's be honest, you're way too smart to hang out with a Spencer."

"That's bullshit, and you know it."

His eyebrows rise to his hairline. I know that we don't have much in common. Mason has colorful tattoos on his arms and a piercing in his nose. He's a free spirit in a lot of ways. But we do have something in common.

"We were always looked at by our classmates differently. I know it couldn't have been easy with what happened to your parents."

He shrugs and looks out at Sammy. "Yeah. It wasn't."

"The attention… it's annoying."

He looks at me, and I know he gets it. His parents died in a car wreck, and the town came together to help his brother raise Mason and his sister Everly. Wyatt was old enough to adopt his younger siblings, but it couldn't have been easy—even with the town's help.

"Yeah. And people always wanted you to be like your father and his brother."

I nod.

"But Liv loves her sister more than anything, with the exception of her kids."

"And you?"

"Getting there," he says with a smile. "I'm a close third behind Avery. I think."

His tone tells me he isn't that upset by the situation.

"So, you'll break my legs if I hurt her?"

A bark of laughter catches me off guard. "No, dude, you don't have to worry about me. I'm easy. You need to worry about the O'Bryan sisters."

"I do?"

"Yeah. Anything hurts Avery, they will descend upon this town ready for your blood."

Yeah, right. He must read my thoughts because he shakes his head.

"A lifetime with Everly taught me one thing. Women are always more vicious, protecting what they love. Those sisters? They will take you apart, piece by piece."

"I'm touched you're worried about me." I can't help the sarcasm in my voice. It's my go-to defense when I'm dealing with emotions I don't like.

Mason doesn't get irritated with me. Instead, he smiles. "And part of it is that I want to tell my woman that you aren't going to hurt her sister. They all worry about her because of some douche she dated in her past."

"That Chet guy?"

He nods. "It was a long time before I met Liv, but I know it was rough for Avery. So, just do me a favor and play nice. I hate dealing with bail money, and those sisters would definitely take the location of your body to their graves."

Chapter Fourteen

Avery

It's one in the morning, and I can't sleep. I lay in my bed, looking up at the ceiling. I'm exhausted since Mr. Egg White woke me up early this morning. My head is spinning with thoughts of my situation, of work I should be doing, and the creepy neighbor. I need sleep and crave it like Houdini craves chaos. Unfortunately, my mind doesn't care how I feel. At all. Stupid mind.

There's only one way to get my brain to let me rest, and that's to pace it out. I look at Meredith snuggled next to me. I hate waking her, but I have to get up and move. It's something that I have done for years. I know that my ADHD goes into overdrive when I'm tired. Right now, I have so many thoughts tumbling through my head. I can't grasp just one. With a sigh, I pull myself up out of bed. Meredith blinks awake. Her gaze tells me she is not happy with the interruption.

"You can stay here. I'm going downstairs."

I would pace in my room, but as much as I don't like my new housemate, I'm not about to bother him either. My entire body is worn out, and I don't have it in me to fight him right now. My eyes burn, and I know I'm about to cry. I press my fingers to my eyes, trying to get my emotions under control. I do the deep breathing exercises a therapist once told me to use, then open my eyes again. I glance back at Meredith, whose eyes are closed. Shaking my head, I realize I picked the only cat in existence who does not get up in the middle of the night. Figures.

I head down the stairs, avoiding all the creaks in the steps. I've walked up and down them the last few weeks enough times to know where they are. Tea is definitely in order. I will try some chamomile, although it doesn't always work.

I set the kettle to heat up and prepare the tea.

You should be sleeping.

I can hear Grannie Pam in my head as if she is standing next to me. Melancholy hits me in the chest. The eye-burning thing is back. How many nights did we spend together? I lost count.

You need rest.

"I know."

Stop moping, girlie. You have things to do and see. What about that hot guy upstairs? You should sneak into his room.

Rolling my eyes, I put a teabag into my cup. Grannie Pam wasn't a prude, but I'm sure she would tell me to pack up and move out.

"Mind your beeswax."

"Who are you talking to?"

I scream at the sound of Jon's voice.

"What the hell?" I demand as I turn to face him, which is a big mistake.

Holy hot nerd, Batman. Every thought in my head is now drained out and has left me completely stupid.

Jon isn't wearing a shirt, and in my opinion, he should never wear another one ever again. There should be a law that says he must show his chest off to everyone. I take in the expanse of golden skin, the sculpted chest, and Jesus, he has an eight-pack and that sexy V thing going on.

"Meow." I look down at Meredith, who is standing beside him.

"Meredith came into my room and woke me up."

I frown at my cat. "How did she open your door?"

"No idea."

When I look at him again, I wince at the scratches on his chest. "Did she wake you up by sitting on your chest?"

He nods.

"I'm sorry. Meredith, you mustn't do that to Mr. Jon."

"Mr. Jon?"

I shrug as the tea kettle goes off. I pour the water over my tea and stare at it like it is the most exciting thing in the world. My hope that Jon would leave me disintegrates as I hear him step closer. I lean against the counter. "I'm trying to teach her proper etiquette."

That gets me an eye roll. "Why are you up?"

All my happy to see a hot nerd feelings dissolve, and I get defensive. And when I get defensive, I get juvenile. "Why are you?"

"I think we established that. Does that tea have caffeine in it?"

"No. I'm not an idiot."

"I never said you were."

"You implied."

"You inferred."

He walks towards me, his gaze focused on mine. I don't know if I have ever seen a man concentrate on my face that way. I know it's weird, but I didn't pay attention if they did. With Jon, it's different. He captures my attention and holds onto it. That's no easy feat.

He stops a few inches from me. Now I can see his mess of curls, the way they fall over his forehead.

"Avery?"

His voice is low and sexy, and, Jesus, I want him so badly. My fingers twitch with the need to slip them through all those curls, preferably when he has his head between my legs.

Nope. That's the insomnia brain talking.

"What?"

"Could you move? I want to make myself some tea."

Mortified, I say nothing but step aside to let him make his tea.

"Do you mind if I have some of your chamomile?"

God help me…that voice. It's low, and there's just a bit of Texas twang. It flies over my nerve endings, leaving my body overly sensitive.

"Avery?"

Ugh, I got lost in my thoughts again. "Sure."

I step away, grab my tea and head to the living room. I love the open-concept houses, but this is a historical home—on the registry and everything—so there was only so much they could do to change it. I do love the cozy living area.

I figure since Jon is up, I can go ahead and turn on the TV. I tend not to watch at night unless I have insomnia, so I've been watching a lot. I pull up the latest true crime series on Netflix and push play. Just as I settle back, Jon walks into the living room. Ugh. I should have known he would come in here, and, yes, I should be more gracious. My Grannie Pam taught me to be nicer to people, but he's trying to get me kicked out of my house.

He settles on the opposite side of the couch. Meredith jumps up on the cushion between us.

"Is this what you watch when you can't sleep?"

"No."

"But you are tonight?"

"Yes."

He's probably got a genius IQ, so I'm hoping he takes the hint. But, just like everything since Grannie Pam died, things don't go the way I want them to.

"This is not going to make you sleep better."

Dammit.

"I'm not worrying about sleep at the moment."

I'm trying to ignore his stupid chest and all the rest of his exposed skin. Who walks around like that, flaunting his perfectly formed pecs? And yes, I know I just went on about how he needed to show off his chest, but my tired brain doesn't always make sense.

"But you didn't have any caffeine in your tea."

I glance over at him. His blue gaze watches my every move. There's a tickle in the back of my throat and a funny feeling in my belly. God, he really is pretty. And built. He must work out all the time. He could not get that definition without lifting some weights, especially since he sits behind a desk to work.

"Avery?"

I blink. Great. He caught me staring at his chest. I look

up at him. "I know when there is no going back to sleep. I passed it about thirty minutes ago."

"And it took you that long to come downstairs?"

"No. Yes. Okay, I know that if I don't fall asleep within an hour of going to bed, there's probably no going to sleep. I just don't always accept that."

He makes a sound in his throat. "Of course."

The narrator tells the story of some young woman who went missing thirty years ago with no links to any crime. That could be me. I get that my sisters and parents would look for me, but no one is waiting at home for me. That it would probably take days before someone noticed I was missing. It hits me in the gut. No one would notice. They would just think I was busy doing something in my thoughts.

"Avery?"

I shake my head and look at Jon.

"Are you alright?"

"Of course."

"You're crying."

"Am not." But even as I say it, I feel a tear slip down my face.

"If you say so."

I roll my eyes and get myself under control. At least as much as I can get myself under control. I have never been able to control my emotions.

"Have you always had a problem with insomnia?"

I glance at him again and realize he's watching the TV or pretending to watch. The light from it dances over his features, and I can't stop the sigh that slips from my mouth. He looks at me.

"What? You just want to sit here in silence?"

I realize he thinks I'm annoyed, and I am so happy about that. I don't need him thinking that I want to jump his body.

"No. And yes, I've always had a problem with sleep. I have ADHD, so it sometimes tends to give me issues at night. This time is one of the worst."

"This time?"

I nod. "I haven't really had a good night's sleep in weeks."

Lies. It's been months, really.

"What happened?"

Out of nowhere, the memories of the last few months hit me, and I bite back a sob. I should be over this or at least handle it better. But for some reason, I can't get past it.

"Avery?"

I blink back the tears. "My grandmother died."

"Ah."

"She helped raise me, but she had dementia these last few years. Thankfully, when she died, it was in her sleep, peacefully."

He nods. I look back at the true crime documentary series. I decide to pull up one of my streaming services and select *Superbad*.

"Why did you change the channel?"

"It's this or Columbo. They were Grannie Pam's favorites."

For a long time, we sit in silence as the movie starts.

About fifteen minutes in, Jon stirs. "This was one of your grandmother's favorite movies?"

I smile and look at him. "Yeah. She even named her cat General McLovin."

A bark of laughter catches me by surprise. His eyes are lighter, and dammit, he has dimples. No. Not fair.

"You're kidding."

I shake my head. "He lives with my brother and his wife now. He actually brought the two of them together."

I sigh as I thread my fingers through Meredith's fur. I have always been partial to cats, to animals in general. They didn't expect anything but love, and in return, they gave you everything. All their days and all their love.

"Avery?"

"Yeah?"

"Have you talked to anyone?"

His voice is quiet with concern, that kind of voice I always suspect mortuary people practice every day.

"Talked to anyone?"

"About your grandmother."

"Sure, I talked to people about her."

"I mean a therapist."

"I don't need a therapist. I'm handling everything just fine."

He gives me a look that tells me he doesn't believe me.

"You're not sleeping."

"I'm worried about being homeless."

He rolls his eyes, and I know that's what people expect of me. They always want me to make them roll their eyes or laugh. It's something that I am very good at.

"Remember, I had you checked out."

"You've been checking me out? Do you want to kiss me?"

I mean it as a joke, but his gaze drops to my mouth for the barest of moments.

"I mean that I had a look at your life. You have a lot of money."

I try not to be irritated because I knew he would do that. "I am in no way as rich as you are."

"Still, I have no idea why you want to stay in this house."

I sigh and turn back the TV.

"Avery?"

It's hard to put my thoughts in order. I'm tired, but I'm also sitting next to one of the most eligible bachelors in the tech industry. He's gorgeous, and dammit, my fingers are still itching to slip through those curls.

"I just like this house. I like where it sits, and I really like that garden. I'd try and buy it off your grandma if she would let me."

There is a long beat of silence. I feel him studying me. I turn and face him.

"What?"

He shakes his head. "Nothing. I just thought…"

"You thought what?"

"I thought you might be doing it just to be facetious."

I bark out a laugh. "That's not what this is, but I will give you a pass. That's *totally* something I would do to be a pain in the ass."

His eyebrows wing up in surprise.

"What?"

"People aren't usually that honest, especially about themselves."

"I'm always honest about myself. Well, no. I'm honest about myself most of the time, but I fib sometimes. I know I'm a lot to take."

Again, his gaze dips to my mouth, lingers, then slides back up. "I can see that."

All of a sudden, the living room is hot. Like boiling hot, but it has nothing to do with the AC and everything to do with the man sharing the couch with me. Even as I feel hot, my nipples harden against my shirt. This is so not good. Not good at all.

"You know you don't have to babysit me."

He studies me for a long time, and I get the sense he's weighing everything and how to respond.

"No, I want to see what happens to these guys."

"You've never seen this movie?"

He shakes his head.

I pause the movie, then pop up from the couch.

"Where are you going?"

"We need popcorn if we're going to watch this the right way."

And if he's going to stay up with me, I might just keep from embarrassing myself if I'm shoving popcorn in my mouth.

It only takes me a few minutes to make the popcorn in the microwave, then hurry back to the couch. Meredith is practically lying on Jon by the time I get back. I settle down and start the movie again.

"Here," I say, holding the bowl out to Jon.

He glances down at it, then back up to me.

"It's not poisoned."

Another eye roll. "I just don't normally eat in the middle of the night."

I shake the bowl. "Come on, be bad for once in your life, Jon."

He glances up at me with an unreadable expression before he takes a handful of popcorn. Then we both settle back to watch the movie. All the while, I keep reminding myself that this man is trying to get me kicked out of the house.

But in less than twenty-four hours since he moved in, I'm starting to realize that I might have a real fight.

Chapter Fifteen

Jon

I head out early the following day after my grandmother summons me. Usually, I would ignore her because I have work to do, but I needed out of the house.

Last night had been full of Avery, seeing her with her family, then spending the night watching that stupid movie. And no, I'm not smiling now thinking about her grandmother naming her cat McLovin.

I learned two things last night. One, Avery likes looking at my chest. Thinking about how her gaze roamed over it last night has my cock thickening.

Fuck.

That woman is starting to get to me. I also learned that she does not like being attracted to me. It made her jumpy.

I might have just figured out the way to get rid of her.

Just thinking about those words has my chest tightening. This is usually the precursor to a freak-out for me. I haven't had any panic attacks since I was seventeen, but the thought of not seeing Avery has my pulse scrambling and my head hurting. What the hell?

I shake my head and try to clear it. I don't even like the woman. She stole my house and forced a cat on me, although I have always had an affinity for cats. Also, I get a little thrill that I seem to be the only man Meredith likes. It irritates Avery, and, in turn, that amuses me. I don't think I have ever had an adversary relationship with a woman before now.

Wait. I don't have a relationship with Avery O'Bryan. She just needs to get out of my house and leave me alone. Then, maybe, I'll be able to work again.

After leaving the city limits of Juniper, the road opens up, and it gives me time to contemplate my next move. She definitely doesn't like the idea that she's attracted to me. Avery makes me think she'd run for the hills if I came on to her. But I don't want to be a creep, so that's out. Maybe if I just walk around with my shirt off? She seemed particularly irritated with that. If I do that, and perhaps if I'm nice to her, she'll leave and go wherever.

Another hitch in my chest has me rolling my shoulders.

I park in the circular drive and make my way inside. This house is a monstrosity that I hope Nancy is forced to contend with someday. I definitely don't want it.

Stepping into the house, I listen for noises to figure out where my grandmother is.

"In here, Jon."

I head to the parlor. She's sitting in one of the chairs closest to the window that looks out on the butterfly garden.

"Good morning."

She turns and, for a second, looks so much older, as if the weight of the world is on her shoulders. She's always been a strong woman. I think my mother once described her as having a steel spine. She had to. It couldn't be easy dealing with all of the Howards. But right now, she looks as if she would rather just not deal with anything.

Then, the look disappears in an instant, and she's the same independent woman. Is she sick? It would be just like my grandmother not to tell us if she's sick.

"Good morning, Jon. How are you this morning?"

"Well, since I was summoned to your house, not that great."

She rolls her eyes. I don't think I ever remember my grandmother rolling her eyes. It's weird. There are a few other things that have me worrying. I've never contemplated life without my grandmother. She's always been there, like the sun. Steady, sure, and she can burn you if you aren't careful.

"Quit complaining. Let's go have breakfast. There are pancakes."

She rises out of the chair, and for the first time, I realize just how small she is. She barely reaches my shoulder. But she'd always been bigger than life during my youth and beyond.

Once we're seated and have our breakfasts in front of us, I dig in. There's a churning in my gut. Is she about to tell me she's dying?

"Why are you looking like that?"

I blink and realize I have been staring at her like a goober.

"No reason."

Another eye roll.

"I want you to be here to help me host the annual charity event next weekend."

My grandmother does a lot of good in the community—more than many people realize. I know she's the one who funded the new hospital, and she's the one who helped start the new animal shelter. This is the first time she has insisted that I help her host.

"You want me to help host?"

Why is that giving me a tickle in the back of my throat?

She nods. "Nancy never took to it, and while she and Travis will be here, along with all of the Hawthornes, I need someone by my side."

"Grandmother, are you alright?"

She sips coffee out of her Meissen China cup and studies me. "Jon, do you want to tell me what's happening with you? Why are you here?"

"You didn't answer the question."

"Neither did you."

If she could play hardball, I could too. I learned from the best of them. And one of the things she taught me is there is strength in the silent stare.

"No, there's nothing wrong with me. Why on earth would you ask that?"

I shrug, swallowing down my relief. Grandmother doesn't like big displays of any sort.

"You're acting weird."

"Like how?"

"Well, you just are."

"Jon."

"Okay, it's weird. You're sitting in your parlor looking at the butterflies and hanging out with the LOLs."

"Is that all?"

"And this whole thing with Avery is odd. I thought

maybe you were doing it for some reason. Like you had a brain tumor or something."

She throws back her head and laughs. For most people, this might not be weird, but remember, I said Estella doesn't like big displays of emotion.

"I'm sorry," she says, dabbing her eyes and not sounding the least bit sorry. "I love that my grandson thinks the only way I can be kind is because I have a brain tumor."

My cheeks heat in embarrassment. "When you say it that way, it sounds bad."

"Yes, it does." She reaches out and pats my hand. "Don't worry. I understand why you feel that way."

"You do?"

"I wasn't easy on you or Nancy, but I saw your potential. I love all of my grandchildren, but you and Nancy…you make me very proud. You are a testament to your mother."

I swallow the lump that's risen in my throat. "Is that why you invited me over today?"

She shakes her head. "It's about the charity event, I really do need a co-host, and while I thought of Avery, she has a lot on her plate right now."

"She does? Because she doesn't seem to be doing much at all."

"I told you she just lost her grandmother."

"Yes. She talked about her last night."

Estella's eyes sharpen as she looks over at me. "Last night?"

"That damned cat woke me up after Avery went downstairs, so I got up. She made me watch *Superbad* and an episode of *Columbo*."

I try to sound irritated, but there was something

comforting about being there with Avery. I thought she would be a chatterbox, but she'd been quiet, at least for Avery. There had been something very intimate about spending time in a dark room watching TV with her.

"Which one?"

I blink. "Which one what?"

"Which Columbo?"

"The one with Spock."

She nods, a small smile curving her lips. "Well, be that as it may, she doesn't have the mental capacity to deal with something like this."

"Are you saying she isn't smart enough? Because I have to tell you, I might not like the woman, but she has got to have a near-genius IQ."

Her smile turns into a grin. "Yes, she does. Five points higher than you."

That has me blinking. "Say what now?"

"Hard to believe a woman beat you?"

"No. There are a lot of women smarter than I am. Just…are you screwing with me?"

She shakes her head. "No. I had her checked out when she started hanging around with Travis and Nancy. You know how I feel about outsiders."

I nod. And now I feel foolish for even thinking that my grandmother would be taken in by someone.

"And I'm also sure you had her checked out." Not a question.

"Yes. I did. I wanted to ensure she wasn't out to get your money."

"And you found out she is pretty well off."

She is. She has more money than I thought she would. One of her brother's business partners invests for her.

"Let's put Avery aside. I need your agreement to help me, or I will ask someone else, and you know how I feel about the others."

And by others, she means my half-siblings and cousins. They are all lazy to varying degrees. I nod. "I'll do it."

"Good. I have a meeting with Mason Spencer, so I need to get ready."

"Why are you meeting with Spencer?"

"He's the caterer for this event. You know I like to use local places, and *The Mason Jar* is one of my favorite places to eat."

It makes sense, so I nod, but she's still being weird. I can't put my finger on it, but something is up with my grandmother. "It's a shame your mother can't attend the event."

I grunt.

"That is no way to respond, Jonathon."

She only uses my full first name when she's irritated with me. I always hated hearing her say it when I was a kid. To be honest, I still do.

"Apologies."

Bessie sets a massive plate of pancakes in front of me. "Thanks, Bessie."

She gives me a wink, and after giving my grandmother her plate, she leaves us to our breakfast.

"You shouldn't be so upset over your mother moving in with a man. A lot of people do it these days."

I blink. "I'm not upset she's moving in with Ted. I'm upset that she hid him from me for so long."

"Yes, I don't know why she was so worried. Ted seems like a very nice man. You know he proposed?"

Glancing at her, I frown. "He did?"

"Yes, but your mother is skittish. Understandable considering her marriage."

That is one thing about my grandmother. She doesn't suffer fools. And there is one thing I know for sure. My father is a fool. He's also lazy and probably cheating on wife number three. Or is it number four? Either way, if he isn't cheating, he's planning on it. It's his one defining personality —other than laziness.

When I pull back from my thoughts, I realize my grandmother is staring at me. It's almost as if she's studying me, seeing my reactions. That's nothing new, but there is a different edge to it.

"What?"

She shakes her head. "Nothing. Just…there's something different about you."

"Lack of sleep. I don't know how she does it."

"Who?"

"Avery. She said she's had a bout of insomnia since her grandmother died."

Estella nods. "Yes, but it's probably been bothering her for months, not weeks."

"That's not healthy."

"No. It's not, but Avery has been unmoored since her grandmother died. They were very close."

There is a wistful sound I have never heard in my grandmother's voice.

"And you envy that?"

Her sharp look almost has me apologizing, but I lock my jaw. I will not cower. Maybe.

"Not really. I was never a motherly type."

But there is that wistfulness threaded within the words that make me think that she wishes she was. I don't know how to deal with her saying things like that in that tone. Howards are not good at emotions. It's like in our DNA.

"Don't freak out, Jon."

"I'm not freaking out. And since when did you use terms like that?"

She shakes her head and sips her coffee. "I just want you to be nice to her. Maybe…take her for a milkshake or something. She loves the diner's milkshakes."

"You want me to take her out on a date?"

"No, of course not. Just…get her out of that house. She gets out, but she's usually with the LOLs, her sister, and her kids."

I sigh and nod. There's no use arguing with my grandmother. She will always win. Just because I agreed doesn't mean I have to do it.

"Now, tell me what I have to do to help you host."

Chapter Sixteen

Avery

The sun is the first thing I see the following day. It's shining in my eyes because I forgot to shut the freaking fracking blinds.

I groan in irritation. Opening my eyes, I realize that it's probably mid-morning. I listen, waiting to see if I hear anything in the house. I have a feeling Jon probably gets started working so early that this is probably mid-day for him. I grab my phone and see a few texts from my family, one from a former client I refuse to work with anymore, and then there is a weird text from Estella.

Estella: *I expect you to be at my annual fundraiser.*

I blink. I heard people talking about it but didn't think anything of it. It's a fancy dress kind of thing, and unless there is cake, I don't like attending those kinds of things.

Me: *No, I did not.*

Estella: *Well, I do. Your sister will be here. Mason is catering.*

I know that. Mason told me, and I was thrilled for him. He has the most successful restaurant in town, which is no easy feat in a small town. People get hung up on their favorites and get into ruts. But Mason has built a substantial following, and he's just thirty.

Me: *I don't have anything to wear. Sorry.*

A lot of people are afraid to tell Estella no. I think it's one of the reasons she likes me.

Estella: *You have time to shop. Some of the money goes to the shelter.*

Ugh, the woman is too smart for her own good.

Me*: I have to wash my hair that night.*

Estella: *I really want you to be here.*

I can hear how it would sound if she were saying the words. Estella is a dragon, a woman who has had to run the family business because her husband was an idiot, and now all her sons are idiots. She doesn't put up with crap from anyone.

But this is different. I know she worries about what will happen to the business when she is gone. I know that her favorite Taylor Swift song is *Clean*. And while I know she probably has another reason for me to be there, it's almost as if she needs me there. She knows I can't tell someone who needs my help no.

Me: *Fine.*

I flop back on my mattress and sigh. Liv has a lot of formal dresses left over from her days as a military wife. They constantly had to go to these things they called dining outs. Unfortunately, Liv is about five inches taller than I am and not as curvy. She's slim, with subtle curves. There is no possible way my boobs will fit into any of her dresses.

Me: *I need a dress.*

Liv: *A dress?*

Me: *Estella is insisting that I come to that fundraiser thing.*

I don't know how much she can raise, but from what people tell me, she gets folks from San Antonio and Austin to attend, like all the movers and shakers. They don't miss it because they are afraid of Estella.

Liv: *gif dancing bear* *Something sparkly?*

Me: *I don't know. The last time I wore a dress, Fritz was getting married.*

And the time before that was when his friend Ed got married.

Me: *Probably going to go to San Antonio to shop.*

Liv: *Oh, fun! I'll go with you.*

My nerves ease a little bit. I am not good with picking formal dresses or dresses of any sort, for that matter. I have never been a woman who dressed up. I like to wear my leggings and jeans, thank you very much.

Liv: *Do you have anything tomorrow night?*

Me: *It's a school night.*

And I know I'm not in school, but I can put off this for at least another day, right? The kids have school tomorrow.

Liv: *Nope. The kids are off for a teacher workday Friday.*

Dammit.

Liv: *I'll check in with Fritz and Savannah. Hopefully, they've rested enough for a visit.*

And I know now I don't have any choice in the matter.

IT'S JUST after three when I hear the front door open. I'm looking out over the yard from the kitchen window, watching the creeper who lives behind us.

Meredith slinks away, probably to meet with her lover

Jon. I don't get why the cat likes him so much. It's annoying. Sure, he's hot in that geeky way, all long limbs and muscles, and he always smells great. Okay, maybe I do get it.

"Good afternoon, Meredith. Where's your mother?"

I ignore him talking to my cat—although it's cute—I keep my eye on the creeper. He doesn't seem to be looking at my house, but I still think he is.

"What are you doing?"

"Watching."

I can almost hear his eyes roll. He comes up behind me. "What are you watching?"

I glance back at him and realize he's closer than I thought. "Don't you have an app to invent?"

He says nothing, just stares at me. God, those eyes. This close, I can see the little gold flecks in them.

"I'm keeping an eye on the creeper."

He frowns, and, God, he's even hot when he frowns. If I'm telling the truth, he's hotter when he frowns. What is wrong with me?

"What creeper?"

I motion my head toward the window. He steps so close that I can feel the heat of him. I want to lean back and feel him wrap his arms around me. Because I know that is a big mistake, I force myself to move a few inches closer to the door.

"Why do you call him the creeper?"

I look outside and watch Creeper Neighbor Dude walk through the garden. A chain link fence separates us, so we can see into each other's yards. The man looks like he's just walking through the yard, but something is off. He's odd. I mean, who rents a vacation house in a small touristy town and then doesn't go anywhere? Also, he spends a lot of time walking through the yard.

"He's weird."

"I bet people call you weird."

I glance back over at him. "Rude, but fair. I am weird. But in a cool way."

His lips quirk, and suddenly I get a need. A big fat need. I want to make him laugh. He seems like he could use one, and there is nothing in this world I want more than to give him this.

"If you say so."

I turn back around and watch the guy. "Meredith hates him."

"She hates all men."

"Except you and Houdini."

"I keep good company."

We stand there watching the creeper for a long moment.

"You don't know his name?"

Jon has stepped closer. I can feel his heat on my back. "No. But I'm sure we can ask the LOLs. You know they'll know or be able to find out."

When he doesn't respond, I glance back at him. His gaze is narrowed in a laser focus on Creeper Dude. "What?"

"I might be wrong, but he looks like he's surveilling the house."

"Yes! Finally. I told Liv that he was a creeper and seemed to be watching the house." Excitement and vindication hit me hard. I turn around so I'm facing Jon. "She says it's just my imagination. I mean, yes, I have a history of outlandish accusations but nothing since I was fifteen."

He looks down at me, and suddenly, I remember how

close we are. I inch backward as he places a hand on the door. "What happened when you were fifteen?"

I can't think. Like my entire mind has shut down and refuses to form words. All I can think about is those amazing lips, those blue, blue eyes, and how I would like to climb Jon Howard like he was a tree.

"Avery?"

I blink. This man is my nemesis, and I must remember that.

"Right. Oh, I thought this guy—Mr. Keller—was trying to steal from this little store. It had little figurines and other things to decorate your house."

"And?"

Did he inch closer? I feel he's closer, although I didn't see him move.

"Well, I watched him for a week, and he kept going in there. Maybe he wanted to buy his wife something, but he went there four times in one week. And he was inside forever. So, I set a trap for him."

"You did?"

I nod, my gaze locked with his. "And when I exposed him, I really exposed him."

"What do you mean?"

I sigh, still not able to look away from Jon. When the man concentrates on you, it's like nothing else exists. No wonder he gets so many supermodels in his bed.

"Avery?"

His voice is deeper, sexier.

I clear my throat. "It seems that Mr. Keller was having an affair with the shopkeeper. I caught them right in the middle of a nooner."

He presses his lips together, his eyes lighting with humor. The chuckle escapes, and it's a glorious sound. Everything in my whole entire body tightens at that little sound, and for a second, I'm transfixed. His face relaxes into humor, his dimples showing.

This is the man who gets supermodels in his bed.

I frown at that thought. Why is that bothering me? What do I care if he wants to sleep with supermodels or other chicks? I just need him out of this house.

"I'm sorry for laughing," Jon says, misreading my expression.

I shake my head. "It's okay."

"What happened? With Mr. Keller and his nooner companion?"

The wording makes my lips twitch. "Nothing much. I mean, calling the cops on him was stupid."

Another chuckle and I feel like I've won a damned prize. "The cops?"

"Listen, I get it. It wasn't a well-thought-out hypothesis. I was only fifteen."

"Did you get in trouble?"

"Not really. Grannie Pam took care of it for me. Like she always did." And unexpectedly, a wash of memories hit me. The times she saved my ass, the fun we had planning all the trips I would take when I was an adult.

"Hey, I was going to go into town to the diner for a milkshake."

I blink and look at Jon. "Good for you."

"You want to come with me? Strictly just to get out of the house. You should give watching your neighbor a break. Besides, he went in." He's looking over my shoulder through the window. I follow his gaze, turning to get a better look at the yard. Sure enough, Creeper is gone.

"Dammit."

"Aw, come on, Avery. Estella says you like milkshakes," he whispers in my ear, his breath feathering over my ear. I suppress a shiver. He's so close that he could tug on my earlobe. Heat curls in my belly then slides down. God, he's sending my hormones into overdrive, and he has no idea. I'm sure I'd disgust him if I turned around and kissed him. But I really, really, really want to.

So, to protect myself, I get snotty. "You gossiping about me? Looking for info to try and get rid of me?"

He sighs, and this time I feel his breath on my neck like he's looking down at me. "No. She was warning me to be nice to you. This is me being nice to you."

I glance back, and yes, he's standing right behind me. Again, I get the crazy urge to lean back and snuggle into his arms. I bet he would be good at snuggling if he tried it.

"I can't leave Meredith."

"I'm sure she'll be okay."

I glance at my cat, and then a shiver of unease washes over me. "I don't leave her alone that often."

"We won't be long. Just a milkshake, O'Bryan. She was a stray a few days ago. I'm sure she'll be fine for an hour."

Another look at Meredith. She's snuggled on a blanket I left on the couch. "Fine. You're buying."

"Of course."

I glance down. I'm in my favorite Camos and Cupcakes shirt and PJ bottoms. "I'll change."

I slip away from him and hurry upstairs. As soon as I can draw in a deep breath, my hormones level out. I know it has something to do with the fact I haven't had sex in a really long time, and Jon packs a potent punch. Smart. Hot. Smells good. All of those things are great. And his eyes… they are starting to get to me.

I draw in a deep breath. I just need to remember he's trying to kick me out of my house. If I can remember that, I might be able to keep from doing something embarrassing.

Chapter Seventeen

Jon

I think that I may have lost my mind. That is the only explanation for why I am sitting in the Mystic Diner drinking shakes with a woman I need out of my house.

"You look constipated."

Yeah, she's been busting my balls the entire time.

"There's a lot of people here."

"It's the diner. At lunchtime."

I look around, irritated with all the chatter and noise from the regular operation of the diner. It gets under my skin, and I can't do anything to eliminate the unease.

"Hey, Howard, pay attention. I was talking about me."

I blink and look at Avery. She's the entire reason I'm here. I want her out of my house, but after my talk with Estella, I realized something about Avery's behavior. Some of it is due to the death of her grandmother.

I've never been hit like that. I was only two when my grandfather died, and according to everyone I talked to, he was just like my father. I doubt I would have mourned his death. Avery's grandmother was like a second mother, from what Estella said. And that little catch in her voice and the sad look in her eyes made me do something irrational. I invited her for milkshakes—which I don't particularly like.

There was also that irrational urge to kiss her. Just pull her into my arms, tell her everything would be alright. Then, I wanted to kiss the hell out of her.

Even now, I can still remember the heat of her body, the sugary sweet smell of her, and the way she looked into my eyes. Any guy would fall for that, right? She's gorgeous in that quirky way, like that actress on *New Girl*, and she's intelligent. I know for many people, that's just a regular compliment. But for me, a man who has always prided himself as one of the smartest—if not the smartest—person in the room, it's a high compliment.

It also makes her a very savvy adversary.

"Here you go," our waitress says. She's a woman who looks somewhat familiar, but I can't place her. I think she's a couple years older than I am, but I didn't attend school here for long. Once we moved away, I spent most of my time with my grandmother at her house. I hated coming into town.

Avery talked me into lunch also. The woman is crafty, especially since I planned on having a milkshake and getting out of here. Also, I'm apparently paying for lunch. She said we needed food in our stomachs before our shakes. When she spouts insane rules, it confuses me. She's usually throwing out nonsense, so it confuses me when she says something that seems legit.

I got a salad, and Avery ordered a patty melt with tots. Seriously, I have no idea where she puts all the food she eats. Don't get me wrong. I love greasy food, but I also have a father who has had a bypass and two grandfathers who died of heart disease. Avery apparently pays no attention to the idea of eating healthy. I don't think seven-year-olds eat as much sugary cereal as she does. Still, she must have a fantastic metabolism.

Avery digs into her lunch just as she does life. Pure wild abandon.

She looks up at me as she chews then swallows. "What?"

I shake my head and start on my salad, although now I want a patty melt. Or a bacon cheeseburger. It's not like I would die if I had a burger. It's just that I have to limit myself. I miss the days of not worrying about heart attacks.

She tears off a piece of the uneaten half of her patty melt and offers it to me.

"No, thank you."

A rude sound vibrates from her throat. "I didn't take a bite off that side. I promise."

I shake my head, opening my mouth to argue with her. Avery has other plans. She pops up off her seat, reaches across the table, and shoves the small bite into my mouth.

At first, I can't believe she did that. What am I thinking? Of course, she did. She's Avery Freaking O'Bryan, and she does what she pleases.

I either need to spit it out or eat it. And right now, I can feel people watching us, as if we're on display. If I spit it out, it will cause more attention to swing our way. So, I chew it.

It's everything I remember from my boyhood. Cheesy, greasy goodness. Lord, it's incredible.

"One little taste isn't going to kill you."

Is she just talking about the patty melt? Probably. I'm still half hard from our interaction thirty minutes ago, and she seemed utterly unaffected. I bet just about everything sounds like a double entendre to me.

"No."

"No, it won't, or just, no?"

"I agree with you, but I have to watch what I eat. Family history."

She nods. "That makes sense."

Then she focuses back on her food. The exchange has left me a little off-center. Let's be honest. I've been off-center since the moment she landed on top of me.

"He followed us."

She's speaking in a furious whisper. I look up, then follow her line of sight behind me. Mr. Creeper has arrived at the diner. He gets seated far away from us, but something is definitely off about the guy. He doesn't seem to be paying attention to us, but I get this feeling that he's watching us out of the corner of his eye.

"Why do you think he's stalking you?"

"Wait, why do you think he's stalking me? He was there before I got there, right?"

"Yes. But he never ventured out after me until you came to town."

"Coincidence."

Although, my gut tightens. There was something off, and while I never directly worked for the CIA or the FBI, I did a lot of contract work with them. Or I did at one time. It held no interest for me anymore, and I didn't need the money.

"There is no such thing as coincidence."

I blink and look at her. Like my grandmother said, Avery is brilliant. Hard to see it under the insanity that seems to revolve around her, but it's there. I decide to call my last FBI contact to see if he can dig anything up on the guy.

"Did you find out his name?"

She shakes her head, then looks around the restaurant, grabbing her phone. After sending a text, she sets the phone back down and starts eating again. Her phone pings, and she looks at it, still shoving tots into her mouth.

"Anything?"

She shakes her head. After swallowing a bite, she says, "Mrs. Petersen will start working on it. Shouldn't take long to get his name."

Before I can respond, the waitress returns with two massive shakes. Vanilla for me and chocolate for Avery.

"Here you go," the waitress says, leaning over to give me a view of her cleavage. Avery makes a rude noise. I glance over to see her roll her eyes.

"If you want him to bed you, just ask for his number."

The waitress straightens and shoots Avery a glare. Avery ignores the woman. Instead, she's sucking down her shake. What is Avery like in bed? Is she just as wild? Does she like to experiment?

Dammit. My jeans have grown tight over my erection. I cannot get hot over a woman I need out of my house, especially since the two of us will be there at night. And let me just say she wears almost nothing to bed.

"So, Jon, how about it? You and me this Friday night?"

I blink and look at the waitress. I vaguely remember her from my youth. She was definitely a cheerleader, and because I was a hot-blooded heterosexual boy, I'm sure I noticed her. The one thing I do remember is a particular incident with Becca Gold, one of the owners of Nerdvana.

"I'm busy."

She gives Avery a hostile glance. My roommate just shrugs. "I'm not going to be here, so don't look at me. Also, weird that you would ask him out on a date in front of another woman. I mean, if that woman was his grandma, that would make sense, but I'm young enough to date him, so it's weird, right?"

The waitress blinks. "You are weird."

Avery gives the woman a blinding smile. "Why, thank you."

Then, she starts eating again, and I can't help it. I laugh. And not just the little chuckle like earlier. This one has me throwing back my head and laughing. People turn and look at us, but I don't care. From how Avery is smiling while chewing her food to how the waitress looks at her, it's so funny.

With an exaggerated huff, the waitress stomps off.

"I wouldn't sit at her station any time soon," I tell Avery.

She shrugs and looks outside. We have one of the booths that line Main Street, so we have a good view out the windows.

"Avery?"

She shakes herself and looks at me. "I usually come in the middle of the night. I like to be here when no one…but…"

Then she trails off, and I cock my head. "No one but?"

Is she meeting a guy here at night? Is it Josh, that jerk? I will say he was never a jerk to me, but I feel he is one based on the realization that Avery might be interested in him.

"No one."

"No one but no one? That doesn't make any sense even for you."

She sighs.

"Are you meeting a secret lover like Mr. Keller?"

Her mouth twitches. "No. You can't do anything like that in this town. Everyone would know. It's just that I like it when it's quiet. In the middle of the night or early in the morning, it's calm. It helps me."

I nod in understanding. From what I've seen, she has ADD or ADHD, both of which would make it hard to concentrate when she gets too many things going.

"Understandable."

Then what she said hits me.

"Where are you going on Friday?"

"Nunya."

"Nunya?"

"As in, none of your business."

She has the comedic sensibility of a nine-year-old. "Avery."

She sighs. "I need to find a dress for that fundraiser your grandmother is doing. Some of the money is for the shelter, and she thinks I should be there."

"Ah. She got me too."

"You have to go. I don't."

"What do you mean I have to, but you don't?"

"I meant that you're related to her. She's your grandma. Me, I'm just a stray who rents her house."

Immediately, the description angers me. "You are not a stray, Avery. Estella really likes you."

She glances up, surprise lighting her dark brown eyes. "Excuse me?"

"My grandmother really likes you."

"Oh."

"So, she invited you because she likes you. She spent most of the morning chatting about all you do."

She snorts. "I don't do much."

"You are very involved with the shelter."

"Well, yeah. I like animals. But it's not like I'm a volunteer fireman or the sheriff. Both of those jobs freak me out. I mean…running into a building on fire?" She shudders. "And I'm not allowed to have a gun again."

"Wait, what happened with a gun that you can't have one again?"

"It's not like…a rule or a law. It's just that Fritz made me promise not to do it again."

"Do what again?"

She frowns at me. "Handle a gun. Fritz said that I couldn't pay attention well enough. He was teaching all of us about guns—"

"All of us?"

"Cora, Liv, Gerry, and me. Are you alright?"

"What?"

"I mean, you seem like maybe your blood sugar is low. Maybe take a hit of that milkshake. Although, why someone would want to drink vanilla is beyond me."

I have somehow lost control of the conversation. I'm not sure why I do it, but I take a sip of my milkshake. Another memory almost overwhelms me as the sugary sweetness hits my taste buds. God, that was good. I take another large sip.

"Good, right?"

I look at her, this little woman, and she is kind of small

since she barely comes up to my shoulder, and I wonder what she's doing to me.

"What?"

"Nothing."

"Not nothing. You're looking at me like, well, I'm not sure what you're looking at me like, but I'm not sure it's something I like."

My lips twitch. "There's a lot of likes in that sentence."

She opens her mouth to respond, but her phone vibrates on the table. "Ah, his name is Norman Adams." She looks at me. "Does he look like a Norman to you?"

"Do any of us look like our names?"

"Yes. I definitely look like an Avery. You look like a Jon."

Then she giggles.

"What?"

"Well, a Jon. Get it?"

I roll my eyes and try not to laugh. It shouldn't make me laugh that she's mocking my name, but the truth is, this is the most relaxed I've felt in a long time, especially in Juniper.

"But I definitely look like an Avery."

"It's a different kind of name."

She smiled. "Like me, so it fits."

He couldn't argue with that. "How did your parents come up with the name?"

"For a long time, I thought they named me after the label company."

"Why did you think that?"

"Fritz. He's such, well, a Fritz."

"Your brother told you that?"

"Oh, don't look so horrified."

"That's mean."

"Yeah, but that's siblings. He was in the minority, and we did not make his life easy. Especially Cora." She chuckles. "That's one O'Bryan you do not want to piss off."

"I will never understand siblings."

"You have some, though, right?"

I nod. "I have a couple half-brothers I don't really know. And some step-siblings."

"And this new dude, he's got kids."

"New dude?"

"The dude shacking up with your mother."

Damn, I'd almost forgotten about that. "Yeah. I guess I'm supposed to meet his daughters at some time."

"That will be good. You need siblings."

"Really? Why is that?"

"When you need help, they're always there. At least mine are. Sometimes too much."

But there was something in her voice, something that I couldn't figure out what it meant. The waitress returned, slamming our ticket down on the table, giving Avery another nasty look.

"You're right. I better not sit in her section again. There would probably be spit in my food."

"That's not a thing that happens."

"You never worked in a restaurant, I take it?"

I shake my head.

"I did. I needed to keep myself busy at school, and I had a lot of scholarships, but they didn't cover everything. I worked at this hole-in-the-wall burger joint. I never spit in people's food, but it happens, believe me."

And now, I don't ever want to eat in another restaurant.

"Don't worry, Jon. That woman wants to swap spit with you, not put it in your food."

My face heats in embarrassment. How does she keep doing that?

"Why do you do that?"

"Do what?"

"You say outrageous things."

She cocks her head and studies me. Usually, I'm not bothered by this kind of attention. I get it all the time. But when Avery does it, my entire system goes into overdrive. Irritation mixed with arousal is not a good look on anyone, especially me.

"What?"

She shakes her head. "Nothing. And I do it because people expect it. And I like making people laugh."

"Why do you worry about that?"

"Because when there's laughter, people don't feel so alone anymore."

And in that one sentence, she almost breaks my heart. That's next to impossible. According to my former personal assistant, I have no heart. There is an underlying tone to her words that makes me think Avery must be lonely a lot of the time.

I want to ask her more. I want to ask her just when she was lonely and why. It pisses me off that she has four siblings and is still lonely. But I know I don't have the right to demand those things.

Instead, I shake my head. "It's still rude."

"Rude is trying to pick up a man out with another woman."

I smile. "True."

"So, you know Estella cornered me about her fundraising thing?"

"She did?"

"I didn't know I was invited. And just because of that, I have to go to San Antonio for a dress."

"You don't have much time. Don't you already have something to wear?"

"Oh, sure, I have a closet just for my formal dresses." It's easy to hear the sarcasm in her voice. "But you should be happy. Liv, the kids, and I are going to San Antonio for a day or two to shop. You get to have my house to yourself."

"Good. I can finally get some work done."

She gives me a look, then glances outside.

"What was that look for?"

"No reason. I just know that's a lie."

"What do you mean?"

She sighs and looks back at me. "I have a feeling if you really needed to work, you would. But you're restless. I can feel it. So that tells me you have a major problem at work, you're worried about your ex, or you really don't have anything else to do than hang out in Juniper."

I hate that she's so close to the truth. I want to do something else, but this is all I have ever known, and it makes me a lot of money.

"You're hanging out in Juniper and not doing much."

She offers me a small smile. "That's not a good defense."

I want to say more, but Mrs. Petersen steps up to the table to gossip. I tuck my thoughts on Avery and her perceptive comments in the back of my mind. I will finally have some time to myself in my house, and I can't wait.

Chapter Eighteen

Avery

I hate shopping. Let me rephrase that. I hate shopping in person, and I really hate shopping for clothes. I think most of it comes from the fact that I'm oddly shaped. I don't mean I have an extra foot weird, but I'm short and curvy. It's hard to find something that looks right on me. Also, a girl can find all the PJs she needs to wear online.

"How about this one?" Liv asks, holding up another dress. It's a slip of a dress, perfect for her. It's a deep shade of blue, almost purple, and yes, the color would look good on me. The shape of the dress…not so much.

All my sisters are tall. They have long bodies that are proportioned properly. I'm way curvier with a long torso and short legs. It isn't easy finding things that look good on me.

The long sheath is simple, and it would accentuate Liv's subtle curves.

"You would look great in that."

Liv frowns. "You would too."

"No, she wouldn't," Savannah, our sister-in-law, says.

She'd found a chair somehow and dragged it over to watch us shop. I smile at her. Savannah is blunt. I think it comes from running a kitchen for so many years.

"See."

Liv looks at her. "That's rude."

She shrugs and digs into her purse. She pulls out a bag of nuts. Savannah just hit her third trimester, and feeding her is a priority. I thought I was the hangriest of hangry people, but I'm nothing compared to Savannah. Fritz says he just throws food at her when she gets hungry because she scares him.

"That would look good on you."

Liv shakes her head. "I don't want to spend the money for one night. I have other dresses."

I frown. I thought we were shopping for both of us. I know that Liv has to watch her money, but a dress for a formal event—the first one she's attended in a long time other than our brother's wedding—isn't going to break her. I look at the tag. It's expensive, but it's on clearance. I open my mouth to tell her I'll pay for it as an early birthday present, but Savannah beats me to the punch.

"My treat. Buy what you want. Both of you."

We glance at Savannah, who is still munching on her snack and making appreciative sounds. Savannah is an odd duck, so she fits in our family just fine. Tall, beautiful, and intelligent, she's way too good for Fritz, but he knows it, so I guess that's okay. Long, thick, black hair frames a stunning face, and she's way hotter than me, even pregnant. In fact, she's one of those women who glows. She's a former chef who hosts a travel show and is a bit of a celebrity.

"We can't let you do that," Liv says.

"You have to. I want to, plus I'm loaded. Pick out anything, and I'll buy it." Savannah isn't exaggerating. She would be a billionaire if she didn't give so much of her money away. This is just like her too. She loves to help just about anyone, friends and family. That's why I can take her bluntness. Under that hard exterior is a sweet woman.

I look at Liv. "She *is* loaded. You're going to support Mason. Pick something out for him."

"Try on the dress. Avery and I will look for a dress for her while you're changing."

Liv looks between us, her hands tightening around the dress. She still has issues doing things for herself, but she's improving. It helps that Mason spoils her. She nods and heads off to the changing rooms.

I look over at my sister-in-law, who is attempting to stand. I rush over to help. "You're good."

"Comes from running a kitchen. People need to understand that I run the show. Once they know who the Alpha is, Betas get in line."

Savannah ran her family's restaurant business for years before she became a travel host on *The Adventure Network*. I smile as we start looking through the dresses.

"You hate shopping." Not a question.

"Yeah. You remember how bad it was for the wedding."

She nods, looking through the rack of dresses. "And I helped you then. Or we could get EJ down here. That woman is amazing at shopping for anything, but especially clothes."

EJ is one of her best friends and is married to one of Fritz's partners. Another tall bombshell, she has the curves of Marilyn Monroe, dark red hair, and that deep southern twang that drives many men crazy.

"But I think this would be gorgeous on you."

She pulls out a dress and holds it up. Holy Taylor Swift. It is almost a replica of the gold Oscar Del La Renta dress Taylor wore in the *Blank Space* video. It's a little darker, which is good for me, with bows on the tulle that drapes over satin material. It's a shorter dress, so I don't have to worry about getting it altered. I want it so badly, I almost cry, but it isn't me. It's fancy and gold, and well, I'm a short, squatty girl who doesn't look good all dressed up.

"I…I don't think that will look good on me."

Savannah rolls her eyes, but before she can say anything, Liv steps out of the changing rooms. The blue sheath dress fits her perfectly, accenting her slight curves like I knew it would. The color is perfect on her.

I walk closer as she looks in the three-way mirror. "Oh, you look fantastic in that."

"You think?" She glances over at Savannah and me. We both nod.

"Mason's tongue will roll out of his mouth like Houdini's when Sammy's eating."

She snorts. "That's a pleasant thought."

She turns and looks behind her. The dress shows a little more of her back than I realized. And I'm right. Mason will lose it when he sees her in it.

"You have to get it. It fits you perfectly, and that color…"

"Okay," she says, smiling. If you knew my sister, you would understand what a big step that was. She was taking on too much and feeling like she was a failure. Thanks to

Mason, she now understands that asking for help doesn't mean she's failing.

She's smiling as she rushes back to the changing rooms.

Savannah steps up once we're alone again, still holding that dress. "It's A-line, and it'll show a lot of boob."

"That's not a big recommendation."

I'm not a prude, but I do have hang-ups about my chest. I developed before a lot of other girls, and being two years younger than everyone else in my grade, it was terrible. I wasn't emotionally equipped for the behavior of hormonal guys.

Savannah presses the dress into my hands. "Go put that on. Perfect for you to wear. It's the kind of dress dudes look at and think about taking off."

For some reason, Jon's face pops into my mind. "That's not my intention."

One eyebrow rises. "There is a lot of chatter about you and this Jon dude."

Embarrassment swamps me. "What do you mean, chatter? On the Juniper Springs Express?"

She rolls her eyes and snorts. "No. I don't mess with that insanity. I have enough of that being married to Fritz."

It's usually only for locals, but Savannah has several connections to the town, so I could see that she could get on the JSE without being a resident.

"So where was this chatter?"

"Your siblings. They're all thinking it is only a matter of time before you jump his bones."

I know it wasn't from Fritz. He wouldn't make comments about my love life. He could care less. I mean, as long as no one hurts us, he's good.

"It was Cora, wasn't it?"

She smiles, rubbing a hand over her belly. "You know she instigates all the problems. Now, go try this dress on."

"That jerk."

"Go."

I take the dress and stomp off to the changing room. I am not the svelte goddess of the quill—Taylor Swift, if you didn't know who I was talking about. I have the exact opposite type of body, but there was no way I wouldn't do as my sister-in-law ordered. Savannah kind of scares me.

I'm definitely going to have to buy another bra for this. I get it on, but can't zip it up, so I call Liv. She knocks on my door, and as soon as I open it, she gasps.

"Oh, that's perfect."

I look in the mirror and realize the gold dress brings out the gold in my eyes. The feel of the dress against my skin is fantastic.

She steps behind me and does up the zipper. I feel like… a princess.

I mean, not an actual princess, but I feel special. The neckline does dip down, but not as much as I thought. The way it cinches in at the waist…I look like a hot woman from the fifties or something.

"Of course, Savannah helped you find something perfect."

I glance at Liv. "What's wrong?"

"Nothing." She sniffs.

"What has you almost crying? Are you pregnant?"

"Good God, why would you say that?"

"You're almost crying."

She sighs. "This is just…I'm really enjoying doing this with you and with Savannah."

I feel my heart soften. Out of all the O'Bryan sisters, Liv is the most soft-hearted. She feels the most, even though she is a tough-as-nails former military wife. She's endured a lot but still gets caught up in these things.

"I like doing this too."

"We should do it more often."

"Sure, next time I have a formal event, I promise to go shopping with you."

She cocks her head, studying me. "Be careful what you say with the company you keep these days."

"What's that supposed to mean?"

"Jon Howard is the kind of man who would have to do many of these things. I bet he's coming to the benefit."

I roll my eyes. "Of course he is. It's his grandmother's charity. I think he's helping her host or something."

"Okay. Well, let's check out and then grab something to eat. Savannah needs food."

I nod, then look at the tag for the first time. When I see the price, I wince. I have the money, but I hate spending it on things like this, and it kind of irritates me. The amount of PJ bottoms and fuzzy socks I could buy for this is insane. I mean, those I can wear all the time. This will probably be a one-time thing, and I hate wasting money. If this was any other person, I wouldn't go. Hell, even if one of my family was handling it, I would donate money and just not attend. Or if I did, I wouldn't worry about a new dress.

Estella is different. First, she's scarier than Savannah. Second, I owe her. She could have easily kicked me out of the house, but she didn't. I will dress up and go to pay her back and show her respect.

I change back into my clothes, then go out to the floor. The sales lady takes my dress, puts a bag over it, and hands it back to me. Liv's dress is already bagged. The woman shakes her head when I pull out my card to pay.

"Your friend already paid for it."

I look at Savannah. "I can pay for it."

She shakes her head. "I said I would pay. Also, you got me out of the house. I can't believe we aren't filming for the next few months."

Their trip to Puerto Rico was the end of the second season of her show. Fritz—and the Hawthorne family, who owns the network—insisted that she take off for her last trimester and the first three months after the baby is born. "I just know that Fritz is going to get worse."

It's been fun seeing my former player of a brother freaking out and going all Alpha Protector over Savannah. She winces and settles a hand on her stomach.

"What?"

"This demon seed is kicking me. Figures I'm having a boy."

Liv and I share a smile.

"Then, let's go eat. My treat."

"That sounds like a plan," Savannah says. "I could really go for a big thick steak."

Chapter Nineteen

Jon

The house is too quiet.

I never thought I would think those words. Still, I realize that two hours into my workday, Avery's exuberance was something I'd gotten used to. I've been here a few days, and she has gotten under my skin already.

Still, I forge ahead and get a lot of work done, but I finish it all that morning. I even got closer to a decision about selling my company to Trevor. But it isn't abnormal for me to get work done early in the day. Avery is usually asleep until about eleven in the morning.

I get up and wander through the first floor. Why do I feel so unsettled? It can't be that I crave the insanity of Avery. I know she has a successful business, but I don't know how she gets any work done. Chaos is something I despise, and that's Avery in a nutshell.

A cup of coffee will get me out of my funk. As I'm filling up the machine, there's a loud quacking out front. Once I hit start, I head for the front door to find Bert and Ernie, the two male mallard ducks that seem to be living an alternative lifestyle here in Juniper, standing on the porch being the assholes that they are. They go from house to house demanding food.

"Give me a second."

As I grab some bread, I realize they hadn't come by since I returned. I wonder if Meredith is the reason. Without her here today, did the ducks sense they were safe? Or maybe they're afraid of Avery? Understandable. She's scary.

I toss out a couple of pieces of bread and shut the door. Thankfully, that's all it takes with those two. They will harass the next house as soon as they gobble the bread down.

Again, I find myself wandering the house again, thinking I could come up with something else to do with my day. I told Avery that she could leave Meredith here with me. Still, she said Meredith needed to meet her cousin, General McLovin.

I shake my head. Since her grandmother named the cat, I will say that she and Avery were a lot alike. He could see Avery naming a cat McLovin. Hell, she named her cat after Taylor Swift's cat.

She was definitely close to her grandmother. To her whole family, really. I know they're constantly texting. While we were eating lunch yesterday, there were at least a dozen texts. All she would say is that there was an argument among her siblings. That alone would irritate me, but she laughed when she said it.

The woman has a way about her.

Uh, no. Not thinking about that. Sure, I had a great time eating with her the day before yesterday. I couldn't help inviting her out. I couldn't take the sad look in her eyes or how her voice caught when she talked about her grandmother. I have never been close to mine, but Avery seemed to think the world of hers. And all I wanted to do was make her the happy woman I knew her to be.

But even that's not true. I suspect she's a happy woman, but something else is happening now. Something I sense beneath the surface like she hasn't dealt with her grandmother's death all that well. That revelation yesterday kind of shook me. Seeing another side of her beneath the shiny, happy surface made her less of an adversary and more of a…not friend. That's not a word I would ever use to describe her.

What word would I use to describe her?

My phone vibrates in my pocket, and I pull it out.

Trev: *What is going on in the great state of Texas?*

Me: *Nothing.*

Trev: *You're so exciting. Sure you don't want to come to NYC?*

Ugh, I could do with some fishing in upstate New York, which is probably what he wants to do. But I still don't feel right about leaving right now.

My grandmother is right, though. I probably need a good vacation. I was thinking about going to Hawaii. Mom loves Hawaii, but I'm unsure if she would go with me—at least not alone.

I bet Avery would love Hawaii. I have only been there once with my mother for a week. The Howards have a house on the island, and we went when I graduated from college. I couldn't live there, but damn, I loved the time I stayed there.

Me: *Still don't have my house.*

Trev: *Damn, you're losing your touch.*

Me: *Fuck off.*

I notice some movement out of the corner of my eye, and I realize it's Creeper Dude. He's not looking my way. Instead, he's rummaging around in the yard. He's a vacation renter, so why would he be fucking with that kind of stuff? Whatever he's up to, he does look a little shifty. I think he's just one of those guys that looks shifty even if they aren't up to anything. Serial killers rarely look like people think they will.

He tosses a look at the house. I immediately step back. Stupid, I know, because I have every right to stand at my door and look out. I watch from the side, hoping he doesn't see me creeping on him. The malevolent look he gives the house is…well, it's weird. I mean, who looks at a house like that? Especially one he has never been in. The Howards have owned this house for over half a century, so there is no way he has been in here. I pull up my phone and take a pic of him, hoping he doesn't see me.

He doesn't respond, so I let loose a breath I didn't realize I was holding. I look down at the photo. It's not that great, but it's a picture I can use. After he stares long and hard, he turns and lumbers back into the house. I stand there, thinking of how he looked at the house and Avery's comments about the man.

I do have friends at the FBI, but I want to do a little checking on him myself before I go to any of them. I call my investigator.

"Howard, how's tricks," Sam Dixon says, his Long Island accent making me smile.

"Not bad. I have another person I want you to look up."

"Don't tell me your mom dumped that football player. He seems like a nice guy. I emailed you the report."

I had seen it in my email inbox but hadn't read it.

"I'll look it over as soon as I can. I have an issue in Juniper, though, nothing to do with my mother."

"That Avery O'Bryan? She's clean."

"Yeah, no. There's something else that has come up. I have a sketchy renter behind me, and I want him checked out."

"Shoot."

"His name is Norman Adams. I would say he's in his thirties, although it's hard to tell."

"Got it. Nothing else, other than he's renting a house you own."

"Nope. He's behind mine, and he's…a little sketchy."

There's a bad vibe about the man. I know that most people would think I've lost my mind, but I just don't like the look of the man. I hate to admit it, but Avery might be on to something.

"Got it. I'll start looking through his life. Or at least try to find him. Call me if you can get anything else, a driver's license, a social security number, or anything else. You know that makes it faster."

"I'm going to send you a pic, although it's not that good."

"That will help. Later."

Then he hangs up. Having someone who works for me and isn't a yes-man is nice. He does his job, but he doesn't give a shit that I own *Lone Star Tech* or that I'm a Howard from *that* Howard family in Texas. All he cares about is getting paid to do a job he loves.

After slipping my phone back into my pocket, I decide to get back to work. I always thrive on long work hours, and yes, I know I have a problem. But as I head back into my office, I realize it isn't as exciting as it used to be.

IT'S the following day before Avery gets home. She apparently decided to stay in San Antonio for a second night. She didn't tell me, but I saw it on the JSE. Rude.

But I'm surprised she's walking into the house at ten in the morning. It means she had to get up before eight to make it here because she is a bottomless pit and would not leave a house without food—unless she had been promised food.

The clatter of little feet and excited voices is what gets my attention. I leave my office and see Sammy and Callie running down the hallway. Meredith is following in their footsteps.

"Kids, don't run in the house. I've told you this a hundred times," Liv says, but her voice has no real heat. Only exasperated affection. She reminds him of his mom.

"Hey, Jon, I'm sorry for the intrusion," she says. "Avery promised the kids could go in the backyard. They love it."

I nod. "No problem."

She follows her kids, and my gaze stays locked on the door. As soon as Avery steps over the threshold, my entire body relaxes. It's as if a piece of my puzzle just locked into place.

Weird.

"Jon!" She sets her overnight bag down on the floor and smiles at me. "I'm so happy you are here to greet me."

I roll my eyes, even as my heart is pounding so loud. I can't believe she doesn't hear it. What is this reaction? Seeing her return to my house shouldn't leave me with a sense of relief. I should still be irritated. Right?

"Find a dress?"

"Yes."

"You're home earlier than I expected."

"Oh. Were you hoping I never returned?"

No. "Yes."

She frowns at me, and, Jesus, my dick twitches. What the fuck is happening?

"We stayed an extra night because we were lured in by cupcakes, Tex-Mex, and the promise of Savannah's ricotta pancakes."

"Of course, food."

"Yes."

Then we stand there with the distant sounds of children laughing and nothing else but silence. It's weird to see Avery so still. She is always going, so…loud.

"Hey," Liv says, walking back into the kitchen. She comes to an abrupt stop. I don't break eye contact with Avery, but Liv studies us as if we are specimens.

"What's going on?"

Avery's lips twitch. Even that has my hormones dancing. It's like she's some kind of damned Svengali. She breaks the stare down first.

"Jon and I were having a staring contest."

Were we? My heart is still beating out of control, and I feel breathless. Beyond that, I'm half-hard dealing with the nearness of her. It's been almost forty hours since she left. When did I start counting the amount of time she had been gone. Oh, fuck, have I become an Avery addict?

"I lost, but there will be another duel soon."

"I take it you found a dress?"

"I thought I just told you."

"Oh, yeah." She did, and I look like a fool in front of her sister. Again.

"Is there something going on?" Liv asks, and again, she reminds me of my mother. But, since she's not my mother, she doesn't know my tells. I hope.

"No."

"Yes," Avery says at the same time. "Jon is apparently good at staring contests."

Her sister shakes her head. "I need to get the kids back to the house. Houdini is apparently depressed without them."

"I told you that you should bring him with us."

"He would have been fighting with McLovin the entire time. See you tonight, Jon."

"Oh, yeah."

Which reminds me, I have to head over to my grandmother's. Although now I don't want to. I want to stay here and listen to Avery tell me about her time in San Antonio. And that's enough to irritate me.

Liv turns and heads to the kitchen door, and to break the spell Avery has on me, I follow Liv. She's laughing, watching her kids dance around the yard. Callie doesn't look like the serious little girl from the other night, and Sammy is…well, Sammy.

"They think the yard is magical. As soon as I can afford it, I want to do something like this to our backyard."

"Aren't you renting that house from my cousin?"

She nods. "I'm going to buy it off her."

"Your cousin and her man are my date tonight."

I blink and look down at Avery. Again, for someone so loud, she is being super stealthy. "What?"

"Liv and Mason have to be there early."

"You could go with Jon."

My head whips around to look at her sister, who gives me a knowing smile. Okay, maybe there is some kind of weird knowledge power base all moms have.

"Nope," Avery says.

"Why not?"

I glance down at her. Her attention is out in the yard, watching the kids. Meredith is following them through the yard as if she's guarding them.

"Yeah, why not?" I ask.

"You have to be there early to help your granny."

"Estella has never been called granny."

She snorts. "Yeah, well, you should try it."

I don't say anything in response.

"I also need a nap. Getting up so early threw me completely out of my regular rhythm."

"You mean staying up until four or five, then passing out until noon?" I ask.

Her sister laughs. "He has you there."

"Go away. You are my least favorite sister. Maybe," she says, looking around me to her sister, "I'll rate you lower than Fritz."

Another laugh. "Sure. You do that. Call him when you

need to talk about your latest Taylor clowning. Kids, let's go."

There were complaints and whining.

"Houdini is missing you," she calls out. They start running full speed to the door.

"What do you say to Mr. Howard about letting you play in the yard?"

"Not his yard," Avery says.

"Thank you," the kids yell out as they rush into the house.

"Sorry about them. See you tonight, Jon. Avery, don't oversleep. You know Estella wants you there."

She nods.

The moment the front door closes, blessed silence fills the house. Avery turns towards the stairs.

"Where are you going?"

"Nap. So tired. Too many people. More tonight."

I watch her go, irritated with myself for feeling slighted.

"Meow."

I look down at Meredith, who is watching me, apparently worried I'm upset. Which is a stupid thought because she's a cat.

Still, I lean down and scratch her behind her ears. "Your mistress is going to bed. You might want to get in on that."

Meredith rubs against my legs, then stalks upstairs. I have no time to nap because my grandmother has already called twice. With a sigh, I head off to grab everything I need for tonight. One thing I know about my grandmother is that you do not keep her waiting. She controls everything, and it's best to just go along.

Chapter Twenty

Jon

I roll my shoulders and try to count backward from ten. It's been hours since I arrived at my grandmother's house, and I'm ready to escape. The truth is, I was ready to leave as soon as I arrived. The idea of being in a room with tons of people makes my skin crawl. I find gatherings like this wasteful of my time. It's one of the reasons I think I get so bored with the women I date. They tend to like the type of events my grandmother throws. Granted, there are probably no party drugs here, but it is Juniper, so you never know.

I nod to the mayor and his wife. In one way or another, he has always been a fixture in Juniper. He taught science, was the principal of the high school, and he was on the city council. His wife is a pediatrician, semi-retired.

"Hey, Howard," Ford Gold says.

I glance over at Becca Gold's brother—stepbrother—although the three brothers are more like blood brothers to Becca.

"Hey."

"Hiding out in the alcove?"

I cut him a look as he drinks his whiskey.

"Maybe. You?'

"Same. I tried to hide in the library, and your grand-mother caught me."

The oldest of the Gold siblings, he has always been the quietest and most serious. He's taking over the family's ranch, from what I understand. Other than the Howards, the Golds are the largest landowners in the area.

"Yeah, she warned me off too. What are you doing here?"

"My folks are out of town on their anniversary trip. Mom said I had to come."

Mom. Millie Gold is his stepmother, but she has always been their mom. It's odd to me to be that close to stepsib-lings, but they are not horrible people like mine.

"And I assume you're stuck here because of your grandmother."

I nod, but before I can say anything else, Becca steps up next to him. She's dressed all in pink from head to toe. And when I say head, I mean she's colored the tips of her blonde hair pink, and they are a riot of curls down her back. Her dress looks as if it was made from cotton candy, molding to her curvy figure. Her makeup is light. It almost feels as if I'm looking at a fairy.

"Good evening, Jon."

I smile. "Hey, Becca."

She is the sweetest woman, and I have no idea how she is friends with Everly. I guess opposites attract.

She settles her gaze on her brother. "Ford, you must come with me."

"Why?"

"Some beauty queen from Dallas wants to meet you."

"Well, I don't want to meet her."

Of course, someone is looking to hook up with him. The Howards are the richest, but the Gold family isn't that far behind.

"I know. That's why I'm helping you out." She gives me a look. "You need to look out for her too. I heard her talking over at the bar. She's all about finding a rich husband. You both qualify."

"Duly noted."

"She's in purple, has hair bigger than Texas, and is roaming the room with a pack of other women. Not hard to miss. Come on."

She drags her brother away to save him, and I find myself smiling. It's the same kind of relationship I have with Nancy. At least when I'm around. I know I've always been… distant because she lives in Juniper. My memories here aren't that great. Those early years of my parents' marriage falling apart and being bullied still get to me. I need to deal with them because I love Nancy and want to be around her more.

I just have to get my house back.

My phone vibrates in my pocket. I pull it out and roll my eyes.

Trev: *Hey, get your house back?*

He has been texting me every freaking day. He's enjoying my predicament a little too much.

Me: *No.*

Trev: *Leave her the house and come to New York before I do something stupid.*

It's the second time today that he's asked me to come to New York.

Me: *Stupid?*

Trev: *Never mind.*

Oh, no, that doesn't sound good. I step further into the alcove and call him.

"I told you to never mind."

"Yeah, but if you weren't worried about your behavior, you wouldn't have said anything."

"Why do you say that?"

"Because you never worry about your behavior."

He snorts. "True."

Then, nothing. A niggle of worry wormed into my gut. "Trev?"

I know he had some issues with PTSD when he returned from deployment, but he told me he got help for it.

"Oh, I just got Jon's worried voice." His mocking tone might upset other people, but I hear the fear under it. It's simmering in the background.

"Trevor. Tell me."

He sighs. "I'm having issues with my…needs."

I frown. "Needs?"

"I just feel out of control."

His PTSD didn't come in the form of violence or depression. He became a speed junky, always looking for the next high.

My pulse scrambles as alarm careens through me. "What are you talking about?"

"It's…a woman."

"Tell me you didn't sleep with one of the socialites."

Trevor's mother has been after him to get married. The

laugh that explodes out of his mouth has my nerves settling. "No. I can't stay far enough away from those women."

"So, tell me."

"It's someone I shouldn't even be thinking about."

I start sorting through our conversations. An eidetic memory is sometimes painful, but it's good in cases like this. My mind works back to a conversation we had a few weeks ago. He has an old Army buddy who asked for a place for his sister. Something happened with her rental, and she desperately needed a place to stay.

"That sister. The one who's staying with you."

"Fuck me." It comes out as a whisper so low I'm not sure he realizes he said it out loud.

"Nope. You are definitely not my type."

"Is that a fact?"

"Too pretty for a man."

Another laugh has my nerves settling. "It's funny that people don't know you have a sense of humor."

"Tell me."

"We…let's just say we've always had this hate thing going on."

"And now?"

As I ask the question, Avery steps into my line of vision, and everything in my brain stops working.

Fuck me.

I don't know if it's out of frustration or a request. Probably both. Jesus, she's stunning. I knew she was beautiful, and hell, I knew she had curves, but I didn't understand what they would do to me dressed up like that. The dress is vaguely familiar. It doesn't even show much skin except her legs. But the color of it leaves her skin looking golden. It molds to her body, leaving no doubt that she has the most amazing breasts and a tiny waist. She has what they call an hourglass figure, and damn me, I want to spend time exploring every inch.

Fuck, I feel my cock twitch, and my palms are sweating. As she turns to say something to Travis, I almost growl. I know Travis has no interest in her, but the fact that she's close to another man has my entire once-dormant possessive side roaring to life.

"Jon?"

"What?"

"What's going on? I just went through what happened, and you said nothing but 'fuck me.' I find it odd since you just told me you weren't into me."

I shake my head to clear it of the thoughts crowding every corner of my brain, but it does nothing to help.

"Listen, you're calling the wrong person for advice. You know, I don't know crap about relationships."

"Jon, I can't talk to her brother, and he's got a kid on the way. Too busy for me."

"I don't know what you want me to do. I'm in Texas, at a formal function that my grandmother bullied me into hosting with her." Although he was still trying to figure out what that consisted of.

As if conjured up my thoughts, I feel a tap on my shoulder. I turn around and then look down. My grandmother is standing there with a big frown—the one that used to make me freak out as a kid. She stamps her cane on the floor.

"Jonathon, what do you think you're doing?"

"Who's that?" Trev asks.

"Talking to Trev."

She rolls her eyes. "Why would you call him during the party?"

Old habits die hard, so I throw Trev under the proverbial bus to save myself from retribution.

"He's having female issues."

One eyebrow rises. "You're hiding out in Juniper Springs, trying to avoid your mother and ex-girlfriend. I don't think you're the man to call unless you're about to open a commune for men who are afraid of women."

"Ha! Your grandmother is brilliant."

"Shut up."

"Excuse me?" my grandmother asks.

"Talking to Trev."

"Give me the phone."

I hesitate.

"I thought you might want to talk to Avery."

I fight the need to look around for her. "Why would you think that?"

She smiles. "So, you're okay with Josh talking to her."

My attention zeroes in on Josh and Avery when she says it. She's laughing, and he's leaning in like he's interested. An emotion I don't understand shoots through me. My body heats, anger whipping through me. I want to beat the crap out of Josh. I have no idea why, but I want to tear his arms off his body and smack him in the head with them.

This is not a feeling I have ever really dealt with. I can't help myself. Okay, that's probably a lie. But the truth is, I'm tired. Tired of fighting the pull she has on me. Tired of telling myself I don't want to touch her. Every day, I wrestle with the feelings she stirs in me.

I look down at my grandmother, who holds out her hand.

"Talk to my grandmother."

I don't know what my plan is, but I've learned that planning anything around Avery is a waste of time. I ignore Trev's sputtering questions and hand my phone to my grandmother. Then I step around her and head off in Avery's direction.

Chapter Twenty-One

Avery

Josh is telling me stories about Everly when they were kids, and I can't help but laugh. I was always kind of a pill—my grandmother's description, not mine—but I was never as bold as Everly Spencer. She's Mason's sister, and I have a feeling she will be my sister's sister-in-law someday, so it will be nice to have someone bolder than I am. Then people can get off my back.

"I didn't know if you would end up hanging around so long," Josh says, sipping his water. The guy is always on duty because that happens when you're a small-town sheriff.

"I like small towns. I actually like all kinds of towns."

I look around and see Estella talking to Jon. Arguing from the looks of it. God, he's so pretty. His tux is amazing and, without a doubt, a custom fit. Estella brought Josh to me because I was hanging with the LOLs. She said that wasn't a good thing. It was odd when she winked at me. Estella doesn't wink at people, but she did, making me wonder what is up with her.

"How is it going with you and Howard in the house alone?"

I glance at Josh. I know he's not interested in me. Rumor is that he's got a thing for one of the Russo sisters, who own the winery outside of town. It's so bad that even my sister has heard about it. I sip my favorite Russo Pinot Grigio—complete with ice cubes, of course.

"Eh, it's okay. He's kind of a stickler for things like eating regular meals. Also, he said that I need to ignore the guy behind the house."

Josh frowns, his milk chocolate eyes narrowing. He's a gorgeous man, and the rumors about the women he dated in town are legendary, and I can say I understand. Square jaw, sexy smile, and dark unruly hair—yeah, it makes sense. Shame that he does nothing to my heart or my body other than to acknowledge he's a good-looking man.

"What man?"

"This guy who is renting the Tolbert house behind us. Meredith doesn't like him."

He blinks, his face going blank. "You're worried about a man your cat doesn't like?" I nod. "She doesn't like me."

"Truthfully, she doesn't like most men. Well, except for Jon. I have no idea why she likes him."

Besides the fact that he's pretty, his blue eyes are amazing, and he smells like a dream.

"Is the only reason you don't like him because of Meredith?"

I shake my head. "No. He's creepy."

"Okay."

I hear the tone. Listen, I know I'm a lot to take. Most people can't deal with my constant struggle to remain on topic or my insane love for Taylor Swift. Also, not everyone thinks Froot Loops is a balanced meal. I get it. But there is one thing I am good at, and that's reading people. One of the reasons I earned my BS in Sociology was because I could never figure people out. I would see their behavior and be perplexed by their motivations. Like Chet, my first serious boyfriend. I thought he was a good guy, but I was waaaaay off on that account. In my defense, I had been eighteen and thought I was in love.

"Avery?"

I glance up at him and smile. "Sorry. Off gathering wool. It's why I don't normally come to these things. I find them very overwhelming."

Although, I do love the dress. It's a dream, clinging to every one of my curves, and for once, that makes me feel pretty.

"No problem. I'm the same way, but I thought I should make an appearance. Estella insisted."

"She did?"

He smiles. "Yeah. She showed up a day or two ago. You know, when Estella Howard shows up to the police station slash city hall, it causes people to freak out."

I laugh. "I can imagine."

"I think Jim almost passed out when she showed up at the desk and insisted on talking to me."

"My grandmother has that effect on people."

I turn, ready to make a sarcastic remark but can't. I'm too stunned to make a sound. If Jon was pretty from across the room, he's downright dangerous to my libido this close. He definitely tried to get his hair under control again tonight, but a few curls have broken free. His tux is definitely custom-made, and he looks like James Bond. That is, if James Bond was a persnickety know-it-all trying to make me homeless.

"Howard."

"Collins."

There's a thread of danger to Jon's voice, and I'm not sure what to think about that. I mean, other than to think about it later when I spend time with my vibrator.

No. Dammit. I need to stop that. He's not the man I should be fantasizing about. He's so particular about things, worrying about every detail. I can tell from the way he lives, and it is so annoying. It's also so freaking hot because all I can think about is how he would be in bed. I mean, if he is that detail oriented about cooking, I bet he's good with his hands.

God, why? Why do I think about these things? I know we have a truce of sorts, but I need to remind myself that he hates everything about me.

"I see you arrived finally."

I frown at him. "Were you looking for me?"

He rolls his eyes. "No. It's just that I thought you would be here earlier."

"I had to be Cinderella'd to get here. Do you think I could get to look this perfect without a ton of help?"

His gaze travels down my body, then rises back up, seemingly fixating on my mouth. It's ruby red, a color I don't always use. Lord, that is hotter than any time a guy kissed me.

"You do look amazing."

"Oh, hey, look over there. Someone wants to talk to me."

I glance at Josh and smile. "Yeah, the Russo sisters are over in the parlor."

"Really?"

I nod.

"Excuse me."

It seems that the rumors about Josh and his crush are accurate. There is always a little truth in every rumor. I almost laugh out loud as Josh ignores everyone else as he beelines to the parlor.

Once we're alone, Jon says nothing. He just keeps staring at me, and it's freaking me out.

"What?"

"You know he's got a crush on Bree Russo, right?"

I snort. "Yeah. Everyone knows that."

"So, he wouldn't be interested in dating you."

"More importantly, I'm not interested in dating him."

He searches my gaze with his and seems to relax.

"Jon," Estella says from behind him.

He turns. "What?"

I almost laugh at his tone. He sounds like he just got caught stealing cookies. And, of course, that makes me think of many other things that could represent cookies.

"Here's your phone. Your friend is kind of a mess."

"Tell me something I don't know."

He takes his phone back.

Estella smiles at me. "Are you enjoying yourself, Avery?"

"Always."

Estella gives me a slight smile. "I have to mingle. You two should dance."

And with that pronouncement, she heads off to terrorize other people.

"I love your grandma. If I ever grow up, I want to be like her."

Jon turns to face me again, and he shakes his head. "Because she ordered us to dance?"

"No. It's because she lives life on her own terms."

He cocks his head as he studies me. "Is that what you're doing?"

"What do you mean?"

"I mean that you don't seem to follow the rules."

"What rules? Where in life did this set of rules get written down?"

He shakes his head as he reaches for my now empty glass, taking it from me and placing it on the platter of one of the servers. He holds my hand as he tugs me to the dance floor.

"What are you doing?"

"My grandmother told us to dance. And you know that when Estella Howard tells you to do something, you do it."

I roll my eyes and allow him to lead me to the dance floor. This is a terrible idea. The songs are not fast, mainly because Estella hired an orchestra to play music.

But, instead of stopping to dance, Jon pulls me through the crowd approaching the band director. He talks to the man, who nods, then steps away and pulls me into his arms. The band stops playing the song everyone was dancing to. Like right in the middle of it, it just stops. Everyone is looking around, confused. The first cords from the piano start with the first dance version of Taylor Swift's *Lover*. What is this man trying to do to me? Does he know that I love Taylor Swift? I try my best not to respond. His mouth curves as if he knows I'm dealing with my attraction.

"What are you doing?"

"I thought that was apparent."

"Jon."

"Avery, it's just a dance." Then he turns us, pulling me against him tighter. God, his body is so warm and hard. Holy guacamole, he smells like a dream. A really hot dream where we're both naked.

"No reason to freak out."

He bends down to whisper those words into my ear. His breath feathers over my skin, sending a wave of need through me. He's so warm, and he smells so good. I glance up at him through my lashes and see the heat in his eyes. I don't think a man has ever looked at me like that. And if I can see it…

I glance around. Yup, everyone is watching us. Not openly, although a few are gawking. There will definitely be a lot of gossiping on the JSE about this. That really shouldn't bother me, but it does.

Looking back at him, I shake my head at him. "They're staring."

"Who cares?"

"You, normally."

He frowns. "What do you mean?"

"I know you hate to be the center of attention."

"That's…weird."

"I think so too. Why wouldn't you want to be the center of attention?"

There is a beat of silence, then a chuckle sneaks out of Jon. It sounds like rust, like he's not used to it. Then, as if he can't help it, a full-bodied laugh explodes out of him.

"You know, you drive me up the wall, right?"

I smile. "You and just about everyone else."

He shakes his head. "Naw. The LOLs love you. They are always talking about you. And then there are your nieces and nephews. They think you are the cool aunt."

"You've only just met Sammy and Callie."

"True, but I bet they all love you. You're like a golden retriever."

"Did you just compare me to a dog?"

He smiles and executes a turn to avoid another couple. I glance over and realize it's the mayor and his wife.

"Yes. But you are happy chaos. That's a golden retriever."

I frown. That doesn't sound very nice. Like here I'm mooning over his tux and what he can do with his hands, and he thinks I'm the female Houdini.

"There is that other part of you."

A timber to his voice has me looking up at him through my lashes again. "Yeah?"

He leans down ever closer. I can feel his cheek against mine, and his breath is now shivering down my neck.

"It's the part that drives me crazy."

"What part is that?"

"It's the part where I can't think of anything other than kissing you."

My entire body goes into overdrive. Heat sears through my blood. "Jon."

"Yes."

"Are you insane?"

He chuckles. "I just might be."

I can't say anything else. My mind is going into overdrive as we finish out the dance.

When the last strings of the song play out, Jon leans down again. "Don't overthink it, Avery."

I blink up at him, but before I can respond, he's leading me off the floor. Suddenly, I'm unsure about Jon Howard and what to do about him.

Chapter Twenty-Two

Jon

"So, you and Avery, huh?" Nancy says as she steps up next to me.

I glance down at my cousin. "What do you mean?"

"Please, I think everyone got a contact high from watching y'all dancing."

Yeah, and I haven't been able to get my hormones to calm the fuck down. I have been attracted to women and danced with them, but my reactions to Avery during and after the dance are off the charts. I have never shared a dance with a woman that left me out of sorts.

When we were on the dance floor, no one else mattered. We were in our little bubble, Swift's music flowing over us. I could feel Avery's heartbeat and the way her breath caught when I whispered in her ear. My cock twitches at the memory.

Now, though, I want to beat the shit out of every man in the room. They all seem to think that they can look at Avery, and while I'm pretty sure she isn't paying attention to them, it irritates the living hell out of me. I toss a few of them nasty looks, which causes Nancy to laugh.

"What?"

"You," she says, sipping her champagne. "I never thought you would be the kind of guy who went all Neanderthal."

"What the hell does that mean?"

I know exactly what she's talking about, but I refuse to admit to it.

"Oh, please, you look like you want to growl at every guy, especially Ford Gold."

"Why Ford?"

"Well, he's chatting up your roommate."

My head whips around, and just like when I saw her talking to Josh, an emotion I can't fight crowds every bit of my body.

"I don't care," I say, but even to my own ears, my words lack conviction.

"Listen, Jon." She snaps her fingers, and I blink. Tearing my gaze away from Avery and Ford, I look at my cousin.

"What now?"

She smiles. "Just know that you need to get your head out of your ass. Don't take things for granted."

"Speaking from experience?"

"Yeah. I ignored my feelings for Travis for years, and he did the same. It almost broke us."

I study her for a long moment. My cousin and her fiancé have the number one home improvement show on cable, but not too long ago, they almost broke it off. They had both denied their feelings for each other. Until Nancy got a stalker who nearly killed her, they both refused to admit their feelings to each other.

"This isn't the same situation."

"Yeah, well, no, it isn't. Every love story is different."

I rear my head back from her. "I am not in love. That's a silly emotion."

Nancy throws her head back and laughs. "My God, you sound like Syd. She was in love with Grady for months, and it took her forever to admit it. Again, it was a different story than mine, but they started out hating each other. That sounds like someone I know." She wiggles her eyebrows at me. "Sounds like the beginning of a rom-com movie. It also sounds like someone I know."

"You have lost your mind."

But I can't fight the worry that tells me there is more to my attraction. Truth is, I have never been this infatuated with a woman. It feels like I have done a three-sixty because I hated her for the last week and a half. Now, I want her? Makes no sense.

"What's going on over here?" Travis asks as he slips a hand around Nancy's waist.

"Nothing. I'm just giving Jon crap about his crush."

"I don't have a crush."

"Oh, Avery?" he asks at the exact moment.

"Yeah," Nancy says as she looks at me over the rim of her glass. "Avery."

A scream is lodged in my throat. I love my cousin—the only cousin I can genuinely say that about—but she knows me too well. I'm infatuated with Avery, and it's stupid. It's close proximity. In other words, we're stuck together, and maybe that's the reason.

The music stops, and I hear her laugh over the crowd. I can't help myself. Looking over to where she was standing with Ford. The rancher is taller than I am and broader than what I remember as a stand-up guy. But just like with Josh, I now want to beat the shit out of him.

"Jon."

I ignore my cousin as I watch Avery laughing, the way she snorts, and something moves through me. It's not jealousy, but there is a lot of that. But it has more to do with the fact that I want to be the man who makes her laugh. I want to make her eyes sparkle.

What the actual fuck is that about?

"Jon!"

I blink and look at my cousin. "What?"

"I said your name a billion times."

"Twice," Travis says.

"What is going on with you?"

"Nothing."

She looks at Travis. "Go away."

"What?"

"I love you. Go away. Need to chat with Jon."

He kisses her cheek. "Come find me, babe."

Then, she grabs my elbow and drags me across the floor and down the hall to the library. This is where I usually like hiding during things like this, but immediately, I want to go back out on the floor.

"What is going on with you?"

"You were bothering me."

She cocks her head and studies me. Ugh, she knows me too well.

"I don't fall in love. It's a silly, messy emotion."

She studies me for a long moment, then straightens. "Jon, don't go by your father's behavior. Love is not silly."

"It's messy. And useless."

"It is messy, but that's part of the great thing about it."

"And you? You're happy with Travis now, but I remember the years of you being all goo-goo-eyed about him. And unhappy. You were miserable."

"Yeah, well, we both had our heads up our butts."

That makes me laugh, and her expression softens.

"But I wouldn't give any of that up because of the end result."

"You didn't know you would end up together."

"It's the hope."

"Hoping for things that never happen is not my usual go-to."

She sighs. "Yeah. Our family is fucked up. But I promise you it's worth it. Now tell me about Avery."

"What's there to tell? We're opposites."

"In a way. But not completely."

"What's that supposed to mean? I'm nothing like Avery O'Bryan."

She snorts. "Oh, sweet, silly man, you two are so alike in important ways."

"Oh, idiot woman, tell me what you're talking about, or I'm out of here."

She shakes her head. "First, you graduated from high school around the same age. You're both brilliant. You're both loners."

"Avery is constantly surrounded by people."

"True. But she's...it's hard to put it into words. She seems like such a solitary soul. She's got this big family, but none of them know what she's up to. Well, other than their grandmother. Liv's been trying to fill those shoes, I think. It's not easy, though, with everything she's got going on."

That makes me swallow a lump in my throat. I remember our night together on the couch, how she seemed out of it, and how she watched old shows her grandmother loved.

"She's definitely working through some things."

"And you are both Taylor Swift fans."

"Come on, half the world loves Taylor Swift."

"Okay, I'll give you that one. But…just don't let your father fuck you up. You would make a great husband and father, Jon. You're solid; when you love someone, you go all out."

I have to swallow another lump in my throat. We might be close, or at least close for the Howards. But we don't talk like this.

"Oh, I surprised you." She smiles. "That's hard to do. And I think there's another person who surprises you regularly."

"We would never work."

"Is that how you start every relationship? You know they will never last, so you're cool with it."

I open my mouth.

"Oh, Jon, you date all those models because you know you would never want forever with them. That's why you're freaking out about Avery."

I rear back. "I am not freaking out about Avery."

She giggles as she sips her drink. "You are, and I'm here for it. It's about time you have someone who upends your world. It's good for you. You've been alone for too long."

"Why is it that when women get their happily ever after, they want everyone else to have one too?"

"Because I love you, and I want you to be happy. Also, you've been lonely."

"I have not."

She sighs and shakes her head. "We both were. I found Syd, but you never really found that as a kid. I know you're friends with Trevor, but I also know that you keep him at arm's length."

"If you have to count on people, they will let you down."

Her smile fades. "Jonathon Jebediah Howard."

"That is not even close to my middle name."

"So, your mother let you down?"

"No."

"Maybe I should text her right now and let her know."

Fear flashes through me. "Don't you dare."

"Jon, dude, please don't tell me that your father fucked you up that much. Thank God you are a good man, more like your mother."

"You think I should just jump into a relationship with Avery? That's absurd."

"Why, because you want to kiss her?"

"I do not." Lie.

"Do too."

"Do not." Still lying.

"Well, this is where the only two grandchildren I invited to the fundraiser are hiding," our grandmother says.

I whip my head around and frown. She has always been a ninja, even with that damned cane tapping on the floor. She could probably teach the SEALs about how to sneak up on people.

"We aren't hiding. I'm giving your second favorite grandchild a talking to."

I scoff. "Second favorite."

"You both need to be out on the floor. Especially you, Nancy. Travis is looking at bidding on something insanely inappropriate."

She sighs. "Oh, well, you're on your own, cuz."

She kisses our grandmother on the cheek and then leaves us alone. They haven't always been that close, but that stalking incident helped them resolve their issues.

"I saw you dancing with Avery."

I nodded. No use in denying what everyone had seen.

"I want you to be careful with Avery."

"What's that mean?"

"Please don't use your mutual attraction to get her out of the house."

"What are you getting at?" A sick feeling swirls in my stomach.

She sighs. "You are a very handsome man. All the Howard men are."

"And?"

"Please don't try to seduce her to chase her away. Avery has been through a rough time."

"As everyone keeps reminding me," I bite out. I wish people would worry about me as much as they worry about Avery. I didn't just lose a loved one, but I never have gotten the same worry from my family. No, they seem to think that I'm an asshole.

"Jon, I want your promise that you won't do anything like that."

I haven't always gotten along with my grandmother, but I at least hoped she knew I was a decent man.

"Do you actually think that I would do something like that?"

She shakes her head. "Not when you're in the right frame of mind. You're acting weird, though."

I roll my eyes. "I promise not to seduce Avery to get rid of her. There, happy?"

She steps closer and cups my face. "I will be happy when you are finally happy, Jon."

She's never said anything like that to me before. "Grandmother?"

She shakes her head and turns to leave.

"Is everything okay? I mean, you're not dying, are you?"

She looks back over her shoulder at me. Her mouth curves. "We're all dying, Jon, but I don't plan on leaving this earth before I get great grandbabies."

Then she leaves me to my thoughts. None of which are good. I didn't think I would ever want to have something to do with Avery. Other than signing a sworn affidavit after she was arrested for stealing my house.

I shake my head. Now, I can't think of being in that house without her. Hell, yesterday had been sad and lonely without her fussing around the house. I'm not sure what that means, but I might have lost my damned mind.

My phone buzzes in my pocket.

Nancy: *You might want to get out here before Ford romances your roommate away from you.*

Me: *There is no romancing her away from me. We are not interested in each other.*

There, I put it in a text to prove I'm serious about that statement.

Nancy: *If you're telling the truth, then this won't bug you.*

Nancy: **pic of Avery and Ford dancing**

Me: *Not in the least.*

But even as I send the message, I stare at the two of them. They are laughing, Ford is holding her a little too close, and dammit, she has no idea what a player he is. Before I can stop myself, I'm stomping out of the library and down the hall. It only takes me five seconds to find them and start marching toward them. I ignore Mayor Albert, who tries to talk to me, and also Mrs. Petersen.

I don't stop until I reach the dance floor. The song ends, and Ford and Avery are only a few feet from me.

"Come on," I say, grabbing her by the wrist.

"Hey, Jon. How are you doing?"

"Fuck off, Ford."

Then I tug Avery through the crowd. I hear Ford laughing and murmurs from everyone in the crowd. I ignore all of them as I tug Avery to the foyer. Liv is there with Mason.

"Hey, Avery, Jon," Liv says before she frowns. "What's going on?"

"Avery and I are leaving. She's worried about Meredith."

Liv looks at her sister. Avery, for her part, slides me a look and then smiles at her sister. "Yeah, and I'm getting a headache."

Liv's gaze ping-pongs back and forth between us. "Avery, are you sure?"

Avery rolls her eyes. "Yes. I've been here forever, and I had some of that wine that gives me migraines."

"Avery."

"I know, but I love the taste, and I thought maybe this once it wouldn't matter."

Her sister sighs. "Okay."

Finally, I can drag her out of my grandmother's house and down the stairs. Other people have to park with the valet, but my car is parked in one of the two spaces in front of the house. Before I know it, we're on our way home, and I realize that I have about fifteen minutes to figure out just what the fuck that was about.

"I JUST DON'T UNDERSTAND what is happening."

It takes ten minutes for Avery to finally say something. The woman who never seems to shut up can play the quiet game well.

"I…you just shouldn't fall for Ford."

There's silence from the other side of the car. I'm not used to this when I'm around Avery. She's a woman who never seems to shut up. And I thought I would be thankful for her to be quiet.

Spoiler alert: I'm not.

I think it's because I'm sure she's plotting something.

"Ford isn't my type."

It takes a second or two for the words to register.

"Sure seemed like it."

What the hell am I doing? I'm not interested in Avery. Or I shouldn't be. Now that I've held her close, I'm feeling…territorial. But, more and more, I can't stop these insane thoughts from taking over my entire mind.

"Dancing is a long way from being interested. Besides, he had lots of stories about Everly and Becca."

"Hmm."

It's all I can say because there is a thread of relief coursing through me. Why? Because Avery isn't interested in a good-looking man? This is the fucking worst. I have no idea what is going on with me.

I park in front of the house. Avery doesn't wait for me to come around the car. She slips out of the car and walks up the sidewalk to the porch. I stride after her and make it to the porch simultaneously. She gives me a look of annoyance, but I ignore it.

Meredith is sitting on the last stair, waiting for us. She has a look of kitty disappointment. Is she mad because we came home or that we were out?

"See, she was missing you."

Avery snorts. "Probably mad because she thinks I took her boyfriend out."

I roll my eyes.

"It's okay, Meredith. Jon was being grumpy, so we had to come home."

"I was not being grumpy."

"You were. I don't know what's happening with you but thank you for the ride home."

"You don't know what is going on with me? I told you."

"Yeah, whatever."

"Why do you think that I wanted you to leave?

She sighs, a sound filled with weary loneliness. "Don't worry about it, roomie."

"No, I think we do."

She shakes her head and turns toward the kitchen. "I feel like some cereal."

I grab her wrist and pull her back. "Stop trying to distract me. Tell me why you think we left."

Her shoulders sag. "You're worried I'll embarrass your grandmother."

I blink. "That's not it at all."

"Okay."

I can tell by the tone in her voice that she doesn't believe me. Trying to deny my real reasons for wanting to leave made her think worse. I don't know why, but that hurts my heart.

"You cannot embarrass a Howard. My Uncle Monty likes to get drunk and wear his underwear on his head."

She blinks and looks up at me. "You're making that up."

I shake my head. "True story. You can ask my grandmother. It's the reason he's not invited to events anymore."

"Still, then, why did we leave? It isn't about Ford because, truthfully, he's not my type."

"I…"

Then I say nothing. I can't. She's looking up at me. We're so close that I can feel the heat of her. She sighs again and turns to leave. For some reason, I think I will lose something vital if I let her step away from me. Something I need to survive. Panic races through me.

"I was jealous."

She stops and looks over her shoulder at me. "You don't have to lie."

"I'm not lying."

"Okay, sure."

Then she pulls her arm away, and for a brief second, I don't react. "I was."

"Okay."

I need her to understand what is going on with me—even if I have no idea myself, so I grab her wrist again and tug her back, crowding her against the wall.

"Stop that."

She looks up at me through her lashes. The hall light isn't on, so the only light on is the kitchen, but it leaves it dark enough to make it feel secluded.

"Stop what?"

"Stop acting like I'm lying to you."

"Jon, you don't like me. You have accused me of trying to steal your house, insinuated that I was spending time with your grandmother because she's rich, and generally been a butthead to me. I'm supposed to think that you are attracted enough to be jealous of another man? I'm goofy, but I'm not stupid."

I lean down. "I don't understand it either. But seeing you with other men…it does something to me."

She's giving me a dubious look.

"It makes me want to beat the shit out of them."

Her eyes widen.

"Yeah, surprised me too."

"Still. It's not like you're interested in me."

This woman doesn't make anything easy. Nothing.

"You've been a pain in my ass since I arrived here and found you squatting in my house."

"Not your house."

"And there you go. You have to argue with me all the time."

"I do not."

I don't point out that she just contradicted me, and that's arguing. I can't think. Being this close to her while we're alone in the house has my body reacting. My head is spinning, my blood is heating, and my cock twitching. I draw a deep breath, trying to calm myself, but that's a mistake. The scent of her sugary sweetness. Then, I do the only thing I can think of. I lower my head and slam my mouth against hers.

She doesn't react for a second, and regret hits me. She doesn't feel the same way. But just a second before I pull completely back, she makes a little sound and then starts kissing me back. Her hands slide up my chest to behind my neck as she opens her mouth. Slanting my head, I deepen the kiss, invading her mouth. God, her taste explodes inside me, and I don't think I've ever tasted anything as decadent as Avery O'Bryan.

I settle a hand on her waist, my fingers flexing against the soft fabric of her dress. I want more. I want her legs wrapped around me as I thrust inside of her. I want it all, her flesh against mine, her moans echoing off the ceiling in my room.

Then, in the next second, she pulls away from me.

"This isn't a good idea."

"What? I think it's an excellent idea."

Her breaths are coming out fast and furious. Even in the dim light, I can see she's flushed.

"Uh, yeah, we're good at kissing, but we live together. Not a good idea."

I open my mouth, but she slips around me and heads up the stairs.

"Let's sleep on it."

"You expect me to sleep after you kissed the hell out of me?"

She turns around and frowns. "You kissed me."

"You were a participant."

"I…never mind. You stay there. I'm going upstairs, and we can discuss this in the morning."

Why is she being so reasonable? Avery O'Bryan is a lot of things, but reasonable is not one of them. Before I can convince her to stay, she's hurrying up the stairs as if the flames of hell are chasing her.

My entire body is humming, need coursing through every inch, and of course, my cock is harder than a nail.

"Meow."

I look down at Meredith.

"Exactly."

Chapter Twenty-Three

Avery

The sun slants over my windshield as I park in front of Liv's house the following day. I left my sunglasses at home, but I couldn't go back there and get them. I snuck out of the house in the early morning hours and haven't screwed up the courage to return.

I tried to go to bed after that kiss. Not surprisingly, I couldn't sleep. My insomnia is legendary, but there was a reason behind it last night. I also couldn't promise that I wouldn't sneak into Jon's bedroom and seduce him. Just thinking about that kiss right now has my entire body lighting up and my fingers itching. I need to touch him, to feel his skin beneath my fingertips.

Closing my eyes, I pull in a deep breath. My nerves have been strung tight since he showed up at the house. Last night about broke the last little nerve I've been holding onto.

There's a knock on my car window, making me jump. I look up and find Mason standing beside my car. He's smiling at me. Sighing, I grab my purse and phone and slip out of my car.

"Kind of early for you, Avery." He takes a sip of coffee as he studies me.

"Did I catch you sneaking back home?"

I smile when his cheeks turn ruddy. God, he's a cutie and perfect for my sister.

"No."

"So, you got up early and are on your way back?"

He chuckles. "Come on. I promised Sammy I would take him to breakfast today."

"Look at you."

We walk up the path to my sister's house. I know there are probably posts on the JSE about my night, before and after the kiss. Not that anyone knows about the kiss. Now I show up at my sister's house at what I consider the crack of dawn. Other people call it just before eight.

I squint against the sun wishing I'd brought my glasses. I really should have gone back for them. And Meredith.

The moment we step inside Liv's house, there's chaos. Well, as much chaos as my sister allows. Little feet scurry, and there's Houdini, who comes running down the hallway, his tongue hanging out of his mouth. You would think he would slow down, but he doesn't. Instead, he speeds up and then hurls himself at Mason.

"Hey, buddy, careful there," Mason says between kisses.

While Mason is occupied with Houdini, I rush into the kitchen to find my sister pouring herself a cup of coffee. Her eyes widen when she sees me.

"What are you doing here so early?"

I raise my hands and then let them drop to my sides. "Why does everyone keep saying that?"

"Who else has said that to you?"

"Your boy toy."

That gets me a frown, but I ignore it.

"I need to talk."

"Hey, Avery!" Sammy is so loud in the mornings. It's a wonder he doesn't wake everyone up on the street.

"Hey, kid." I notice Callie walking in behind him, the same expression of concern her mother is wearing at the moment. "Hey, Callie. I heard you have a very handsome chauffeur today."

"Yeah. What are you doing here so early?"

A frustrated scream lodges in my throat. She's like her mother, so I should have expected the question.

"I have a problem, and I need your mother's help. You know your mother is the smartest."

"If you say so," Callie says.

Liv chuckles. "You guys remember the rules, right? No running off without Mason. Ranches are fun, but they can be dangerous too."

They both nod. After kisses for the kids and Mason, she sees them to the door. When it closes, she turns to me with a smile, and in that moment, I am envious. I have never really wanted another half. Romance—long-term romance—isn't for me. I learned that early in life. But seeing Liv, who was widowed almost six years ago, find love again makes my heart yearn. I don't begrudge my sister for her happiness. In fact, I take credit for helping them on their bumpy road to happily ever after.

"I thought they were going to breakfast."

"They are, then they are going out to the Gold Ranch. Do you want some coffee?"

"No. I've had five cups today."

"Okay…wait. You've had five cups today?" Her eyes are wide and filled with worry.

"Yeah."

"You have been up that long?"

"Yeah." I sigh. "I didn't sleep last night, so I went to the diner, and they kept filling my cup."

There's a long beat of silence, heavy with judgment. Usually, I can ignore it and just move on to my next adventure. I don't have it in me this morning to shrug it off. This morning, I need understanding.

"Don't judge."

"Oh, Av, I'm not judging. I'm concerned. There's a difference."

I sigh and drop down into one of the kitchen table chairs. "It's because I did something stupid. So stupid, in fact, that everyone, including you, will hate me."

She sits in the chair beside me. "Did you kill Jon Howard? Because if you did, I think we might need Cora for this. She would know the best way to hide the body."

"No." I blink. "No, nothing like that. That actually might have been better."

I would know just how to hide the body. I spend enough time watching MDK—Murder, Death, Kill—shows, although Cora knows the law better than I do. She's married to a Department of Public Safety officer.

"Then what happened?"

I draw in deep breaths and open my mouth, but nothing comes out. No words or even a sound. Once I tell her, I will never be able to return to being the girl I was before I kissed Jon Howard.

Just thinking about it has my stomach tightening and my

body shimmering with heat. I cover my face with my hands, and that's a mistake. The moment I do, I close my eyes, and the memory of that kiss hits me hard. The feel of his mouth against mine, his taste as his tongue explored my mouth, and the way his fingers flexed on my waist as he deepened the kiss.

"Avery, are you okay?"

My sister's voice pours cold water onto my fantasy. I peek through my fingers.

"I kissed him."

"What? You're mumbling, and your hands are in the way."

I move my hands and say, "I kissed him."

Then I slap my hands over my face again. It's stupid and childish, I know that. It's not like I can keep the memory at bay. I can't go back and make it not happen.

"Him? Him who?"

"Jon Howard."

There is another long beat of silence. It's so long that I peek through my fingers again to see the stunned expression on my sister's face.

"You…when?"

I sigh. "It was after the party. I had a little wine, and we got into an argument. Before I knew what was happening, his mouth was on mine and…I just couldn't stop."

"Were you drunk?"

"No."

"So, he didn't take advantage of you?"

"Oh, no. Nothing like that. I mean, once he kissed me, I felt as if I had had a whole bottle of champagne with a bottle of tequila along with it."

"What does that even mean?"

"It means it left me weak in the knees, with my head spinning, and I felt like I was going to throw up." I draw in a deep breath as the memory of the kiss floods my body. "It was like starlight."

She cocks her head and crosses her arms as she leans back in her chair. "Dammit. I can't believe I lost that bet."

"I'm sorry…wait, what?"

"Cora and Gerri bet me you would fall for Jon in a month. I can't believe they were right."

Panic churns in my gut. That isn't what this is. "I haven't fallen for Jon Howard." No way. He's my enemy, with dreamy eyes and that sinful mouth. And from the feel of things last night, a really big cock.

"Really? You're using a Swiftie term."

I shake my head. "No, I'm not."

"*Starlight*? I'm not the Swiftie you are, but I know *Starlight*. I know that it's one of your favorite songs of hers off *Red*."

Oh, no. "No. No. No."

My head is spinning. I can't be falling for a man like him. He probably dreams about spreadsheets and egg whites. If I fell for him, he would never be interested in me, and I would be in love and then sad. So sad. And I have spent a lot of time being sad lately, and I don't like it. And pathetic. I would be sad and pathetic, and I don't like that idea one bit.

I pop out of the chair and start pacing.

"You keep saying that, but it doesn't change the fact that you used a term from one of your favorite Taylor Swift songs."

"It was the kiss. It messed with my mojo. I mean, he's all fussy and gets up at the same time every day."

"How do you know that?"

"He told me." I wave that away as I continue to pace. "But he's all those things, along with probably folding his underwear, so I didn't expect that kiss. I mean…" I come to an abrupt stop because I can't continue. I get a little dizzy whenever I think about the kiss too much.

"Was it marvelous?"

I give my sister a narrowed look. "Stop using words from *Starlight*. He is not Bobby Kennedy."

She giggles. "No. You're more Bobby, and he's more Ethel."

I stare at her. My sister rarely giggles like that. Not since she became an adult. "Oh, I'm so happy you find this amusing."

"It's just that…are you going to have ten kids?"

My family knows me too well, and apparently, my sister knows the lyrics to Starlight. I walk over to the chair and collapse. "What am I going to do?"

She sobers and leans forward. "What do you mean?"

"I have to face him. I have to live with him!"

I know my voice is turning hysterical, probably because I'm about to lose it. It's like when the whole thing with Chet happened, and I felt out of control. I did some out-of-control stuff that would probably be considered illegal. Okay, they were illegal. But Chet deserved it.

At that time, Grannie Pam had talked me down off the cliff. Without her around, I feel out of control most days and today most of all.

"Hey," she says, putting her hand on my knee. I look up

at her, and this is Mama Bear Liv. "You are Avery Freaking O'Bryan. There isn't anything you can't do. You conquer every fear you have."

I want to scream. I love that my family thinks so much of me, but right now, everything in my head is like the Upside Down in *Stranger Things*. It's been that way since Grannie Pam died, and this development is like Vecna showing up. I want someone to see me and understand what is happening with me. Part of it is my fault. I haven't talked to them about what's happening in my head. Mainly because I can't figure it out myself.

"I guess."

"Listen, why don't I tell Nancy I will be late?"

Usually, my sister doesn't work on Sundays, but Nancy and Travis are about to head out to start filming their show again. I know they were getting together to ensure everything was good to go while they were gone.

"I don't want to make you late for work." I know she would do it for me, but Liv is a stickler for doing things on time.

She shakes her head. "You're my family, and Nancy always says family comes first."

"Thanks, Liv."

She leans over to give me a one-arm hug. "I'm just happy I get to do something for you since you help me so much with the kids."

The backs of my eyes burn, but I say nothing. My emotions are pushing against my brain and making me feel completely out of control. I'm afraid I'll start sobbing, not from sadness.

"But only if you tell me you told people you were a duchess and Jon was a prince."

"Har, har."

"Let me text Nancy, then we'll go to the diner. Does that sound okay?"

I nod and let her go. Pointing out that I was just there wouldn't do any good, and besides, all I did was drink coffee. Okay, I had a midnight donut. Don't judge. Or do. I don't care. I needed it.

My phone buzzes in my hand, and I look down. It's Jon.

Unknown Number: *Please tell me you are okay and just in a sugar coma somewhere.*

Unknown Number: *This is Jon, by the way.*

I roll my eyes. I admitted to having a donut at midnight, but he doesn't know that. Then I realized he had my number, and I never gave it to him. I assign the number to his name before texting back.

Me: *How did you get my number?*

Jon: *You signed a lease.*

Jon: *Also, I am a computer genius.*

Me: *I'm fine.*

Jon: *Good. Meredith was worried.*

I fight a smile because, seriously, who would think Jon Howard had a sense of humor.

Me: *Right. That skank probably went to sleep with you.*

Jon: *Not sure, but she did wake me up to feed her.*

Me: *She is demanding.*

Jon: *And I have the scratches to prove it.*

I will not think about his bare chest.

Me: *Sorry.*

Jon: *No, you aren't, but if it has you thinking about my chest, it was worth it.*

Oh, no. I can handle uptight Jon. I can handle even funny Jon. Flirty Jon? That might just kill me.

Me: *Oh, was that your plan? Entice me with your chest?*

Jon: *Would that work on you? It would work for me if you wanted to use that strategy.*

My face flames hot. I don't get embarrassed, so this has to be arousal. I've been a walking hormone since I saw him in that tux last night. Strike that. I've been simmering with hormones since I landed on top of him a few days ago. This flirting is going to kill me. Dead.

Me: *Stop that.*

Jon: *Come back and make me.*

Me: *Is this your way of trying to get rid of me?*

Three dots appear, then disappear, then they show up again.

Jon: *I'm weird, but I'm not **that** weird.*

Jon: *Unless you're into that.*

"What has you smiling?"

I almost screech because Liv is standing next to me. I didn't even know she was there.

"Nothing."

"Not nothing." She cocks her head and studies me again. "You would tell me if there was something wrong, right? You know I'm here."

"I do. What do you think is wrong with me?"

"There is nothing wrong with you, Avery. You're perfectly imperfect."

I snort. It was something that my grandmother said all the time to me. Growing up and being different, it was hard to accept that I didn't fit in. As a teen, you want to fit in so badly, and every time someone points out that you don't, you die a little inside.

But Grannie Pam reminded me that every day there are imperfections. In those imperfections, we could craft the perfect life for us.

"I love you, Liv."

"Now I *am* worried."

I laugh. "You're an ass. Let's go eat some carbs."

I slip my phone into my pocket and grab my purse. I need some sugary goodness.

Chapter Twenty-Four

Jon

When Avery doesn't answer my text, I try to work. But I'm worried. I don't want her to go away. Yeah, I know I started this with the idea that I wanted her out of my house, but my panic is beginning to take over. The thought of being here alone makes my eye twitch.

I rise out of my chair and start pacing in my office. Meredith is watching me, as she has all day. With her mistress away, she seems to be out of sorts.

"I know exactly how you feel, Meredith."

"Meow."

"Exactly."

I breathe deeply to calm my nerves, but it isn't helping. Not one bit. My phone vibrates on the desk, and I rush over, realizing it's a phone call from my mother. I've been avoiding her for hours, but she'll keep calling me until I answer.

"Mom."

"Darling boy."

There's a sarcastic edge to that name. She's irritated with me, and I have no idea why.

"What's up?"

"Nothing much, but I wanted you to know I'm heading to Juniper. Take I-35, babe."

"What?"

"Sorry. I was telling Ted which way to go."

"He's coming with you?"

"Yes. Your grandmother wants to meet him."

"Travis Fillmore wants to meet him too."

She chuckles. "Yes, I got a text from Nancy about it."

I collapse into my office chair and look over at my laptop. I have the JSE open and notice that Avery and Liv are at the diner. My soul seems to settle down now that I know she's safe again.

I run through a few of the posts and frown. Only Juniper Springs' residents can access the app, but this is a safety issue. If someone hacked into it, they could stalk someone.

"Are you listening to me?"

"Sorry, I was just working something out."

She sighs. "I wanted to do dinner tonight, but your grandmother said there is some kind of town meeting."

He had seen the notice. A Juniper Springs town meeting was always an exciting time. And by exciting time, I mean irritating. They constantly went off script, and things always got out of hand. I know there was one time a fistfight broke out.

"She's going?"

"Yeah, she said something about a proposal for more money for the animal shelter. That young woman she has living with you is very interested in it, so she was going to show her support."

"Are we sure she didn't have some kind of stroke? She's acting weird."

"Weird, how?"

"She's spending time with the LOLs, knitting, drinking."

"Oh. My. Gawd! The horror!"

Once again, it's easy to hear the sarcasm in my mother's voice. "It's not like her."

"Those are very normal things to do."

"Not for her. And let's be honest, she's never been normal."

"Tsk, tsk. I never knew you were so judgmental."

"I'm not." But in that instance, I know I am. What I can't tell her is that I don't trust the other women. My mother would laugh at me for my worries about Estella, but she's not acting normal. As people get older, they get taken advantage of.

"Well, I think it's good for her. Getting out of that massive house and spending time with people around her age is important."

"That's what Avery says."

"Avery?"

"The woman who stole my house."

A beat of silence. "Do you have something to tell me?"

"What does that mean?"

"There was something in your voice."

I roll my eyes. First Trevor, now my mother. "There's nothing in my voice."

You and I know I'm lying, but I don't want to discuss this insanity with my mother. No other woman has gotten under my skin like Avery has. They've tried, but none have succeeded. Avery tried to get under my skin, but it was more about getting me to leave than capturing my attention. She's been a complete asshole to me, and I can't stop thinking about her.

What does that say about me? Nothing good, I'm sure.

"You're not listening to me again."

I blink and pull myself back from those thoughts. I can't start brooding. That leads to depression, which is never good. It can get me off track for weeks. I've dealt with it for over a decade and know how to pull back from it.

"Sorry. I was up late because of the party last night."

"Yes, you looked very handsome."

I smile. "Mom, I know you didn't see me."

"There were pictures of you on the JSE. I told you."

Dammit. Okay, it isn't *a* big deal, but I'm also realizing the security issues. I should have foreseen this issue, but for some reason, I did not. All I wanted to do was create the app and be done with everyone from Juniper bothering me. Getting them off my back, especially the LOLs, had been my main focus when creating it.

"We should be there in time for the meeting."

"Is bringing Ted to something like that a good idea? He might go running for the hills."

"True, but he's looking forward to it. He has a weird sense of humor."

Another mumble, and my mother laughs. She sounds happier than she's ever been. It makes my heart somehow lighter. While I didn't like how she sprung Ted on me, I was coming around to the idea that he might be good for her.

"I'll see you when we get there."

"Okay. Be safe."

"Always."

Once I'm off the phone with my mother, I look at Meredith, who is now sitting on the arm of the sofa, giving me a glare.

"I didn't tell her to go out."

I've never had a woman run away from me like that. I didn't expect more than that kiss last night. Not that I didn't want more than a kiss. I wanted to taste every inch of her body and how it felt to have her legs wrapped around my waist.

I roll my eyes, trying to get my body to settle down. Just thinking about Avery has me acting like a thirteen-year-old with no control. I could call Trev, but he's still pissed at me from last night. The texts I got complaining about my grandmother were funny and quite profane.

I can't work, and I can't call my best friend. Maybe I should do something else. I could sit here and obsess, which is never good, or get out of the house. I opt for the second idea and head out to do something, anything, to get Avery off my mind.

AN HOUR LATER, I'm wandering the aisles of Nerdvana. The store is whimsical but well-maintained, with lots of places to relax and read. If it had been opened when I was a teenager, I would have spent all my time here.

"Jon Howard!" Everly yells out, waving me over. She's one of the store's owners, and honestly, she scares me a little. She's a tall drink of water with black hair and blue eyes. As I approach, I see her shirt and smile. It reads, 'Customer service is not something I agreed to.'

"It took you long enough to stop by and see me."

As she says it, a man steps out of her backroom with a baby on his shoulder.

"Been busy."

The woman's wit is sharper than my grandmother's. The smirk she gives me is more of a warning than anything else. Estella stings with her barbs. Everly leaves gaping wounds.

"So, I've been reading on the JSE."

I roll my eyes.

"And you would be?"

I look at the man who doesn't fit in this shop. He's wearing a tailored shirt and tailored dress slacks. His hair is perfectly in place. He's the kind of guy who would love to be on the cover of GQ, and he could pull it off.

"I would be Jon. Are you Everly's worse half?"

"Worse?"

"There is no way I was about to say better half. She would kick my ass."

"Damn right," Everly says. "This is not my man. This is his brother Carter Hawthorne. Carter, this is Jon Howard."

"Oh, of the Avery slash Jon poll?"

Everly smiles. "Yes."

I blink. "Wait, what?"

He hands Everly's little girl over to her. She cuddles her daughter to her chest and smiles. This is so different from the Everly I remember from my youth. She's a couple years younger than me, but I remember a rough and tumble girl who didn't take crap off anyone. She grew into a sarcastic and confident woman. And now she was making goo goo noises at her daughter. It's kind of sweet.

Carter walks around the counter to stand next to me. He holds up his phone.

"They have a poll on who they think will end up with the house."

I look at the poll that I somehow missed and frown. It's running fifty/fifty, so that's at least something. But still. I'm the hometown boy or man.

"I own the house."

"Not what your grandmother said at the last LOL meeting."

This snags my attention. I study him for a long moment, but he only smiles at me.

"Carter is an honorary LOL. Only your roommate and my man's brother have been honored with the title."

"She's not my roommate."

Everly chuckles. "Sure. Anyway, there's a lot of discussion on who will move out first."

"Did you vote?"

She nods, a smile curving her lips.

"You voted for Avery?"

Another nod.

I roll my eyes, "No loyalty."

"Only against the patriarchy. Also, she's a woman, and we are the stronger sex."

"She's got you there. Women kick our asses every day of the week and twice on Sunday," Carter says, chuckling. "Of course, there's more discussion on what is actually going on in the house."

"What the hell does that mean?"

"Well, those pictures from last night are really getting people excited," Carter says. "You did kiss her, right?"

"Carter Phineas Hawthorne," Everly says. "Didn't Syd talk to you about those kinds of questions?" She looks at me. "Sorry, but Carter doesn't always think before he talks."

"Why is it important to you?" Is this another man out for Avery's affection? Another dude who is going to try and steal her away from me?

Wait, is she with me? I mean, we kissed and living together, but are we *together*?

"I'm invested in romance," he says with a shrug, but his eye catches on something at the doorway. His entire expression changes as he smiles. I turn and see a redheaded woman come striding into Nerdvana. She's zeroed in on Carter. She's tall, slender, and there's something vaguely familiar about her. Her pale green eyes hold a wealth of intelligence.

"Phin, what are you doing here? You left while I was sleeping." There's no anger in her voice.

"I kissed you before I left. After the delivery last night, I knew you needed sleep."

"I think I'm the best judge of when I need sleep."

He pulls her into his arms and gives her a smacking kiss. "I knew my brother was trying to finish writing a chapter before we all head to Mom's for dinner. So, I helped out with Esme."

"You stole her from her father, brought her here, and have been bugging me," Everly says.

"My love, this is Estella's grandson Jon. Jon, this is the love of my life, literally, Dr. Piper Abernathy-Hawthorne."

"Nice to meet you."

"Same. Estella is always going on about you. And about Nancy. For the longest time, I thought she only had two grandchildren."

I chuckle. "If you met any of the others, you would understand."

"We've met Monty of the underpants on his head," Carter says. "Are they worse than him?"

"He's amusing. The others are just jerks."

"We're going to miss the meeting tonight," Carter says out of the blue. I blink, trying to follow his direction. Both of the women share a look. He looks troubled by it.

"Yes, but you knew that," Piper says. "It's your father's birthday."

"Oh, right." He leans over and kisses his wife's cheek. "You're so smart." Then he looks at me. "So, how about it, Howard? Tell us you kissed the girl."

"Phin, stop. Jon doesn't seem like the kind of man who would kiss and tell," the doctor says.

I throw his wife a thankful look. Being a Howard, I should be used to the scrutiny, but this is different. I never dated anyone in the town. Wait, I'm not dating her. We're living together. That's it. I might have an itch to explore more than just one kiss, but it's normal.

And, okay, I will admit, I can't think of anything else than her today. I came away with her on my mind. Makes sense since I had to take an extra-long shower last night with my fist around my cock.

Now I'm standing in a store, aroused and irritated. All of them are looking at me like they want me to say something.

"What?"

Everly smiles. "Nothing."

"I don't know why my father has to have his birthday today," Carter says out of the blue.

While I'm confused by the comment, his wife is not. "You don't need to go to the meeting."

"But I should support Avery."

I frown. "Why?"

"She's presenting a proposal to the city council tonight. She needs our support."

Piper smiles. "Phin, Avery has already told you to chill out about it. She says family comes first, always."

"So, she's proposing something to the city council?"

Carter smiles. "Yeah. Your woman is going to get money for something. Was it the animal shelter?"

Piper nods.

She does spend a lot of time there. Estella told me Avery was keen on building up the social media component for the shelter.

"Well, I gotta get going. Mom's gonna be here today."

"Tell her I said hi," Everly says.

After saying goodbye, I escape, realizing I didn't get to look around the store.

As I head back to my car, I decide to attend tonight's meeting. I have no idea why I need to be there, but Avery will need support, and I want to give it to her.

I start driving back to the house, thinking about Avery and my feelings for her. Less than a week, and I'm losing my mind over the woman. That should scare me, but for some reason, I feel…settled. More than I have felt in a long time. Her crazy behavior seems to calm me on some level.

Once I get home, there's no Meredith waiting for me.

I've found it comforting to walk into the house and see her sitting on the bottom stair.

Me: *Did you take Meredith somewhere?*

Avery: *Yes. She's volunteering with me.*

Me: *You're avoiding me.*

Avery: *Well, yeah. We both need to make sure we haven't gone insane.*

Me: *Who are you, and how did you get Avery's phone?*

Avery: **middle finger emoji**

Me: *Aw, you do like me.*

Avery: *Go away. I have to work on some TikToks for the new puppies.*

I find myself smiling, realizing that I might have lost my mind, but at the moment, I really don't care.

Chapter Twenty-Five

Avery

I make it to the meeting early. I hate being late for things. Most people would say it was out of character for me, but it's not. My anxiety goes through the roof if I don't show up on time. I think it comes from being the youngest in my family. There's always this feeling that I missed out on good stuff before I was born. I didn't say it was normal, just that I had that feeling.

Leaving Meredith with her new friend worried me, but they seemed to be settling in quite well. Yes, I brought another cat home. I felt terrible about leaving her all alone. I'm home most days, but it makes me sad to leave her there all alone. So, I got Benjamin.

They seemed to like each other. I hope they don't tear up too much stuff in my room. I made sure to shut the door behind me when I left.

"Avery, dear, how are you this evening?" Mrs. Petersen asks.

Dammit. The LOL Queen snuck up on me. I love the LOLs, but they have been chomping at the bit to discuss what is going on with Jon and me. I do not want them to get any ideas. Hate kissing someone is a far cry from being involved. Although, when I think about it, there was a lot less hate and a lotta heat in that kiss, at least on my side. I'm pretty sure Jon Howard still hates me.

I smile at Mrs. Petersen. "I'm fine."

"Ready to fight for some money for the shelter?"

I nod. That wasn't the true reason I was here. It was only the first week of the month, and the rescue charity already made their monthly quota. Since I took over their social media, their donations have gone through the roof.

I'm here with another proposal. Estella and I have been talking about how there needs to be more programs at the Senior Center. I wanted to get it on the agenda, but Estella said it was better to do a sneak attack. Just the thought has my stomach turning over and over. I can do the presentation, but I hate any pushback.

I wave at Becca, who is urging me over to sit with her.

"I'll talk to you later, Mrs. Petersen. Becca has something she wants to tell me."

Mrs. Petersen looks behind her and smiles at Becca. It's hard not to. She's dressed in red and black, her hair up in two space buns, and it's black. Since her hair was blond last night, she must have changed it today. It's nothing big since she changes her hair color regularly.

"Of course, Avery."

I scoot around her and make my way to Becca. "Hey, like the black?"

She rises and gives me a big hug. "I just felt like black was my color."

That's not a color I would associate with the comic

bookstore owner. She and her best friend Everly run one of the best comic and graphic bookstores in Texas, if not the entire country. Every day, Becca dresses like she's at a con. She's about as happy as a person can be.

"Bad week?"

We sit down, and she shrugs. "Men are assholes."

I chuckle. "That they are."

"You know I'm going to grill you later, right? I want to know all about you and Jon."

Before I can respond, I get hugged from behind. I turn around and find my nephew.

"Hey, Sammy. I didn't know you were coming tonight."

"Mom said we needed to be here for more nail support."

I blink.

"Moral support, kiddo," my sister says with a laugh.

"Hey. Where's Callie?"

"She's at her dance lessons. Mason is going to pick her up when she's done."

I nod and realize that the entire room is watching my every move. It's weird, but it doesn't bother me like in my old hometown. As my gaze scans over the room, I see the weird guy who lives behind us.

Wait, when did *we* become *us*? We are not an us.

A commotion at the back of the room draws everyone's attention. Estella walks in. I wasn't sure if she would come because I know this isn't usually her thing, but she agrees with my ideas for the center. It warms my heart that she came here to support me.

I've never seen the woman beside her, but she looks vaguely familiar. Where have I seen her before? As I take in her features, I recognize those high cheekbones and those blue eyes. Oh, no. Is that Jon's mother? I get my answer when I see the tall, bulky guy beside her. That's why everyone is freaking out. It's not every day a former Cowboy shows up for our little town meeting.

I blink at my wording. This isn't my town. I'm here trying to figure out what to do next, but I'm definitely not staying in Juniper Springs. Maybe. Like before, I'm thinking of that house as mine, and it isn't. As it is, I might have to run away from the town to keep from kissing Jon again.

I roll my shoulders, trying to settle my mind because I need to get my thoughts in order when I see the newest person arrive. Nancy and Travis come strolling in with Jon. That has the breath backing up in my throat and my nipples pressing against my bra. How does he look so cute all the time? It's like all he does is jump out of bed and look perfect. Me, I'm a walking disaster. I watch as his gaze moves over the crowd. I figure he's looking for his mother.

"Oh, exciting. Jon showing up, and Carter is missing this," Becca says with a laugh. I glance at her quickly. She's typing out a text to Carter Hawthorne.

"What's he looking for?" My sister asks.

"I think his mother," I say.

"Uh, I don't think so," Becca says with a laugh.

I look in his direction and find him staring at me. That intense look has my whole body vibrating with excitement. Oh, damn. The buzzing in the room grows.

"Avery," Estella says. "I want you to meet Jon's mother and her beau."

I smile at the old-fashioned term. Then I pop up out of my seat. "It's nice to meet you."

I study Jon's mother. I see the resemblance in the high

cheekbones and her smile. Her blue eyes dance with happiness. It's hard to believe that grumpy Jon came from such a happy woman.

"It's nice to meet you too, Avery. I've been wanting to meet you forever."

"Oh?"

She laughs. "I'm on JSE. I'm also a big fan of what you're doing for the shelter. And Nancy. I know it isn't easy wrangling people for social media."

"Thanks."

"Mom," Jon says. His mother turns and hugs him. There is genuine affection in their exchange, which melts my heart a little. I learned with my first real boyfriend that the relationship with a mom is essential to pay attention to. If you get someone like Chet, you learn a lot of things to avoid.

I notice Travis inching his way over to Ted, and I laugh.

"Avery," Jon says.

His voice dips, slipping over the syllables. It waltzes over my nerve endings, sending a wave of heat through my body.

"Jon," Estella says, "I understand you know Liv and her boy Sammy."

His gaze stays on mine for one moment longer, but he then looks at my sister, the heat banking just a bit in his eyes. "Hey, Sammy, Liv."

As Estella introduces Jon's mom to Liv, Jon steps around that cluster to sidle up to me. "You've been missing most of the day."

"I went home before the meeting. I had volunteer duty today at the shelter."

He nods. "I saw the posts."

Then silence. We stand there staring at each other.

"We need to talk."

My palms are so sweaty. I'm amazed they aren't dripping. "About what?"

He cocks his head and studies me for a long moment before saying, "You're denying what happened?"

"Hmm." I'm not trying to be coy. I really can't come up with words. I never have issues with words other than I can't control them from spilling out of my mouth.

"I guess I could put on a demonstration right here in the middle of the meeting."

"No. I…listen, I have a presentation I need to do, and you're messing with my mojo."

"I want to do more than just mess with it."

I laugh. I can't help. His humor is as dry as a Texas summer.

"Jon," his mother says, "You didn't tell me your roommate is *the* Avery O'Bryan."

His head whips around. "I said her name was Avery."

"You didn't tell me her entire name." She looks at me. "I loved your article about the importance of socializing for seniors and how social media could help."

I smile while fighting a blush. Most people in my life pay no attention to my writing. A lot of it is dry and aimed at academics. I was especially proud of that article.

"Thank you."

"That's why she's been teaching all the LOLs about other apps," Liv says.

"It's important that senior citizens understand how they can be dangerous. It's a great way for them to connect, but there are scammers out there."

Jon stares at me like I grew an extra head or a third eye. Why do people seem so surprised when they discover I'm smart? Hell, I get regular requests from universities and think tanks to come to talk to their students and employees. My Alma Mater wanted me to teach for a whole semester. Which sounds like a nightmare because they expect you to be on campus and wear a bra, but still.

"I would love to chat with you about your ideas of social media and social justice as soon as you get a chance."

"Of course, anytime. Are you in town for long?"

"No. Just a couple days, and Estella wants to have a family dinner. Do you want to exchange numbers?"

"Sure." I rattle off my number for her as there is movement onstage. The entire thing seems to be about to start on time, which isn't normal for Juniper Springs. Most times, things begin about ten to fifteen minutes late.

Once everyone is settled and they call the meeting to order, my phone buzzes in my pocket.

Jon: *So, you are alive.*

I roll my eyes.

Me: *We established that in our conversation, and I sent you messages today.*

Jon: *There was no proof of life.*

I look up, trying to make it look as casual as possible, and look over the crowd. Jon is staring at me, a smirk on his sexy mouth.

Me: *Why did you want to kick my cats to the curb?*

Jon: *Cats?*

Dammit, I thought I might be able to keep that a secret a little longer.

Me: *Yeah. I brought home a grey Russian. Benjamin.*

Jon: *Are you going to name all your cats after Taylor Swift's cats?*

I blink. He knows the names of Taylor's cats? I know that many people know things about her, but I didn't think anyone but Swifties knew her cats' names, at least not off the top of their heads.

Me: *Maybe. Means I need to get at least one more.*

Jon: **gif Taylor Swift eye roll**

That has me smiling. He's been kind of understanding about Meredith, who apparently has a crush on him.

Me: *You slept with her last night.*

Jon: *Only because her mistress turned me down.*

Jon: *I'd rather create a private oasis with you in bed.*

I blink. That's another Taylor Swift reference and not a single she put out. That's from *Dancing With Our Hands Tied.*

I glance over at him again. He's still staring at me. Those hot blue eyes are burning. I shiver and turn around.

Me: *What is going on with you? Are you trying to get rid of me?*

Jon: *Truth?*

Me: *That would be nice.*

Jon: *I don't know. All I can think about is kissing you again.*

Heat flares deep in my belly, and I know there's a good chance my panties are wet. I shift in my seat. Yep.

"Avery?"

I look up at Mayor Albert. He's in his late fifties, missing most of his hair, and his gut spills over the waistband of his pants. He looks like he's been cast as the stereotypical mayor of a small town.

"You have a proposal?"

I glance around and realize everyone is watching me. Great.

"Yes. Sorry."

I slip my phone into my pocket and make my way to the stage.

Once I step on the stage, my brain starts working on sabotage. I have had a fear of public speaking for my entire life. Small groups don't bother me, or if I'm online. When there's a packed recreation center with the entire town staring up at me…that freaks me out.

I start using my breathing exercises as my gaze moves over the audience. As if I can't help myself, I seek out those Pacific blue eyes of my housemate. The man who made me lose my mind last night. He's watching me with a calmness that settles my own nerves.

"Good evening, everyone. I wanted to let you know that my original idea to speak to you tonight was about the animal shelter. Thankfully, our efforts on that front have been very lucrative. Thanks to the staff and their TikToks, we have received more donations. Also, the volunteer roster is full, although they are always happy with more people to help."

"Then why are you here?" That question comes from Freddy Jones. He's annoying. He owns the gas station on the way to I-35, and no one said he had to come tonight. Also, he's always a loudmouth.

"I will be truthful. I did not expect the social media campaign to explode the way it did."

"I did. You do such a good job," Mrs. Petersen says with a smile. God love the LOLs. They see me as one of them and do not let anyone bully me.

"Thank you. But what I want to move to is this recreation center. I know that the LOLs raised the money to fix this building into a multipurpose space, and with the generous bid from Nancy and Travis, it was done in almost no time flat. But, a year later, it's still not being used to its fullest extent."

"That's not our fault."

I'm going to fucking strangle Freddy. Seriously, how can he be only in his thirties and so cranky? I try not to scowl at him and open my mouth to tell him to stick it. It's hard to control my need to stand up for myself. I've been doing it for so long.

"I think you need to settle down, Freddy," Estella calls out. I glance at her and smile but find myself transfixed by Jon. He isn't looking at me. No, he's looking at Freddy like he's going to tear Freddy a new butthole.

I draw in a deep breath. "We need a director. Someone who can handle the schedules, and then we'll need input from the town on what kind of classes and meetings you would like to hold here."

That causes a lot of discussion, and I let it go on. I know Juniper. They need to discuss things ad nauseam.

"Hey, everyone, I get you want to discuss it. I encourage that, but how about we set a date to talk about it next month. If the town is interested, I can put together a proposal."

Once more questions ring out, Mayor Albert rises from his chair to get people to behave. This shouldn't be getting to me the way it is, but I can't seem to keep my anxiety at bay for some reason. I glance around the room and notice CND—Creepy Neighbor Dude—glaring at me.

What the actual fuck?

My chest is hurting, and my entire body tingling with anxiety. I know what this is. I haven't had a panic attack in years, but I'm close to hyperventilating. I don't understand it, but the room is starting to spin right now. Then I feel my phone buzz in my pocket.

Jon: *Breathe.*

I look up and find him staring at me, sympathy in his gaze. He seems to understand.

I draw in a deep breath, then a second and third. By the time I release the last breath, my pulse is calmer, and I don't feel like running away screaming.

Jon: *Freddy sounds like an eight-year-old.*

A laugh escapes me.

Me: *Right?! He definitely complains like one.*

Jon: *Are these meetings always like this?*

Me: *Not sure. This is my first one.*

"Avery, I think we can wait to vote on this next month," the mayor says. I look up at him and nod.

"I'll post some ideas on the JSE for everyone to read."

As I make my way to my seat, I glance at Jon, who is watching me, his gaze moving over me as if to check for any injuries. I settle in my chair.

"You were daydreaming up there."

I glance at Liv. My grandmother was the only person in my family who knew about my panic attacks. They started when I went to college, and I didn't want anyone else to know. I haven't had one since I was twenty, so that was a little weird.

I don't respond, but I realize Jon might have been the only person in the room who recognized my freak-out.

Me: *Thank you.*

Jon: *You're welcome.*

I expect a smart remark about me moving out, but it doesn't come.

Me: *Aren't you going to tell me that I must move out because you know my secret?*

Jon: *All of a sudden, I don't feel the need to get rid of you.*

I smile, my entire body lighting up. This isn't good, this feeling he gives me, but at the moment, I can't bring myself to get upset by it. In fact, it's damned nice that he seems to get me.

With a happy sigh, I concentrate on the rest of the meeting, knowing I can deal with Jon and all my feelings later.

Chapter Twenty-Six

Jon

Dinner is longer than I'm used to. My grandmother insists we go to *The Mason Jar* for dinner, and of course, she holds court there. I could be an ass about it and insist on leaving, but I'm enjoying the night. My mother and Ted seem to fit together well. When he gets up to go to the bathroom, my mother smiles at me.

"So, how are you liking Juniper Springs this time around?"

"Okay."

"Wow, no comment about how your house was stolen by a woman and her cat?" Her tone is darkly comical.

"Cats," I say absentmindedly. Sadly, Avery is not here. Liv, Mason, and her kids are, but she apparently went home. She never answered me after the comment about kissing her, and I hope I didn't step over my boundaries with her. I want my house, but I don't want her to feel harassed.

"More than one?"

"Yeah, apparently, she adopted another one today."

And I did check out the Insta of the shelter. She'd posted

a video of Benjamin saying she was taking him home with her.

"Something is going on."

"What?"

"With you and Avery."

"No."

She gives me the same look she gave me when I was accused of hacking into my father's bank account and moving money around to freak him out. I didn't steal it. I just put most of his money from his bank account into his savings account. My father is not a smart man.

"I would rather not talk about it."

"Okay. I'll let it go. Tell me what you think of Ted."

"Does it matter?"

"Of course."

"I just don't want you to get hurt. Football players have reputations."

"Yeah, but Ted has a reputation in the other direction."

"What do you mean?"

"He's been married just once."

"And why did they get divorced?"

"They didn't. She died of breast cancer three years ago. This is his first dating experience since then."

"Well, then he hit the lottery."

"My sweet boy," she says with a smile. "If people knew how sweet you are, they would take advantage of you."

I roll my eyes. I have a reputation for being a ruthless businessman regarding my apps and programs. There are a few reasons for that. Number one, my father. The bastard tried to get me to sign him on to my first venture, then he tried to initiate a takeover of my first company. He failed, but it taught me that no one could be trusted.

"I bet Avery O'Bryan could use someone like you in her life."

"Mom."

"Sorry. I just loved that you two sparkled around each other."

I feel my face heat. "I don't sparkle around Avery."

Ted sits down. "Stop messing with him, Clarice."

"Thank you. Nice to have your support."

"Oh, don't get me wrong. I agree with your mother. Reminds me of when we met."

I don't want to hear about this, but, on the other hand, I also want to hear about it. It's a weird clash of thoughts.

"He doesn't want to hear about that."

"No. Tell me."

"We were working for a charity together. It's the one that helps homeless vets get medical help. Anyway, she's all sweet. You know your mother. She has the best-damned smile in the world."

I nod because it's true. Even through the mess of my father leaving us, my mother could always find reasons to smile.

"Anyway, I asked around. I hadn't dated since my wife died, and I realized I didn't know how to go up to a woman and ask her out. Your mother draws people to her, especially men. So, I wanted to ensure I wasn't stepping on toes, if you get my drift." I find myself nodding again. When he glances over at my mother, I see it. There is sheer love. There is no doubt that this man is head over heels in love with my mother.

"Took me most of the night to work up the courage to approach her and ask her out." He looks at me. "I changed my clothes about five times the night we went out. I had to call up Fiona and ask for help."

"Fiona?"

"My oldest. She dragged my three grandchildren over to help me pick out clothes." He shakes his head. "It was worth it. You just have to decide if it is."

"What?"

"If this Avery is worth any pain she can cause you. Your mama is for me."

Oh, he's a sneaky S.O.B. He drew me in with a sweet story—and it is, and I feel much better about him and my mother now—then hits me over the head with a two-by-four of truth.

He's smiling at me like he won some kind of lottery.

"Proud of yourself?"

"Well, yeah. I mean, you are a genius."

I snort. "Please don't play the stupid jock card with me. I, of course, had you checked out."

"Did ya?" The twinkle in his eyes tells me he isn't the least bit bothered by it.

"I know that you have an investment firm you run."

"I do. Although, I'm stepping back and letting my daughters do most of the work now. I want to slow down to spend more time with your mother."

The truth was, I looked over the report and made sure he wasn't a gold digger or married. I forgot to pay attention to any of the reports about his dating life. Yes, I'm an asshole, but I wanted to make sure he was on the up and up.

"I do have a question."

"Okay."

"If you had me checked out, you would have probably run a background check that told you I haven't dated in a while. What did you think I was doing?"

"I thought you were being discreet."

That's a bit of a lie. Like I said, I barely looked at the report because I've suddenly become infatuated with my housemate, and she's all I can think about.

And I definitely can't think of anything else but that kiss. Fuck, I missed three meetings today because I was obsessing. Thanks to the JSE, I could keep up with her.

"Ah, that makes sense."

Dinner finishes without any more interrogating, thankfully. My mother is having a grand old time with my grandmother. I guess I have to give it to them. My father is a shit. I know. He's been married four times, and my grandmother ensures all her grandchildren have what they need. My mother is the only one of her ex-daughters-in-law Estella likes. They talk regularly, and they genuinely like each other.

It's another hour before we finally leave the restaurant. I find it amusing that my grandmother is now in with the LOLs, but I will say that she seems happier than, well, ever. I help her to her car, although I know she doesn't need it.

"I tried to get Avery to come to dinner."

"She's tired."

She stops by the passenger door. Ted is waiting to see if she needs assistance. Estella waves him off.

"And why is that?"

"She was out all night last night."

I know she knows about that. Hell, people were keeping up with Avery and speculating about us dancing together at the fundraiser. I followed along because I freaked out when she left the house. Without the JSE, I wouldn't have made it through the night. I would have called Josh and demanded he look for her.

"Yes. And why was that, Jon?"

I look down at her. "I have no idea."

She rolls her eyes. "You are the worst liar. Just make up with her."

"What makes you think we had a fight?"

A snort escapes, and my eyes narrow. "Jon, you would never intentionally hurt someone, especially a woman."

"Haven't you heard? I'm the worst billionaire to date."

"Yes, I'm sure you aren't fun to be around."

"Rude."

She throws her head back and laughs. That is so out of character for my grandmother, I blink. "You sound just like Avery when you say that."

Do I? "I don't." But she might be right. Good God, what happens if I start eating sugary cereals and sleeping all day?

Another chuckle slips from her lips, and I frown at her.

"Oh, Jon, you are in for a bit of a reality check and very soon."

"What's that supposed to mean?"

"We'll talk about it later. What do you think of Ted?"

I blink at the change of subject, but I know better than to challenge her. Estella runs every conversation, and everyone else is along for the ride.

"I like him. I checked him out."

"Yes, as I did."

"You did?"

"Do you think I would let someone get close to your mother without having a background check done? I care too much for her and for you to let anyone with a sketchy background near you."

I'm strangely touched. Estella never discusses things like this, and it makes me feel cherished. I know that she approved of me. I make my own way in the world, but I always thought she took a hands-off approach.

"Now, I'm ready for bed. My bones hurt, and there's rain coming."

"Not in the forecast."

Another snort. "I can tell you we will have rain tonight."

I help her into the car then watch as she heads home. Of course, she came in her own car. Estella likes to be on her own. I think it has a lot to do with her upbringing and constantly being told to let men take care of things. Avery might be right because she mentioned just that last week.

The moment she pops into my mind, I know I must search her out. I have to see if she wants anything more than that kiss.

Unfortunately, as I turn to go, my mother is standing there, a mischievous smile brightening her face. "I thought maybe we could have dessert."

I glance at Ted, who is looking anywhere but at me. "Is that a fact? Didn't you have some kind of dessert after dinner?"

"Well, a milkshake isn't really a dessert."

"That's not what you said when I was growing up."

Ted coughs, but I think it might be to cover up for a laugh. My mother sends him a look that would make lesser men run. Ted just smiles at her, and it's then that it hits me.

They are different in a lot of ways. I don't know Ted that well, but I come by my OCD issues from my mother. He seems like the kind of guy who can take what life throws at him. And dammit, that might make him perfect for my mother.

"Watch it, buster. I'll have you sleeping in the other wing."

"Why is that horrible?" Ted asks, amusement threading through his voice.

"Cousin Clara is there."

"Oh, please, I know how to handle a woman's advances. You know I have no interest in another woman."

"That would be my ex-sister-in-law you would want to avoid."

I nod at that. Nancy's mom is handsy with every available man she doesn't share blood with. And yes, she is married.

"Then, what's the problem?"

My mother looks at me to explain. "Great Cousin Clara is a bit out of touch with reality. She sees every man as her ex, and one thing that my grandmother always says is that all Howard men are reprobates. She hates him, even thirty years after he died. When she's in residence, only women work that wing."

"Why is that?"

"She threatened to kill Josh when he was at the house once."

"The sheriff?"

"Yep," I say, popping my p. "Then, there was the time she tried to kill my father. I think grandmother put him there on purpose. Just be glad Estella likes you."

"How do you know that?" Ted asks.

"She didn't put you in the wing with Clara."

"You were right, love," Ted says. "The Howard family is insane. Present company excluded."

"Thanks for that, but I'm living with a woman who stole my house and keeps adopting cats."

My mother chuckles.

"Ted, can you give me a second with Jon."

"Of course." He winks at me. "Good luck."

Once we're alone, my mother studies me. "What's going on?"

"What do you mean?"

"Something is going on with you and Avery. Please tell me you didn't upset her."

"She stole my house. I would think you would be on my side."

Oh, no. It's the look. The one she gives me when she knows I'm obsessing about something at unhealthy levels. Which, okay, is true, but it seems to have changed. Before, I was angry about it. Now, I'm just obsessed with getting more kisses like the one from last night.

"What is going on with you?" she asks again.

"You keep asking that, and I keep saying the same thing."

Sure, I'm thinking about selling my company, hiding out from my ex, who might be stalking me, and obsessing over a woman who not only stole my house but is entirely and absolutely wrong for me.

She sighs. "I'm going to let it go for now. I believe your grandmother is having a dinner tomorrow night that she invited Avery to."

"She didn't invite me."

An eye roll from my mother is not a good thing. "Jonathon Fredrick Howard, stop being so cheeky."

"Ah, you've been watching Doctor Who again."

She can't stop the chuckle. "Ted had never seen them before. He loves them now."

Of course. My mother can convince anyone that it's the best show in the world. "I'll be there. Just tell Estella to send me a time to show up."

I kiss her on the cheek and watch her get into the car with Ted. He waves at me, and I watch them pull out of the parking spot. Someone walks into me, and I turn around. I get the back of a massively built man, at least an inch taller than me, and he looks like he weighs about one hundred to one hundred and fifty pounds more than I do. Oddly, he doesn't stop to apologize, which is the norm in Juniper.

"Hey, Jon," Josh says as he steps up next to me. "Got a problem?"

"No. Just…do you know that guy?"

He looks at the man as he gets into the car. "He's renting the place behind yours."

"Oh, you agree that it's my house and that Avery has stolen it."

"You didn't act like you had a problem with her last night."

"What the hell?"

He rolls his eyes, and I'm getting irritated with people doing that to me.

"Everyone noticed you just about took my head off for talking to her. Just know it's been noticed, and the LOLs will pay attention."

With that, he heads off in the direction of the diner. Jesus, this town. If I were smart, I would run out of town tonight and avoid all this. Avery would probably rejoice.

Avery.

With her on my mind, I hurry to my car.

Chapter Twenty-Seven

Avery

It's been an hour since I arrived home, but I can't seem to settle down. I know, surprising. Benjamin and Meredith seem to be doing really well together, so I can't even blame my cats for the problem. I just keep walking through the house, my entire body still humming. I don't think I really want to face the reason for it because then I would have to admit I have a crush on my housemate.

Jon is such a hot man. I mean, who wouldn't want to jump that? I can see why so many models date him. Sure, some people would say it was his money, and I'm sure that helps. But beneath the surface, there was passion. I felt it just beneath that fussy exterior. That kiss. I stop by the sliding glass door and close my eyes. Every nerve ending in my body goes on alert as a rush of hormones floods my system. My nipples tighten, and I shift my legs. God, just from a kiss, I'm so turned on that I might need the help of my vibrator.

There's a knock at the door, and I frown. It could be one of the LOLs, but I thought most of them would go to *The Mason Jar* or the diner. But you never know when one of them just wants to chat. I step up to the door and look through the peephole. Whoever it is, she has her back to me, but it is definitely a she. A fall of perfectly styled golden curls tumble down her back, which is no easy feat in this humidity. When she turns, I gasp.

How did Sienna know where to find Jon? Also, how dare she show up here? Okay, I don't have a right to be so irritated by her appearance. All I shared with Jon was one kiss. I'm sure she's shared a lot more with him.

Now I want to hit her.

"I hear you in there. Answer the door."

She stomps her foot, and I roll my eyes. Seriously. Models. I've worked with a few, especially when starting and needing social media capital. I'm pretty damned dramatic, but nothing compared to a couple of models I've worked with.

"I will stay here all night."

That's a lie, but there is a tiny part of me worried that if Jon shows up and sees her standing there on the porch, he might think twice about kissing me again. Which is insane because I don't want to kiss him again.

"Jon," she whines.

Oh, God, how did he ever have anything to do with this woman? She's a complainer, but maybe he just tuned her out. I'm like that a lot. I get to thinking about one thing, like a class that teaches younger people how to keep their finances in order and track how much of their money they're spending on things like eating out. A balanced budget is more critical today with the price of housing and food.

I blink when Sienna starts pounding on the door. I

realize she's been losing it on the other side of the door while I was thinking about the class. I would ignore her, but if the LOLs haven't seen her yet, they will, and then it will get blown out of proportion.

I open the door causing her to stumble back.

"You bellowed?"

"What?"

"Is there a reason you keep knocking on my door?"

Her blue eyes cloud over with confusion as she stares at me. I don't know if she is confused by my words or has never had anyone be rude to her.

"I thought this was Jon's house."

"It's not. It's Estella's."

"That's an odd name."

I blink. Had Jon never told this woman about his grandmother or introduced her? There's no way she had been in town and Estella had not met her. Maybe she's an airhead. I know most people think that models are stupid. Don't get me wrong, some are not that bright, but the ones I worked with were actually bright. They saw themselves as businesswomen, and they understood the business of modeling more than many CEOs know their own business.

"I'm not Estella. I'm renting the house. And you are?"

I know who she is. I've been obsessing about her all day. I know. It's so unhealthy, and while I know that kiss means nothing, it irritates me this woman has shown up looking so tall and pretty.

"I...you don't know who I am?"

I shake my head and try not to smile. Irritation colors her expression,

"I'm Sienna," she announces with a toss of her head. Her curls ripple over her shoulder. Damn, she's good.

"Just that? Sienna? Like Madonna or Cher? I guess it's not like The Weekend. Do you go by The Sienna?"

She blinks. I bet she's deciding if she should start going by The Sienna. Inwardly, I roll my eyes.

"I'm here to talk to Jon."

"Jon?"

"Jon Howard."

Pursing my lips, I pretend to think.

"I know he's in there," she says, pushing past me. I shake my head and roll my eyes for real.

I see that Benjamin and Meredith are sitting on the bottom stair. Their expressions tell me they are not happy with Sienna.

"I know. She's rude."

"Who are you talking to?"

I glance at her. "Meredith and Benjamin."

She looks down at my precious babies with disdain, then back up at me. "Where is Jon?"

"Probably having dinner with his grandma, according to the Juniper Springs Express."

"The what?"

"It's an app Jon developed."

"He developed an app?"

It's my turn to blink. I know Jon is known for his security background for various government agencies. Still, he made his big bucks developing apps. Does she not know how Jon earned his money?

"Sienna, what are you doing here?"

She must understand that I know who she is.

"Are you the reason he wouldn't come to Milan?"

"Uh, no. I rented the house from his grandma, the aforementioned Estella."

"Oh."

"Come on. Let's go sit down."

She follows me into the kitchen, looking at it like it's disgusting. Oh, so she's one of those people who love the sleekness of new things. I get that. Me, though, I love historical things. I think that's why I love this house so much. It was built even before Estella met her husband. They owned pretty much all the land of Juniper Springs at one time.

"Would you like some tea?"

"Yes. Thank you."

No offer to help. She just sits her boney ass in one of the chairs.

I plug in the kettle and get the cups prepared. "I have green tea if that's okay with you."

"That's fine."

It takes me a few minutes to get the tea ready. I don't really drink it. I keep it around because it reminds me of Grannie Pam. She would have tea every afternoon when I got home, and we would talk about our days.

Blinking, I mentally order myself not to cry. Once I add milk and sugar to mine—the only way I can drink it—I bring the cups to the table. "I figured you didn't like to have anything in yours."

She nods, but she doesn't sip it.

"Really, Sienna, what are you doing here?"

"I came to make up with Jon. To forgive him."

I tamp down on my panic. Why would I worry if they made up? If they did, Jon would leave, and I would have the entire house to myself. That's what I wanted. To be left alone.

Why does that make me sad?

"Listen, I get it. He's a good-looking dude. But don't you find him a little…boring?"

"Personality-wise, yes. He hated going to parties with large groups of people. He also hated when I talked about the shows I walked in."

That does sound like Jon. The problem is that she never had a man act like that before. I bet most guys hang on to her every word. If I was a guy, I probably would too. She's gorgeous in a shiny, sparkly way. Like, I bet she wakes up without morning breath.

"Can you tell me what Jon does for a living?"

Again, another blink. "I thought he was independently wealthy."

He probably is. The Howards are legendary in Texas, and from her twang, Sienna grew up here. The only other rancher with a bigger reputation is the Waggoner family. They have owned a considerable part of South Texas for a long time. Rumor is they were here before it was even a nation. And yes, Texas was a nation. Look it up.

"He's one of the best-known people in the tech industry."

"Uh."

"See, I don't think the two of you know each other that well. That's why he bailed."

"He didn't leave me."

"First, I don't see it as leaving unless you lived together or married. Second, he did. He freaked out when you wanted more."

"It's like you know him."

No, but I'm starting to wonder how much we have in common. Whenever a guy wanted to get serious with me, I always figured out a way to leave town. I didn't realize it until now, but that's precisely what I did.

"No. But I have a degree in sociology, and I don't think you want him back."

She frowns. "I do."

I shake my head. "You like the idea of him. Of a man who will take care of you. You have a demanding job, and I bet you started before you were eighteen."

"Fifteen."

I nod. "I get it. Wanting a man to take care of things, of you. But, Sienna, my Grannie Pam always told me that you have to love yourself. If you don't, then your relationships will falter. They won't be real."

Her eyes fill with tears, and I panic. I don't like crying, and it freaks me out when other people I don't know well do it in front of me.

"But I want someone to be there for me."

I sigh. "When is your next job?"

"I have a little break now that the fall shows are over."

"I suggest you take a little time for yourself. A spa vacation. There's this spa in Arizona I have always wanted to go to. They have treatments and activities, and I know they have a good staff to help you. I know one of the therapists. You need to take some time for Sienna and not anyone else."

She cocks her head. "Why are you helping me? Trying to get Jon for yourself?"

I snort. "First, do you think I want to be the woman

who follows Sienna? And second, I can't bear to see a woman who should be confident as fuck doubt herself. Stop trying to find the next guy, the next show, the next, whatever. Spend time on Sienna."

"Have you done that?"

I nod.

"It's scary."

"Oh, absolutely. I did it when I felt I should be in Texas, but my Grannie Pam insisted. I'm not working right now because I need time to myself."

"But you're in Texas."

"Yeah. I was planning on Hawaii next, but I came to Juniper to help my sister with her kids, and I fell in love with the place."

"With this place?" There is a look of disgust on her face. "Ugh, I could never stay in a little town like this. It would drive me crazy."

"I can see that. You need a bigger city with more fun. Me, I've always been a homebody. Or at least someone who didn't like too many parties, things like that. They make my head hurt."

"Meow."

Meredith has joined the girl talk.

I look down and see her slinking under the table.

"So, what do you think, Sienna? Do you think you can spend some time on yourself?"

She blinks. "It's…"

"Scary, yes, you said that. But it's imperative. Jon isn't the man for you. He hates parties and spending time in large groups, and he couldn't give a shit about fashion."

"He used me."

"No. You used each other. Would you have gone after him if he had been Jon Howard computer science teacher?" She shakes her head. "It was mutual, and there's nothing wrong with that."

Another blink. "Yeah, I guess."

"So, why don't you head back to Dallas, and I won't tell him you were here. Unless you want me to?"

She opens her mouth to say something, but the door opens.

"Avery?"

Jon has the worst timing.

"Well, I guess we don't have a choice now," I mutter.

He steps into the kitchen, and his gaze narrows in on Sienna. "What are you doing here?"

"I came to win you back, but that's unimportant."

He rounds the table to stand by me. Meredith meows at him and looks at him like he hung the freaking moon. Skank.

"It's not."

"Jon, be nice. Sienna is a product of a society that has convinced her she needs a man. She doesn't. She's a strong woman who can stand on her own two feet."

"And that's your analysis?"

"Yes. You know, I do have a degree that helps with this."

He rolls his eyes. "And I dated her."

"Oh, please, mansplain stuff to me, Jon."

I'm readying for an argument because, well, because. I don't want to look at my reasons too closely. Yes, I do have that sociology degree. It's not really for self-reflection, though.

"Woah, I think this is where I leave," Sienna says as she

rises from the table. Jesus, with those heels on, she's almost as tall as Jon.

"I'll see you to the door," I say, wanting to escape whatever the hell is going on between Jon and me. "Come on, Meredith."

Meredith ignores me as she rubs against Jon's ankles. What a complete skank. Jon leans down and pulls her into his arms. I frown at him but want to ensure that Sienna leaves, so I hurry after her.

"Thanks, Avery."

"Any time. Find me on social media if you need any more chats."

She offers me a friendly smile, and I see the girl then. The ordinary girl who just wants to be accepted, just like the rest of us.

"Sure thing."

I stand on the porch and watch her leave, and it has nothing to do with the fact that I'm avoiding Jon. At all.

Once her taillights disappear around the corner, I'm forced to go and talk to Jon. Because while I hoped he would hide in his room, I know better. He's sitting in the kitchen waiting for me, probably with Meredith.

And while I'm at it, I wonder where Creepy Neighbor Dude is? He hasn't been out at all.

I step back into the house. It's quiet. I peek into the kitchen, but it's empty. Frowning, I turn out the light and head to the living room. There's a pool of light from the lamp beside the sofa. And there, with Meredith in his lap, sits the man who has been giving me problems for the last ten days.

"So, you got rid of my ex?"

Of course, he doesn't even turn around, and I realize he can see me in the reflection of the window on the opposite side of the room.

"Yeah. So, you owe me. Move out. That will be payment enough."

"Are you going to keep standing there like a coward?"

He isn't nice, and I know he's doing it to get me riled up. Still, I can't help but take the bait. It's immature, but I stomp over.

"I'm not being a coward."

His smile is not especially friendly, but it sends a shaft of heat coursing through my blood, and I curl my toes.

"What do you call running away from me last night, hiding out all day, then scurrying away after the meeting?"

Oh, he is so sure of himself. My fingers itch to smack him, but my lips tingle with the memory of our kiss.

"You think that's the reason?"

One eyebrow rises. "You have another reason?"

"Sure. I know you're infatuated with me. I was trying to let you down gently."

There that sounded like a reason, right?

He cocks his head, studying me in a way that makes my right eye twitch and my nipples harden. Ugh. Of course, my adverse reactions to him have me befuddled, and he uses it to his advantage. He rises so fast I don't have time to react before he pulls me down to the couch, then covers my body with his.

"Let's put that theory to the test."

Then he slams his mouth down on mine.

Chapter Twenty-Eight

Avery

The moment Jon's mouth touches mine, my brain goes completely blank. Like completely shuts down, just like last night. And tonight, I have had no alcohol. It's all Jon's mouth on mine, his tongue in my mouth, and, oh, God, his cock. He's hard, and again, even through our clothes, I'm impressed by the size.

He hums against my lips, and I feel it all the way down to my lady parts. How does he do that? It's like he knows what gets me going, and I can't understand that at all. He breaks the kiss only to attack my neck, and my pulse scrambles. His heart is beating hard against my chest, so at least I'm not alone.

"Jon, we shouldn't. This is insanity."

He scrapes his teeth against the sensitive flesh just beneath my jaw. I shiver, my mind going blank.

"Tell me to stop."

"I did."

"No, you said it was insane, and we shouldn't do it. You

didn't say stop." He murmurs the words against my neck. God, that's sexy. "So, tell me to stop, and I will."

I open my mouth to do that, but I can't. Because I want this. I want him—on top of me, his mouth on my body.

Fuck.

And I don't use that word often, but I think it works in this situation.

He rises up to look down at me. His face is as flushed as my entire body feels. "This is your last chance."

"Last chance?"

"Yeah. Otherwise, I'm taking you upstairs, stripping you out of these clothes, and putting my mouth on every part of your body, especially your sweet pussy."

I blink briefly, trying to get my brain to function, but I never pegged Jon for a dirty talker. But, geez.

"I take that as a yes."

He pulls away, slipping off the couch, and for a moment, my entire body rebels. The cool air replaces his hot body, and I almost gasp at the sensation. But he doesn't give me the time to recover. Instead, he leans down, pulling me into his arms.

"Jon, put me down."

"Nope."

"I insist."

He stops at the base of the stairs. "Are you telling me no? It's okay if you are, but you have to tell me no right now."

I blow out a breath. It would be easy to tell him no, to tell him that I'm not into this idea at all. Or at least it should be. But my body is humming with need just for him.

"I can't say no. I…just think this could be a big mistake. We should think about it."

He starts walking up the stairs. "I *have* thought about it. Even before last night. Getting off to the idea of you has become one of my favorite pastimes since I arrived."

My eyes widen.

"Then, after last night, God, that's all I've thought about. The taste of you and just how sweet that pussy of yours could be. I want to be inside of you."

He steps into my room. He sees the cat and looks at me. "I guess that's Benjamin."

I sniff. "Meredith needed a friend."

He says nothing. Instead, he sets me on my feet. This is usually where I get awkward. I'm not good with intimacy, thanks to my ADHD. Other thoughts usually crowd my mind, and I can't concentrate on what is happening. But in this instance, I don't feel like thinking about anything else. Nothing seems important other than how he's looking at me. It's like I'm the most important thing in the world. Like I'm precious. I have never felt like this, even when I was young and stupid and dated guys like Chet.

I slam that door shut. I will not let a man like that ruin this moment. I'm not sure it should even be a moment, but the way Jon's intense blue gaze moves over my body tells me that if this is a mistake, it will be worth it.

He slips his fingers beneath the hem of my t-shirt, urging it up and over my head. I'm wearing a plain black bra, and for once, I regret wearing something so comfy. Jon slips his fingers over my breasts, trailing over the skin just above the fabric.

"I've been obsessed with your breasts for what seems like forever."

"We've known each other for less than a week."

He snorts. "Doesn't seem to matter when it comes to you."

Something flutters in my stomach. Hope. That's not something I usually want or need regarding sex. In fact, I try not to go beyond the good feelings. This is somehow different. There's just something about the way he looks at me. It's like I can feel it down to my bones.

He says nothing as he tugs my pants down, and I undo my bra and toss it on the floor somewhere. When Jon straightens, his gaze zeroes in on my breasts.

"Fuck."

The word is whispered, but it's as if he shouted it. He's so proper, so hearing him cuss is sexy. He slides his fingers over my breasts again, his thumbs teasing my nipples. The heat that had been simmering since I tackled him that first night explodes. Impatience grinds into my arousal. I growl. He glances up from my breasts, surprise in his eyes, a smile curving his lips.

Damn, that is probably the sexiest expression I have ever had tossed in my direction.

"Frustrated?"

"Yes. I'm naked except for my panties, and you're just taking your sweet time."

He tugs on one of my nipples, and I shiver as I moan. Jesus, this man.

"You're always rushing places. You need to slow down, Avery."

I open my mouth to let him have it, but he drops to his knees before me.

"Your skin is so soft." He sounds mesmerized by it. I don't understand that since he's a man who has dated super-models, who I know have super soft skin. Or I assume because they are pampered. Also, why am I thinking about other women he's slept with? That's just insane.

Thankfully, Jon can't hear my jumbled thoughts. He takes a nipple into his mouth, grazing the tip with his teeth before swirling his tongue around it. Over and over, he teases me and tortures me as he plucks at my other nipple. I feel it all the way down to my clit. He doesn't hurry. Instead, he takes his time, seemingly intent on driving me crazy.

He urges me to sit down on the bed. I do it without questioning him. I am so hot right now that I would probably commit murder if he told me to.

I mean, not really.

Then, he kisses my belly, and I stop thinking about anything but him.

The way his mouth feels against my flesh. My nerve endings vibrate with need. I need him on a level I've never felt before, but this is different. This isn't hot. Out of control. I thought it would be because of the heat between us, but this is something different. He's taking such care with me as if I am precious to him. I've never felt that with any other man. But the care he is taking with me is something I have never had with a man.

It's as if he has all the time in the world to pleasure me, and I am here for it.

"Lay back," he orders, and I obey. I am not one for having a man tell me what to do in bed. But there is something in his tone that makes me eager to do whatever I can to please him.

I fall back, and he takes me by the hips, yanking me to the edge. He places a palm on each of my thighs, spreading them impossibly wide. His blue gaze zeroes in on my center. I want to close my legs because while I'm not a prude, I'm not sure I've ever had a man look at me like this. He's still fully clothed, and I'm completely naked. There's an intimacy to this I have never had with another man. It's not the act of oral sex because I've had that. The way he's doing it, the time he takes with me, makes me feel precious. He leans down, and instead of going straight for my pussy, he kisses my inner thigh.

"Oh," I gasp.

His mouth curves against my skin. "Like that?"

He doesn't wait for me to answer. Instead, he drags the flat of his tongue up my thigh. Anticipation is high, but he bypasses my pussy for my other thigh. I growl, but he ignores me, taking his time.

By the time he makes his way back up to my center, I'm shaking, my legs shifting against the side of the mattress.

He pauses, sliding his hands beneath my rear end and lifting me off the mattress.

"Jon." It's half demand, half plea.

When he looks up at me, his eyes are blazing hot. "I've been thinking about how you would taste for days, and I want to take my time."

Then, with his gaze connected to mine, he leans forward, touching the tip of his tongue against my slit. The featherlight touch shouldn't drive me insane, but I'm impossibly sensitive, thanks to him. I watch him as his tongue dips inside of me. His gaze turns blurry, and a look of complete bliss moves over his expression.

Jon closes his eyes as I fall back on the bed again and just feel. For once, I let loose, allowing Jon to control my pleasure.

Oh, mama, it's amazing. Jon has one talented mouth. He teases my clit with his teeth and thrusts two fingers inside me. Everything I have been wanting, and needing from him, rushes forward. I'm so close to coming that I can barely think straight.

"Let go, baby. You can do it," he says, his mouth moving against that tiny bundle of nerves.

It's as if his saying those words gave me permission. All of the tension splinters, and I explode, shouting his name. Pleasure rushes over me as I shake from the force of my orgasm.

"So beautiful."

The words are so soft I barely hear them, but I do. It almost sends me over the edge again.

Jon lets go of me and rises to his feet. He tears off his clothes, his hands shaking.

I did that. I made him so crazed that he can barely get naked. His body is perfection. He's all lean muscle and golden skin. His thick cock curves up against his stomach.

Fuck, that's pretty.

"Why, thank you."

My gaze shoots up to his, and the smile curving his lips tells me I said that last part out loud. I smile up at him and see the curve of his mouth, and something shifts inside me. Another kind of warmth fills me, one that surprises me and scares me simultaneously.

Pushing those thoughts aside, I sit up and wrap my hand around him. As I stroke him, he leans his head back, his eyes closing, and he groans.

As I pump him, I lean forward to lick the drop of precum. The salty sweetness of his come slides down my throat. I want more. I want him to lose control, but he has other plans.

"Nope. When I come, it will be with your sweet pussy wrapped around me."

He urges me up on the mattress, then curses. He turns to grab his pants, giving me a fantastic view of his ass. God, that man is put together perfectly for me.

He pulls out a condom, rips the package, and rolls it on before joining me on the mattress. With one hard thrust, he enters me to the hilt. Even though I am swollen from my release, I can't complain. I love feeling so full of him, the weight of his body. Then, he starts to move.

I wasn't sure I could come again, although I almost did just a few minutes ago. I've never been a woman who had major orgasms because my mind tends to wander.

With Jon, it's different. I feel safe, as if nothing in the world can hurt me, and for some reason, that makes it so easy to let go. As he rises to his knees, he drags me up with him. His fingers bite into the flesh at my hips. His thrusts are faster and harder, and I enjoy every minute.

Heat swirls and drops to my pussy, and I am coming again. This time I scream his name as I come.

As I am still coming down from my second orgasm, he pulls out of me and flips me over onto my stomach. I can barely think straight as he pulls me up to my knees and enters me from behind.

He starts thrusting in and out of me, faster and harder than before.

"Touch yourself, Avery. Come on, baby, I want to feel all those muscles on my cock."

Again, I do as he orders, pressing my fingers against my clit. I come again, my entire body convulsing with pleasure as he thrusts into me once…twice…three times more before he shouts my name, his fingers digging into my flesh as he lets go.

Moments later, before I collapse on the bed, our heavy breathing is the only sound in the room.

Chapter Twenty-Nine

Jon

I toss the condom in the trash and glance at myself in the mirror. I shouldn't feel this good, this centered. I just fucked Avery O'Bryan, and it was glorious. I didn't think this would happen when she tackled me less than a week ago. She should be my nemesis, stealing my house, disrupting my world. Instead, I feel calmer than I ever have in my life.

"Uh."

What the fuck is that about? And why am I worrying about this when there is an amazing woman in bed?

I push all my worries aside, then return to the bedroom.

"I don't think you need to give me the stink eye, Meredith. He's a human. He wasn't going to marry you."

Meredith sits on the chair beside the bed, staring at Avery like she stole her boyfriend.

"Seriously, you would think you're plotting my death."

"She might be."

Avery looks over at me, her gaze traveling down my

body. She sighs. "You are amazingly put together, Jonathon Howard."

"Why, thank you. Right back at ya."

She smiles at me, her eyes dancing. "Going to snuggle with me, or are you one of those people who needs space?"

I want to deny her. Usually, I tend to like my own space. It's one reason I like to return to my place, even when I'm dating someone. But I need her in my arms, to feel her body against mine.

What the hell is that about?

"I won't be mad. I completely understand. I'm usually the first one to leave."

I feel it has more to do with leaving the relationship than leaving the bed. Opening my mouth to tell her that, but it doesn't happen. Instead, I snap my mouth shut and head to the bed. I slip beneath the sheets. I pull her against me.

"I would rather snuggle."

She hesitates before completely relaxing. "I want to warn you, I do not sleep well with someone in my bed."

I know it's stupid, but jealousy whips through me. Jesus, one of my exes showed up here, and Avery was cool as a cucumber and got the woman to leave. But, no, I lay here upset she had a life before me. Mature, Jon. Real mature.

"What are you thinking about?"

"Why?"

"Your fist is clenched."

Sure enough, I look down and notice my fist clenched against her shoulder. "Sorry. I was just jealous."

She rises up off my chest to look down at me. Even in the dim light, I can see her. Her hair is a mess of curls, and her face is still flushed from our lovemaking. "Of what? Sienna finding someone else?"

I frown at her. "Why would I care about that?"

She shrugs. "She's gorgeous."

She doesn't sound jealous. It's as if she's just stating a fact. One thing about Avery is she doesn't lie. Sure, she might cloud the truth by not telling someone what is precisely going on, but I'm learning that she does that because she thinks she's protecting the other person. Avery isn't meeting my eyes, and that's weird. Another thing about Avery is that she believes in eye contact, even in uncomfortable situations.

"She is, but I don't care who she ends up with."

Her gaze finally touches mine, and a small smile curves her lips. "Sorry. It's not like I have a right to be upset with you. It's just that I've had a bad track record back to my first boyfriend."

I open my mouth to ask her about him, but then she makes a rude noise.

"God, I'm lying in bed with the man who gave me the best sex of my life, complete with multiple orgasms, and I'm talking about my first boyfriend. This is why everyone calls me awkward."

It takes me a second to work through that sentence.

"First, part of your awkwardness is what makes you attractive."

She rolls her eyes. "Sure."

Irritation moves through me. "Stop that."

"What?"

"Stop doubting yourself."

She opens her mouth to argue with me, but I stop her.

"I get that everyone sees you as this brash, funny genius. And you are that. But I've been here the last week. I've seen you up at night, not able to sleep."

"I sleep during the day."

She sounds defensive, and now I understand what is happening with her. She does show the world she's a funny, smart girl. But there is that part of her that's hurting.

"Having insomnia doesn't mean that you're a failure. Dealing with depression isn't easy."

She might not move away from me, but she's building a wall. If this was a normal relationship, I would let it go. This time, though, I don't want that.

"I am not depressed."

Each word is drenched in anger, but I hear the fear beneath the comments. I realize that pushing this issue would push her way. For the first time in a long time, I don't want space. I want to crawl inside of her and know every bit of her. Alarm bells sound in my head, but I ignore them.

"So, tell me about this Chet dude."

I remember that her sister mentioned his name the other night. She hesitates for just long enough to make me think I might have ruined any chances of a second round. But, at that last second, I feel her relax against me.

"He was my first boyfriend."

"And?"

"He cheated."

I hear more beneath the surface once again. Usually, she shares way too much information. If she's keeping some of it hidden, that tells me there's more to the story than she wants to reveal.

And in that instant, I realize I want to know. There's so

much that makes this woman tick. As I thought before, I want to discover it all. If I figure out what makes her the way she is, maybe I can work her out of my system and vice versa.

"That's not the whole story."

She tries to pull away, but again, I refuse. This woman is always trying to get away from me. I wanted her gone when I first arrived, but now, I want her around. All the time.

I blink at that realization, but I refuse to worry about it. Not right now. Right now, I need to know more about Avery.

"Yeah, well, he was stupid."

"He was if he let you go."

She looks up at me, surprise coloring her expression. "Thanks."

"Now, tell me what went on with this idiot."

And do I have to find him and ruin his life? It wouldn't take much to screw with the man.

I blink. What the actual fuck? I think I'm just reacting to her behavior. The shame in her voice whenever this guy is mentioned, makes me want to ruin his life.

"I mean, he didn't protect his phone very well. I had worries about his behavior. He had things to do in the middle of the night, or so he said. He was a big man on campus. The quarterback at TCU the year they were expected to make it to the championship. And he was in a frat, so I thought maybe that was why. I was naive for twenty."

She didn't have to explain that to me. I was the same way, unable to figure out the opposite sex and, worse, being so much younger than everyone else.

"I got into his phone one night and realized he was sending dick pics to other girls—who had asked for them. I mean…there was no reason for him to be so proud. I could see people asking you for dick pics, but let's say he had really tiny hands."

I try not to smile. "Go on."

"Then I found horrible texts and discovered he was only dating me because I was helping keep his grades up. I was tutoring him in statistics."

I do not have an easy temper, but I like to burn everything down once it gets going. This Chet asshole sounds like he deserves all my anger.

"There were worse things."

I feel dampness on my chest. Great, Jon. You got her to talk about something that makes her cry. So suave. But something in her voice signals she needs to tell me what those things were. I sigh and hug her tighter, brushing my lips over her temple.

"Go ahead."

She draws in a deep breath, letting it out slowly. "There were videos. I know some girls do them happily, and I don't judge."

"Were there any of you?"

"No, he knew better." Something in Jon's chest loosened. "But the ones I knew the girls had no idea about were the up-skirt clips."

"What the fuck?"

"Right? I know everyone has their own kinks, but that's illegal. And gross. So, I turned him in."

I blink up at the ceiling. "You turned him in?"

"Yeah. And it didn't go well for him. One or two of the

girls were considered minors. So, that was a whole other charge."

There is something she's not telling me. She was honest about turning him in, but there's more to it.

"And?"

"And what? What's the rest of the story?"

She sighs. "I don't want to tell you."

She's not looking at me, so I slip my finger beneath her chin and gently urge her to look up at me. "Tell me. I won't think any worse of you."

Another sigh. "One of the girls who had been texting with him was someone I had considered my friend. Like one of my very few friends. You know how hard it is to make friends when you're the one ruining the curve in class and, worse, you're a couple years younger than everyone else."

I nod.

"She said some really horrible things about me. They had been texting that night, and he had already taken a pic of his dick. Me showing up for our date apparently made him have to wait. So, while he was in the bathroom, I switched his mother's name with Tabitha's. He never checked. Just sent the pic along."

I blink. Jesus that is a bit evil and a bit brilliant. "Holy shit."

She nods. "I shouldn't have done it, but I was pissed. I had already forwarded all the info on his phone to the local cops. I got out of there just as his mother called. I don't think his life was ever the same."

"His own fault. I mean, the mother stuff, that was freaking fantastic."

"Yeah?"

I nod, a smile curving my lips. "But the other stuff, it's important that you did that. Scum like that shouldn't be allowed to roam free. It was his fault for being an asshole."

She smiles up at me, one of her brilliant smiles that seems to hit me right in the chest. God, she's stunning.

Without warning, she rolls over on top of me, rising up to straddle me. The only light in the room comes from the hallway, but it's enough to see her. Her face is flushed, her nipples hard, and fuck, she's the epitome of temptation. I don't think another woman has enticed me as much as Avery.

"What?"

"You're just…"

Words fail me. It's impossible that I just met this woman, and I have more feelings for her than some of my exes. She's smiling down at me, but it starts to fade when I can't come up with anything to say. It's lodged in my throat, partially because of my own hang-ups.

I slide my hands up her torso to her breasts, tugging on her nipples. Her quickly drawn in breath has me smiling.

"You're so fucking responsive."

She swivels her hips, the heated core of her moving against my cock. I drop my hands and suck in a breath. Fuck. The woman just has to look at me to get me hot, but…this is different. I want to consume her, to know that every little sigh of happiness is because of something I did.

She gyrates her hips once more, and my eyes almost cross. There is no doubt she's wet and needy, and I want to be inside of her now.

"Fuck. I need a condom."

"Are you clean?"

I nod. "I've never had sex without a condom and just had a checkup."

"I'm on the pill and just had a checkup last month."

The idea of being inside her without any barriers has my head spinning. My fingers twitch. "You're okay with no condom?"

She nods and rises, taking my cock into her hand. After pumping me a couple of times, her slender fingers moving over my flesh causes my eyes to roll back in pleasure. She positions herself over my cock, then slides down on it.

"Fuck." My fingers tighten on her hips, digging into her flesh.

For a woman who rushes through life, she takes her time taking me in. By the time I'm fully seated inside her, I'm shaking with the need to take over. I hold back, just barely.

"You feel so good inside of me."

Her breathy comment shifts through me. I don't know what it is about her, but she tempts me to be bad in the best of ways.

She starts to ride me, keeping a slow pace that drives me insane. It's enough to get me close but not let either of us gain relief. I slip my hand between our bodies, teasing her clit as she bounces on my cock. Fuck, she's gorgeous. Her skin is pinkened, her hair is a mess from my hands, and I don't think I will ever get enough of her.

Soon, she's moving faster, her moans filling the room as I feel her muscles quivering against my cock.

"Come for me, baby."

It's like my words spur her into pleasure. She throws back her head, screaming my name as she comes.

Beautiful.

I roll us over the mattress, taking control of the lovemaking. I rise to my knees, dragging her hips up off the bed. I set a punishing rhythm, thrusting into her again and again. The headboard smacks against the wall, intermingling with our moans. I'm close to coming when Avery screams my name again, her tiny little muscles clamping down hard on my dick.

I thrust into her once more, letting the pleasure take over. My fingers are digging into her flesh as I pour myself into her.

I collapse on the bed next to her, our rough breathing the only sound in the room.

"That was fanfuckingtastic," Avery says.

I smile as I look over at her, and at that moment, I feel my heart clutch in my chest. She's looking at me, that stunning smile of hers lighting up her entire face, and I don't think another woman gets me like she does.

That should scare me, and it does, but a part of me knows there is no way to fight it. She's under my skin, and I need to let it happen.

"I agree," I say, pulling her into my arms.

"Do you want to talk about this? Worry about what's going to happen?"

I look down at her and realize she knows me better than other women I have dated. She gets me in a way those women never did.

"Naw. I'm tired. I need a little sleep before we go for round three."

Her eyes widen. "Three?"

I kiss her forehead. "Yeah. Now sleep."

For once, she does as I tell her. She settles against me, her head on my shoulder, her hand over my heart.

This will not be an easy situation, but now, with her next to me in bed, I don't give a damn.

Chapter Thirty

Jon

The text I get the following day tells me I have no choice but to meet my mother and Ted for lunch. And she's insisting I bring Avery. I'm not sure what that's about. The truth is, I would rather stay here at the house, snuggled with Avery. And that's odd for me. I'm definitely a homebody, but this is different. I don't want to stay here to think about things. I want to be here, wrapped around Avery.

I frown. That's somewhat unsettling. Maybe it's the whiplash of going from trying to get rid of her to wanting to spend all day in bed with her. The memory of slipping inside her, the sound of my name on her lips…I get hard. Again. Closing my eyes, I count down from ten, then do it again. I'm becoming obsessed. I don't think I was this infatuated with Maisy Griffin, and she's the first woman who let me touch her boobs.

Once I have my body under control, I open my eyes. Meredith and Benjamin are sitting on the kitchen table, staring at me. That's another thing. I rarely put up with anything that gets in my space without my permission. But I'm getting attached to the cats. I frown.

"Why do you look like that?"

I glance up, my pulse scrambling. Avery is…well, she's gorgeous in my favorite way. I like anything unique, and she is definitely that. She's wearing a shirt that says "Rolling with the LOLs" tucked into jeans that hug her hips. I can't wait to see her ass in them. As my gaze travels back up, I realize she looks rested for the first time since I met her. It's not the makeup hiding it. She barely has any on except for the rosy lipstick. It just makes me want to kiss her.

"No."

"What?"

"Well, you went from frowning to staring at my lips. I need to look nice for your mother and Ted."

My frown returns. "I don't know why we have to go out."

"Because your mother wants to talk work with me."

"How do you know that?"

"She texted me."

"When?"

"When I was getting ready. It was right after I told her that her son knows exactly how to rock a woman's world, and yes, that rumor about hands and dick size is true."

My eyes widen. She laughs.

"The look on your face." She's giggling so hard she bends over at the waist.

I want to be mad at the teasing, but I can't. She's so happy, and while she's always making jokes, I don't think I've ever seen her laugh like this. I rise out of my chair and approach her, backing her up against the wall.

"You think you're pretty funny?"

She smiles up at me as she slides her hands up my arms to my shoulders. My cock hardens. Fuck.

"Yeah. I'm hilarious."

I lean down to kiss her. I meant it to be just a simple kiss, a brush of my lips against hers. She makes a little mewling sound, and I lose control again. Then she makes another sound.

"What?"

"You're going to mess up my lipstick."

Hmm. I lean down and attack her neck. There is something so addictive about her skin. Soft and fragrant. She shivers against me.

"We can be late," I say against her neck.

"We can't."

I sigh and pull back but keep my hands on her waist. "Fine."

She smiles and pats my face. "I'll make it up to you, promise."

After she explains to the cats where we are going, we head out. It's a nice day, balmy for October in Texas. As we ride into town, Avery settles back in the seat and looks out the window.

"Is something wrong?"

She looks over at me with a frown. "Why would you ask that?"

"You're quiet." Too quiet. I think the only time I have ever seen her this still, and quiet was while she was sleeping last night. And yes, I was a creeper and stared while she slept. I just couldn't help myself.

She shrugs and offers me a small smile. "I feel settled.

Not sure what that's about. Maybe Juniper is going to become my permanent home."

That leaves me unsettled. Why would she live here? She likes to travel. She's mentioned she has a trip to Hawaii planned. I don't say anything because I never do well with messy conversations, like, come live with me forever in my big, stupid, cold house in Highland Park.

Odd, I've never thought of my house as cold. Granted, I rarely thought about it, except it's where I slept. And I didn't even furnish it. I paid someone. Besides my computer and pictures, most of it was picked out by someone who barely knew me.

I pull into a parking spot next to what looks like Ted's SUV. As we step out of the car, I feel as if everyone is looking at us. Avery meets me on the sidewalk.

"Hey, what's up, buttercup?"

I look down at her and lose my concentration again. "Don't you feel everyone looking at us?"

She glances around. "It's a Tuesday, so there aren't that many people out and about."

"That doesn't bother you?"

"The fact that there aren't that many people? No, kids are in school."

I growl, and she laughs, rising to her tiptoes. "Jon, I know this is an issue for you."

"I hate being the center of attention."

She cocks her head. "Then why did you date all those supermodels? They're always being photographed."

"Yeah, but people aren't looking at me."

"Ohh, burn on me."

"What?"

"Well, you think they are looking at us but not specifically at me. I get it."

"No. That's…" I groan. "That's not what I meant at all."

"Sure," she says, stepping around me and reaching for the diner's door. I grab her and back her up against the side of the restaurant. I place one hand on the window above her head.

She looks up at me, her face flushes, and another small smile curves her lips. "You drive me insane."

"Good. You need to let loose, Jon."

"I thought I was pretty good at that last night. And this morning."

A faint blush colors her cheeks, and it is the cutest thing I've ever seen. "No complaints."

"I would think not, as loud as you were."

Her eyes widen. "Jon Howard! I can't believe there are people who say you aren't funny."

"Who says I'm not?"

She slips under my arm. "Lots of people. They're wrong, though. You're an acquired taste, that's all."

I open the door for her, and we step into the diner. Everyone is looking at us, and I feel the old panic. Being my father's son didn't make it easy on me when we were in town. A lot of people do not like him.

She leans closer and says, "I can hear your sphincter closing up, Jon. Just remember, you just mauled me in front of them."

"I did not maul you," I whisper to her.

She heads off to the table where Ted and my mother are sitting. She's beaming at me, as is Ted.

"Hey, sweetie," my mother says. "Avery."

We get settled in the booth, and the waitress steps up. "Would you like something to drink?"

"I would like a coffee with cream," Avery says.

"Coffee, black."

When she leaves, albeit slowly and with a nasty look thrown in Avery's direction, my mother smiles at us.

"I'm so excited to talk to you about your work."

"Seriously. She's talked nonstop since she met you last night," Ted says with a chuckle.

"I was wondering if you would like to talk to my students?"

Avery nods as if she's not surprised and like this happens every day. "I could do that. What's the class?"

"Social Media and the generational divide."

"Ah, yeah. I spoke to a similar class at the University of Texas last year. What do you want me to talk about?"

"I think discussing the piece about elderly people and social media."

"That is something I know well."

The report on her said she wrote a few papers, but I had no idea she was so sought after.

"I take it you're working with the LOLs on that?"

As my mother and Avery go into their version of nerdy —talking about sociology—I shared an amused look with Ted.

"I think the gals are just a little smarter than we are."

Avery glanced over at Ted. "There are different kinds of smart. Like Fritz, he has a hair trigger sense or something like that. He said he knew when things would be bad when they went out for the day."

"Went out for the day?" Ted asks.

"Oh. Sorry. I forget that not everyone knows my whole life story. My brother is retired Army."

"He's one of the owners of Camos and Cupcakes in San Antonio."

"Oh, my, I love that place. I don't get into San Antonio often, but I always go over there," my mother says. "And that little bookshop across the hall?"

Avery notices that Ted and I are being left out of the conversation.

"They're housed in a historic home in the King William district in San Antonio." She looks at my mother. "EJ is the owner of the bookshop. She's engaged to one of the other owners of C and C, Harry."

"Is he the big baker?"

"Oh, no, that's Ed." She sighs.

"What was that?" I ask.

"What?"

"That sigh."

"Well, it's Ed." And that's all she says. Like that breathy little sigh explains everything.

"And?"

"He's like six-five, drives a motorcycle, has tattoos, and bakes. They call him the Ginger Jesus because he can create happiness with sugar and flour. I think that every heterosexual woman would sigh over that." She smiles at me. "Don't worry. He's older and married to his Sunshine."

"Sunshine?" my mother asks. I glance at her, and her eyes are dancing.

"His wife, Allison. He calls her his Sunshine. Isn't that sweet?"

Before anyone can answer her, our food arrives. We all dig in, and even though I had breakfast, I am famished again. Avery's the same, although you couldn't order more different meals. I have a salad with grilled chicken, and Avery orders a patty melt with fries, again.

The talk turns to the charity Ted and my mom work with, and it's hard to remember that just a few days ago, I was sure he was after her money.

"I have a question for ya," Avery says.

"Shoot," Ted says.

"You're moving in with Clarice? Not the other way around?"

He nods.

"Hmm."

"What does that mean?" I ask.

"It's interesting because Ted could probably have a mansion."

"I have several, but only one in Texas."

I glance at my mother, who is sipping her water as if this is normal. I mean, when I asked him questions, she got upset.

"And Clarice, please don't be offended. I'm assuming your house isn't that big?"

She shakes her head.

"Hmm."

"What the hell does that mean?"

She tosses me a look. "You know it's a love match. I mean, I've known a few football players."

"Is this about that Chet?"

"God, no. He was a two-timing small-town jerk. He didn't have the talent, and more importantly, the drive, to get into the NFL. I was talking about Demarcus Fallon and Wes Jenkins. I taught them social media, so they could promote their brands and charities."

"Oh."

"But as nice as those two were, they were football players and thought the world revolved around them. Ted is rearranging his life to fit into your mother's life. That's damned amazing if you ask me."

I look over at my mother, who is smiling. "Is that why you're moving in together in your house?"

She smiles. "It's closer to the university."

Avery smiles at me. "See. So, stop worrying about your mama."

"What makes you think I'm worrying about my mom?"

"You worry. It's one of your defining characteristics. Most people would find it nosy to get your top-level detectives to check me out, but I don't. You're a caregiver."

I'm staring at her like she's lost her damn mind. My mother's laugh cuts through my sudden shock. I glance at her.

"Sorry, Jon, but you must admit she's right about you." She looks at Avery. "He was always like that. Always wanted to take care of me. He was a good boy. A good man."

"Of course he is, He had you raising him."

I blink at her, confusion clouding my thoughts. The waitress steps up with the check. I have so many questions crowding my head. And I know when that happens, I tend to brood.

Soon we're on the sidewalk in front of the diner.

"Your grandmother is expecting you for dinner."

"What?"

"Oh, no. This is a very peopley day for you, Jon," Avery says.

"She definitely wants you there, too," my mother says to Avery, who smiles.

"Two dinners at the Big House!"

My mother chuckles. After I get a kiss from my mother and a handshake from Ted, they head off.

We get in the car, mainly because I know Avery wants to get home to the cats. The whole way home, she's quiet again, smiling and looking out the window. When I pull into the driveway, I look over at her. She's a puzzle, and I'm not sure I will ever have all the pieces to completely understand her.

"What? Do I have food on me? That is just something you have to get used to because I get food on myself all the time. I mean, with these boobs, it's hard not to."

Of course, that makes me glance at her chest, and my entire body goes hot. The memory of her gasping my name as I dragged my teeth over them sends a shaft of heat straight to my dick. Fuck, I have never been this out of control. At least not since I turned eighteen. Now, I seem to have no control over my body where Avery is concerned.

"What makes you think I'm a good man?"

"Uh, you care about your mother, your cousin, and whether you want to admit it or not, you care about your grandma."

"She is not a *grandma* type."

She snorts. "What type is a grandma type?"

"Bakes cookies. And she's nice."

"So, to you, every grandma is supposed to be a jovial baker."

I hear the laughter in her voice, and I shake my head.

"You must admit that she's not the traditional grand-mother type."

She cocks her head, studying me. "You know, because you're sexy, I'll let you slide on that one, but I want to explain something to you."

"What do you mean let me slide?"

"I was about to explain that."

"Well?"

She rolls her eyes. "Don't put women in boxes. Your grandmother may not be the baking cookies type, but she does other things to ensure you have a good life. She runs the Howard Dynasty, which I know isn't easy. And she loves you in her own way. She's always bragging about you to the other LOLs. It's just…I don't think she knows how to show affection. When you think about it, it's kind of sad."

A lump forms in my throat. I never looked at Estella that way, but being with my bastard grandfather did a number on her.

"Let's go in. It's a bit warm out today to sit in the car."

She hops out of the car and heads to the house. It takes me a second or two to follow her. The cats practically pounce on us when we step into the house. After giving them both treats, Avery smiles at me.

"I wasn't putting my grandmother in a box. It's just that I don't see people calling Estella grandma. She's the grand-mother type. She told me to call her that when I was younger."

She nods. "She likes people to think that, but she's cooler than you think."

I want to know what the hell she means by that, but I can't get distracted. I need to know.

"I want to know why you think I'm a good man."

"You don't think you're a good man?"

"I..."

It's hard to explain to another person, but I can tell Avery isn't going to let it go. "The Howards don't have a good track record. Especially the men."

She snorts. "You can say that again. Estella has told me stories about your grandfather."

"Oh?"

"Yeah, I would have figured out a way for him to have an accident early in the marriage."

I nod.

"But you aren't like that."

"How can you tell? I only care about my company." It's a refrain I have heard from more than one of my exes. I've lost friends because I was driven to get *Lone Star Tech* off the ground. I think Trev and I are only friends because he understands my workaholic ways.

"Of course you do. It's your baby. There's nothing wrong with that."

I follow her through the house as she approaches the back door. She steps out on the porch.

"I thought you were too hot."

She glances over her shoulder at me and wiggles her eyebrows. "I am totally hot."

I should laugh, but the memory of last night and this morning flood my system. God, I want her. It's like a fucking sickness. I shake my head and try to focus again. This has never been a problem.

"Avery."

She turns with a smile, and then it fades. Stepping close to me, she cocks her head. "What's going on in your head?"

"How do you know I'm a good man? I was trying to get you kicked out of here. I date models because they don't need much attention, and I rarely come to visit my grandmother. And all I care about *is* my business. You agreed with that."

"Well, you're focused on it, although you haven't been doing much work since you've been here."

That's true. "Avery."

She sighs and slips her hands up my arms to my shoulders. "You are a good man, Jon. You could have been pissier to me. Don't get me wrong, you have been a bear, but you could have been sexually aggressive. Other men wouldn't think twice about harassing me until I left."

I snort. "Maybe I'm scared of you."

"You are not, Jon. At least not that way. But you are good. You could go anywhere. Hell, I bet you could go hang out with Asher Kincaid wherever he is."

"How do you know about Asher?" I have two friends or at least two people I can trust. Trevor is one, and movie star Asher Kincaid is the other.

"Your grandmother."

I nod. "He's in Hawaii right now."

"Oh! That's my next destination."

I knew she had talked about it once or twice, but it sounds like she's going there soon.

"You're leaving?" Panic sets into my chest. She's leaving me?

"No. You're not that lucky." I open my mouth to tell her

that's not why I asked, but she places a finger over my mouth. "You are not like your father. Your father would have done horrible things to get rid of me. He doesn't check in with your grandmother like you do. And you love your mother. You are a good man."

I don't know what to say. I dated Sienna for six months, and I don't think she ever thought about my family. Granted, I didn't talk much about my family, but she wouldn't have listened otherwise. She wanted arm candy, a wealthy man on her arm to make her look like she'd arrived.

Avery has known me for less than two weeks and is getting under my skin.

And fuck, if that isn't sexy and scary at the same time.

Just then, Avery glances over the fence at our neighbor's house.

"He's watching us."

I look in the direction of her gaze, and I don't see anything at first. I mean, don't get me wrong. The guy is creepy as fuck, and him being at the meeting last night, well, that was just weird. But being weird only means he fits in with Juniper.

"I don't see anything."

He's not in the backyard like last time. In fact, no one is around. It's a quiet afternoon with the kids in school, and most everyone else is at work. But as I turn to look at Avery, I see movement by one of the curtains. Just a flutter, but it's enough to have me squinting toward the window. Again, I see nothing. Then, a shadow moves behind the curtain. I blink.

"Tell me everything you know about this guy."

Chapter Thirty-One

Avery

I open my mouth to tell everything I know about Creepy Neighbor Dude, but he settles his hand over my mouth. The glare I give him just makes him chuckle.

"Let's do this inside."

I nod because his voice is lower, and damn if that doesn't get me. He's just a shade above baritone, and I feel it beneath my skin every time he talks. It shimmers through me, touching every nerve point I have.

We herd the cats into the house—Meredith isn't happy about that—and I sit at the kitchen table.

"When did he move in?"

"It was about a week after I did. I was surprised he's stayed so long, truthfully. Before him, I think all they had were vacation renters."

He nods, and he starts pacing the kitchen. The stern expression shouldn't get to me, but it does. The slight frown, the dark concentration in his blue eyes… it's a turn-on. I think because when we're in bed together, he has that same look. Only then, I'm the focus. And it's incredible.

My phone buzzes in my pocket.

I pull it out and shake my head.

Liv: *I think I lost the bet.*

Cora: *Of course you did.*

Gerri: *I'm sleeping.*

Cora: *Fine, Liv, let's leave Gerri off this discussion.*

Gerri: *NOOOOOO!*

Yeah. Gerri works horrible hours as a doctor in New York, but she always has FOMO if we leave her out of things.

Me: *How about y'all get your own sex lives?*

Gerri: *Too busy saving lives.*

Liv: *You know I have one.*

Cora: *I have proof of one. I have four kids.*

Me: *Four kids means no sex now.*

Cora: *Pfft. We did it in his patrol car last night.*

Me: *TMI*

Cora: **Gif calling the kettle black**

I smile.

"Avery!"

I blink and look up at him. "Sorry. Girl talk."

"What do you mean?"

"My sister's bet that I would end up sleeping with you."

"That's what you call girl talk?"

I shrug. "That's what the O'Bryan sisters call girl talk."

My phone buzzes again. I know it's probably to congratulate Cora.

"Want to get that?"

I shake my head. "We have to talk about your stalker."

"My stalker? Why do you think he's my stalker?"

I shrug. "It's your family home, and you are known for staying here."

"But you rented it, and he showed up a few days after you."

"How would he know that I lived here?"

"The lease."

"And how would he find out about the lease? No, I think this might have to do with your family. Specifically, you. Didn't you work for the CIA?"

He settles his hands on his hips, and his frown turns darker. My nipples go hard. Jesus, I'm forever going to get hot now when I see a frowning hot guy. "Where did you hear that?"

"Oh, you know, around."

He rolls his eyes. "I did work for the government to get seed money for my company."

"You're rich."

He gets what my comment meant without missing a beat. "I wanted to make it on my own."

Of course, he did. He is the antithesis of his father, from what I understand. His mother raised a good man.

"You're so sexy."

His cheeks turn ruddy. "Stop trying to change the subject."

I can't help it. I love pushing his limits, and this is one of those limits. Granted, he talks dirty in the bedroom. Still, he blushes a little whenever I mention anything about it outside of it. And that just makes me want to jump his bones.

I have no idea why, but it's just something that seems to get me going. I think it's the yin and the yang of it.

"Why are you looking at me like that?"

I rise out of the chair and saunter over to him. "I told ya. You're sexy."

"We're talking about the guy you think is stalking me."

I stop when our toes are touching and close my eyes. I take a huge sniff of him. God, that scent. It's so tempting. I open my eyes and look up at him.

"So, you don't want me to fall to my knees and suck your cock?"

He stills. His sole focus is me now. His heated gaze slips to my mouth as his nostrils flare.

"Well…only if you insist."

Excitement gathers in me as I drop to my knees. Thankfully, we're standing on one of the throw rugs, or I probably would have killed my knees. I unbutton and unzip his jeans, pulling his cock out. After giving it a few pumps, I slide my tongue along the thick vein, up the top, circling the crown and tasting the salty sweetness of his precome. Then, I take him in completely, sucking and licking him.

He spears his fingers through my hair, his hands molding to the back of my head as I push him closer to the edge.

Soon, he's yanking me up off the floor. We tangle our fingers trying to get my jeans off me, and soon I'm off the floor as he lifts me once again to settle me on the table, letting my legs dangle off the side.

He dips his fingers inside of me and hums.

"So, fucking wet. Is this just for me?"

My entire body is vibrating with need. "Always."

His gaze locks on mine as he adds a second finger, pressing his thumb against my clit. Dammit, I am so close, and he's barely touched me.

Soon, Jon replaces his fingers with the broad head of his

cock. I moan as he thrusts into me with one hard, swift move. Every little nerve ending in my body is shimmering.

It doesn't take long before I'm coming, screaming his name. He follows me soon after, my name on his lips as he empties himself into me.

Jon collapses on me, and I wrap my arms around him. We stay like that for a few minutes before he's levering himself up to look down at me.

"I don't think I'll ever be able to see this table without thinking about this."

I smile, then wince as he pulls out of me then lifts me once again off the table. Instead of putting me down, he walks out of the kitchen.

"Where are we going?"

"Upstairs. I think we need a nap, then I want to make love to you again."

As he carries me up the stairs, I try to ignore the warmth spreading over me, through me. I want to panic. I feel it there on the edges of my sanity, the need to pick this apart and figure out what it means. And then I realize there isn't much I can do about it. Jon snuck under my defenses, and my heart turns over at this simple gesture.

I realize I might be in a lot of trouble.

Chapter Thirty-Two

Jon

Dinner at my grandmother's is…okay. Usually, I'm so irritated about being there, but for some reason, I'm not. Maybe because Avery and I've been in bed fucking each other's brains out all day.

"So, Jon, your mother says you're working on a new social media idea." Ted draws my attention away from Avery.

"Yes. I wanted to make something that was just for people under the age of eighteen. Something safer. But we still have issues."

"What issues? That sounds like a fantastic idea."

"It could become a hunting ground for monsters."

I look at Avery and smile. Of course, she would understand me right away. I don't think another person would, other than my mother.

"What would you do to figure it out?" Nancy asks.

I look at Nancy. "Not sure. We are working with the FBI to come up with solutions."

"Oh, look at you, working with the government again."

Avery says it slightly mockingly, but it makes me chuckle. It's hard to be mad at her. Not now. Not when I know what she sounds like when she moans my name.

Someone clears their throat, and I tear my gaze away from Avery. Everyone is looking at us. Avery giggles, and when I glance at her, she's got a cute slight blush working. Inwardly, I sigh. I don't think I will ever not be infatuated with Avery. She just has something that calls to me, even though I know it will probably end in disaster.

Just like her worries about our neighbor had me spending the afternoon doing more digging on the guy. There is nothing there. It might be that he's a creep, and no matter who lived in my house, he would stare at them. I have no idea, but it's something that I shouldn't have been worried about. But Avery was worried, so I worked on it. Of course, after we had lots of fantastic sex.

I needed to remember that this was fun and not anything serious. Otherwise, I would be freaking out. A woman like Avery has the ability to divert my attention with her insanity.

Dinner passes slowly. I want to get her home, in bed, and moaning my name, but my grandmother is a cock-blocker. Travis and Nancy are talking about wedding plans, which makes me think she's doing it on purpose. I mean, she will not shut up about her dress and the bridesmaids' dresses. Avery seems to be just as irritated by the situation as much as I am.

She's quiet on the way home, and I frown.

"What's the matter?"

I feel her glance over at me, but I keep my eyes on the

road. There's always a chance of some kind of wild animal out on this road.

"Nothing. Just thinking about our neighbor. Did you find anything out about him?"

I shake my head just as we're hitting the city limits of Juniper. "Nothing more than I already had. Norman has lived a normal and very boring life."

She makes a harrumphing sound but says nothing else. I know she's working things over in her mind.

"I just don't think that's his name. There is something off about him, and when he was at the meeting last night, he seemed completely pissed off at me."

"Maybe because you're convinced he's some kind of stalker?"

"He has no idea. I think he's a stalker. I've only told you and my sister. So don't even try that with me. I know that something is off about him."

There's something weird about the guy. But without proof, there's not much we can do about it. I glance over at Avery. Again, she's looking out the window. She's having second thoughts, I know. She thinks she's complicated, and she is. Don't get me wrong on that account. But I have my own issues and don't usually have to break off relationships. I drive them away with my brooding or distance. At least, that's what they typically say to me. Sienna was that exception.

I pull into the driveway and put the car in park. I look over at her again.

"Avery?"

She shakes herself and smiles at me. "Sorry."

I hate that smile she gives everyone to make them think she's okay. "Stop."

Her smile fades. "What?"

"You don't have to smooth things over with me, Avery."

"I'm not trying to smooth things over. What are you talking about?"

"You don't think I see how you use your personality to make sure everyone doesn't know you're hurting?"

She blinks. "I'm not."

"Hurting? Yeah, you are. You aren't sleeping."

"I have had insomnia since I was in my teens."

"Before last night, when was the last night you had a full night of sleep?"

She chews on her lip, and I don't think she will answer. I open my mouth to apologize, but she cuts me to the core.

"I can't remember. It's been months."

I hear the tears in her voice, and I can't stand this distance between us. I undo my seatbelt, then undo hers. In the next instant, I pull her closer.

"You're killing me, Avery."

"I would apologize, but this is your fault."

Her words are muffled against my shirt. I smile as I stroke my hand through her hair. "I take full blame."

She pulls back before I'm ready to let her go. "I can't deal with all the sadness. And no one wants to see me crying or depressed."

"I do." And I realize I am being honest. I usually shy away from big emotions. They overwhelm me, and I can't deal with that. I need to stay in control. But for some reason, I want that. I want to be there when Avery has worries and big emotions.

She chuckles. "Well, that sort of makes you a jerk."

"If someone cares about you, they should want everything. Don't you want that from your friends and family? You want them to tell you when you're in pain like this."

She frowns at me. "I hate when you're logical."

"I'm always logical."

She snorts. "Except when you said I stole your house. I mean, how does someone steal a house?"

"Squatters steal houses."

She gasps, and I smile. I can't help it. Her overreactions are starting to really amuse me.

Wait. When did that happen? Then I remember my thoughts. I want the whole of her emotions. My first reaction is to freak out. This isn't something I've dealt with before. I allow space for my mother and Nancy. And I guess my grandmother and Trevor to an extent.

"I'm not a squatter."

"You are, but you're cute."

Her frown turns darker. "I am not cute. No woman wants to be called cute. I want to be known as sexy."

"You can't doubt I find you sexy. I think I proved that last night."

"And this morning."

I chuckle. There's a meow from the backseat.

"We need to go in. Meredith is irritated."

I shake my head and slip out of the car. She gets both the cats out—leashed—and walks up to the porch. I follow her, trying to keep my gaze off that cute ass of hers, but it's hard to do that. She's wearing jeans that mold to her perfectly heart-shaped ass. Her gasp has me looking up with a smile until I see what shocked her.

The door is slightly ajar. That was closed when we left.

"Stay here," I tell Avery.

"Jon, let's just call Josh first."

"No. Let me check it out."

I ignore her protests and go in. The door creaks as I push it open. That's not ominous at all.

"Jon Howard, stay here."

I glance a look over my shoulder at her. "I got this, Avery."

Then I slip inside the house. There's a stillness to it, and I know there isn't anyone in here. No creaking floorboards, but there is a feeling.

I work my way through the first floor, then up to the second floor. My room is neat as a pin. Avery's looks like a tornado hit it, including the bed. My cock twitches, and I roll my eyes. I have no control when it comes to Avery. The idea of what we did together on that bed still has me so fucking turned on. Just seeing the bed has me ready to come.

It takes less than five minutes to navigate the entire house. I was right. There was no one there. I step out on the porch. Avery is in the yard talking to Mrs. Jenkins. Of course, an LOL has to know what is going on, no matter how small. As I hear the sirens, I realize there is no doubt that all this is being reported on the JSE, and everyone will start showing up within five minutes.

How did I ever think I could slip in and out of town without anyone knowing? It was a fool's errand to even contemplate doing that. I roll my shoulders, trying to loosen the tightness of my back. It feels as if it is strung tight, and someone is twisting the rope tighter and tighter.

Avery slides her hand up my spine.

Instantly, my nerves start to settle.

"Don't worry about the Nosey Noras." Her voice is just loud enough for me to hear. "They're more interested in the situation than you."

I glance down at her standing by my side. "When did you get so smart?"

She smiles. "I've been like this since birth."

The chuckle catches me by surprise. Usually, in situations like this one, I'm strung tight. It isn't something I let people know. When you run a company like mine, you have to know how to handle stress.

"So, you had an intruder?" Josh says.

I shrug. "Not sure. Nothing was disturbed."

"But the door was open?"

I nod.

"Well, let's take a look around then."

With a grim look, he heads into the house, and I turn to follow him.

"You don't need to come with me."

"But I can tell you if anything is disturbed."

He nods, but Avery stops me.

"I can do that better."

I frown. I know there's no threat because I went through the place myself, but I don't want her in there. Not until Josh gives us the all-clear.

"You need to stay here for the cats."

She glances over at them, watching us from the car.

"Okay."

She bites her bottom lip, and her worried look fills me with warmth. I can't remember the last time someone was concerned about me like that. Other than my mother, no one checked on me, worried if I was in trouble.

Avery does.

I step closer, slip my arm around her waist, and yank her closer to me. "I'll be fine."

She nods, and I bend my head to kiss her. Just a brush of my mouth against hers. Just a simple kiss, but the need to make it more almost overwhelms my better senses.

Drawing in a breath and some of her intoxicating scent, I step away from her. I have to hurry to catch up with Josh.

He's in the kitchen frowning over the place, his hands on his hips.

"So, you and Avery?"

"Yeah." Then I remember his flirting with her. "Sorry."

He glances at me, surprise lighting his eyes. "Why are you sorry?"

"I thought you were interested in her."

"Yeah, she's gorgeous in a quirky way, but she was never interested in me."

I get the feeling that there is more to that rumor about his crush on the Russo sister, but he turns and looks around the kitchen.

"Nothing missing in here?"

I shake my head, even though I feel it's wrong.

"No, there's something."

I glance at Josh and remember he once worked for the Texas Rangers. He's definitely more perceptive than a lot of town sheriffs.

"There's just something off. Nothing was taken, but it almost feels like someone was here."

He nods, and we start going through the house together.

Again, nothing is gone that I can tell, but things feel off. As if items were moved, but nothing overt.

"Is there a chance you just didn't shut the door all the way?"

I shake my head. "I saw Avery close it, and she said she locked it when I asked."

He nods, and I step into the doorway. I find Avery and the cats pacing the porch.

"Come on. I want you to take a look around too."

Avery says nothing but follows me into the house.

"This feels off," she says as she enters the kitchen.

Josh and I share a glance.

"What do you mean?" Josh asks skepticism in his tone. He didn't question me when I said the same thing. Why now?

She shrugs and walks around. "Just is."

She opens the fridge and gasps.

I hurry over, expecting something horrible like a severed head, but she's shaking her head. "Someone moved the cream."

"What?"

"I always keep it on the shelf. Grannie Pam said it was dangerous to keep it in the door. Something about not keeping it cold enough."

I frown. I do remember always seeing it on the shelf. "Maybe you just forgot."

She glances at me, and I feel a shift. She didn't physically move away from me, but it feels as if she did. "I always put it on the shelf."

Avery

Josh is not taking this seriously. There was someone in our house. I know it like I know my middle name. It's a feeling I have. It's like I've been violated. It's the peace that I found after moving in. I might not have been sleeping, but there was this sense of sanctuary. It doesn't feel like that anymore.

"So, the door was open. You're sure you locked it?"

I nod, and Jon hesitates. "What?"

"The door has a habit of not completely closing unless you slam it."

"I tested it, Jon."

He nods, but I can tell he's questioning me. I look at Josh.

"I don't want to have to call Estella about this," I say.

He sighs. "She probably already knows. It hit the Juniper Springs Express already."

"Ugh, it is the one time I don't like JSE."

"This is the one time?" Josh asks, his tone skeptical.

"Yes. I love it normally, but I don't want Estella worrying."

"She won't worry much," Jon says as his phone rings. He rolls his eyes. "Okay, she lives to prove me wrong."

He steps away to take the phone call as I continue to talk to Josh. My phone vibrates, and I pull it out.

Liv: *What is going on over there?*

Me: *The door to the house was open when we got back from dinner.*

Liv: *Come over here. I'll keep you safe.*

Me: *I can take care of myself.*

I pride myself on that.

Liv: *I know, but you don't have to.*

My sisters drive me a little crazy sometimes, but damn if they aren't the best sisters in the world.

Me: *I'm fine. And Josh is staring at me like I'm annoying him.*

"Finished telling people about this?"

I frown. "My sister was worried."

"Sorry. I'm so used to people getting on that damned app to tell everyone what just happened."

"I can imagine, but no. Liv saw what happened on the JSE and was worried. Like I can't take care of myself."

Josh's gaze flicked to Jon. "I have a feeling you don't have to worry about safety. Howard can take care of you."

"I'm an adult who can take care of herself. I also have attack cats."

"Okay."

"Really? Do you doubt them? You're afraid of Meredith."

"I am not."

I snort. He gave my cat a wide berth when he showed up.

I glance over at Jon, who is watching us while talking on the phone. He has a weird look on his face. That intense look sends a wave of heat coursing through my veins. I'll have to ask him about it later.

"Hey, O'Bryan, you said you had an idea of who this might be."

I tear my gaze away from Jon. "Yeah. The creeper who lives behind here."

"The one renting the Tolbert place?"

I nod. "He's creepy. Plus, he's bald."

"And?"

"Fabrizio Salerno says that the bald dudes are always the toughest. I mean, creeper dude doesn't seem tough, but maybe that's what he does to spy on people."

"Who the hell is Fabrizio Salerno?"

"A YouTuber I watch. At least, I think that's what he said. Anyway, that's the way I remember it. "

He rolls his eyes.

"What's the matter?" Jon says, stepping up.

"I was telling him about the creeper dude."

Jon makes a face. "He's not who did this. I told you I checked him out."

"Why do you think he would break into the house?"

"Jon." Their expressions tell me that they didn't pick up on my insinuation. "Creeper has been watching this house waiting for him. Then, once Jon showed up, the dude is in town all over the place."

Josh flicks a look at Jon. "Is that true?"

Jon shrugs, and I want to scream. "It could be that, or it could be a small-town situation. You know how you can hardly avoid anyone in this town."

"You need to check him out."

"I already did, Avery. I told you."

"I know there is something off about that guy. Just really off."

Jon sighs and slips his arm around my shoulders. I shouldn't let it relax me, but it does. I usually have issues with people in my space, especially men. Even if I'm sleeping with a guy, I typically want them gone as soon as we're done, but for some reason, I like clinging to Jon.

Chapter Thirty-Three

Jon

"I don't disagree with you that nothing about this guy sends up any warning bells."

Avery is still irritated about last night. Granted, she didn't let it bother her when I coaxed her back to bed. The memories of our second night together still leave me half-hard.

"I just think we should take a peek at his house when he leaves."

"First of all, that's a crime. Second of all, the guy never seems to leave."

She opens her mouth, but I pull her into my arms. "Listen, I'll have my investigator do another deep dive."

"I don't know why you don't believe me."

"I'm having my investigator do another deep dive on the guy."

"But you don't believe me."

I hesitate a little too long, and she steps away.

"I don't need you to placate me."

Her voice is no longer warm.

"Avery—"

"No. I need some space."

"What the fuck does that mean?"

"It means I need you to get out of my face."

I panic, mainly because this is out of left field, and I have no idea how to deal with complications like this.

"I have no idea how to deal with that."

She looks at me but with no warmth. Not even hatred. This is indifference.

"I don't know why you're doing this."

"Doing what?"

She does look perplexed now.

"Fine. You need me out of your face. I need you out of mine. I'm going out."

I don't like personal confrontations. Isn't that why I ended up here? How I ended up hiding out in a house with Avery?

"Jon, what's going on?"

I pull in a deep breath. "You're talking about breaking and entering, then you get pissed at me for not doing exactly what you want."

"No. That's not why I'm irritated with you."

"And you want to break off things because I don't agree with you."

"I don't want to break things off. It's just that…sometimes I need space to think. I thought you would understand."

I draw in a deep breath, the panic easing just a bit. I study her for a long moment and realize from her expression she truly is confused. She isn't talking about breaking off our arrangement, whatever that is.

"I do understand that."

She cocks her head and studies me for a long second. "You do?"

The skepticism in her voice sinks into me. I get it. We're two of a kind in this situation. We might not have much in common, but we both need quiet sometimes.

I pull her into my arms. "Yeah, I do. I'm sorry, but I don't want you to get hurt. Breaking and entering is the wrong thing to do."

She blows out a sigh. "Yeah, you're probably right. Also, I thought your grandmother wanted to see you today."

She did, but I was going to avoid her.

"You know you can't avoid her."

I smile and lean down to kiss her. I mean to keep it sweet, but something about Avery always pulls me into a vortex. I can't seem to control my emotions around her.

"Always, but I will be back, just so you know you aren't getting rid of me."

The smile she gives me worries me. It doesn't light up her eyes. It isn't even one of her evil smiles when I know she's plotting something. But she has asked me for space, and I will give it to her.

I kiss her, lingering over the taste of her. Then I force myself to leave.

It doesn't take long to get to my grandmother's house. Low traffic in Juniper, expected higher volume during the high tourist season, is one of the things I love about the place. As I sit at a light, I frown. I don't love Juniper. It's annoying and filled with busybodies who want to know everything about your life. Of course, as soon as I think that, I see Everly Spencer and her man walking down the sidewalk. I smile as the pair apparently are out to walk their baby. They stop to talk to Josh, which makes me frown, still not over his interaction with Avery.

Avery. I sigh. Talk about falling in love.

I blink. I don't love Avery. Right? I mean, I just met her a little over a week ago, and in that time, I have hated her, plotted her ousting from my house, then ended up in bed with her, and, Jesus, I don't think I will ever get sick of that. I have never felt so connected to a woman like Avery. She understands me. I understand her.

Oh, fuck.

A horn pulls me out of my stupor. I glance up in my rearview mirror. Mrs. Petersen is right behind me, beeping her horn. Then I realize the light has turned green. I drive the rest of the way to my grandmother's house on autopilot. I ignore all the texts that are coming in. It's Trev's ring, so there is no reason to answer. He'll just irritate me today. I walk into my grandmother's house.

"Jon, there you are."

It's my mom, and she's staring at me weirdly.

"What's wrong?" she asks.

"I…"

Oh, fuck me. I'm in love with Avery O'Bryan. She drives me crazy, but she makes me laugh, and she's so damn funny. And I know why she's in Juniper. I know that she's still not over-losing her grandmother. She won't say it or tell her family, but the sadness shimmers just below the sparkly Avery she shows the world. I love her even when she's irritating me.

"Jon?" She steps closer and slips her arm over my shoulders. "Did something bad happen?"

I turn my head so I can look down at her. Mom has always been a rock, loving me unconditionally. I guess that's what mothers do, or most of them. All this time, she was teaching me what love was. She never said anything against my father because he's a part of me. And she couldn't separate the two of us.

"I think I just realized something."

"Ah."

"What does that mean?"

She smiles at me. "I know my boy. I know all your moods, your quirks, the way you use your intelligence to keep people at bay. So, it makes sense that I would know when my baby boy falls in love."

Tears fill her eyes. Oh, God, I don't know if I can take my mother crying. Panic hits me.

"Is everything okay?" Ted asks as he steps off the last stair. He frowns, and damn, he looks like he wants to murder someone. From one second to another, I realize it's me he might be mad at. I would fight dragons to keep Avery from crying.

"Oh, nothing," my mother says, squeezing me before stepping away. "My baby boy and I were just having a conversation."

"Ah," he says as if that explains everything.

"Why is everyone milling about in the foyer like common idiots?"

And my grandmother has joined the party. Before I can answer her, the front doorbell rings. Thinking it might be Avery, my heart does a little tap dance. I stride to the door and pull it open. Standing on the porch is Trevor Smith.

"Trev?"

"Yes. Trev. I have been texting your ass for the last hour, and you've ignored me."

"Trev," my mother says.

Trev looks around me. "Clarice, so wonderful to see you again."

My mother practically sighs. No matter who the woman is, they react this way around my best friend. It's the dark good looks and his pretty boy manners.

"What's going on?" I ask. "You hate Texas."

"He can leave any time he wants to."

Yep, the one woman who is not charmed by Trev is my grandmother.

"I had to get out of New York. That's why I was texting you. I've been trying to get you to meet me in LA, but when you didn't respond, I had the jet come here."

"He's not leaving his woman," my grandmother says, which makes me frown. It's probably true. I plan on dragging that woman everywhere with me, or vice versa. Right now, all I care about is her being by my side.

"Come on in, everyone. Let's have lunch and talk things over. Trev can tell you why he's here," my mother says. She's always been the one person who could calm any situation. She knows exactly what to say.

As we walk into the dining room, Trev stops me. "Where is this woman?"

"It's a long story. But I'm assuming you're having a crisis. It is the only reason you would step foot in what you called the arsecrack of America."

"That was mainly due to my assignment in Killeen. It was so fucking hot."

"Watch your language, young man," Estella calls out.

"She heard me?" he asks in a stage whisper.

I nod.

"Damn."

"Mr. Smith, if you don't come in here to eat, how are we supposed to discuss whatever scared you?"

We step into the dining room, and I smile. The look of irritation on Trev's face is hilarious.

"Yeah, tell us why you ran away from New York."

"Piss off."

"Language," my grandmother says.

Trev's eyes widen. He looks at my grandmother, then back at me. "Is she for real?"

"You talked to her on the phone. You should have expected this."

He scowls, then follows my grandmother into the room. I turn towards my usual chair when my phone goes off. It's Sam Dixon.

"Give me a second. I need to take this."

I step away. "Hey, Sam. Do you have something for me?"

"Not much. I mean, your guy is pretty clean. Although he doesn't have much of a social media footprint. He's an insurance adjuster who has been on leave for a month. The woman I talked to said he was on emergency leave to see to his grandmother. The funny thing is that I couldn't find a grandmother on record."

"Weird."

"Yeah, but people lie a lot to take a vacation. His

company has up to six months compassionate leave, so maybe he just wants to screw over his boss."

"Hmm."

"But the fact that I couldn't find anything less than five years old had me digging. And I found out that the guy changed his name. I don't know why he picked Norman, but there must be a reason."

Something cold slinks down my spine. I start walking toward the front door. I don't understand why, but I just know something is wrong. It's as if I have a premonition that whatever Sam will tell me, it will be bad.

So very bad.

"Yeah?"

"Where are you going?" My grandmother calls out, but I ignore her. The sense of foreboding is hitting me hard. I hear steps behind me, but I ignore them.

"His real name isn't that much better. But he got a slap on the wrists and lost his football scholarship."

"What is his original fucking name?" Even though I know what it was and why he was watching our house. It has nothing to do with me and everything to do with Avery.

"Chet Baxter."

I don't say anything. I just hang up and stop when I see Trev's rental blocking my car.

I turn to yell at him, but he's right behind me. "Let's go."

I nod and hurry over to his car. "Head to Juniper."

He nods as I try calling Avery. I need to know that she's okay and to hear her voice. Her voicemail picks up, but that's probably nothing. I mean, millennials don't like talking on the phone. Right? We hate it.

"Tell me what's going on." Trev is speeding along the road that leads into Juniper.

"Avery, you were right. Chet is Norman. He's there for you. Lock all the doors. I'm on my way home."

I text her the message I just left in the voicemail in case she doesn't check her voicemail.

"What is this all about?"

I glance over at Trev. "Avery had an old boyfriend she turned in to the police about eight years ago. Even though not much happened to him, he lost his football scholarship. He's apparently been stalking her since she moved into my house."

"Fuck."

I call Josh.

"Collins."

"Josh, it's Jon. Avery might be in trouble."

"Listen, Jon, I get it. You want to believe her—"

"I do believe her."

"Just because she's your woman doesn't mean I have to believe her."

My woman. I like that.

"No. Norman Adams *is* an old boyfriend of hers. She told me about him."

"Then why didn't she tell me that."

"I have a feeling it's because he changed his name and, more than likely, looks different than he did eight years ago. His name was Chet Baxter. He legally changed it. And I'm worried. I'm on my way to our house, but she's not picking up. She hasn't read my text message either."

"You're driving right now?"

"No. My friend is with me. He's driving. And it might be

nothing, but I think something's really wrong. If I'm wrong, I'll apologize, but I might need backup."

"On my way."

I hang up just as Trev hits the city limits. I just pray we get there in time.

Chapter Thirty-Four

Avery

I'm finally getting some work done. Good sex and sleep with my sexy nerd are good for my work mind. I've been chatting with a few clients and checking in with them. My sister-in-law's brother Austin is having a meltdown. He's gorgeous and a charmer, but he freezes up when he tries to do live broadcasts on his social media.

By noon, I'm feeling more centered, and my stomach growls. We came home with leftovers last night, so I head to the kitchen. The whole fight—if you can call it that—seems silly now. I can talk about a lot of things. I rarely get speeding tickets. Breaking and entering would be a totally different manner.

I walk down the stairs thinking about my argument with Jon. Granted, it wasn't a real argument. With the O'Bryans, especially this one, fights mean dramatic exits. I have a feeling rich people like the Howards don't do that. And especially not Jon. He hates public scrutiny like I hate bras.

Still, I go back to that tiff. I heard the panic in his voice and saw his reaction. He was definitely freaked out about not being with me, which makes most of my anger fade. In the past, guys happily walked out the door. Yes, most of the guys I dated have been happy with a surface kind of relationship. Decent sex, some laughs, and everything was fine. I thought Jon would be the same way.

Of course, he's difficult, but in the best way. No easy relationship with him. My heart clutches. I'm falling for a man who drove me insane just a few days ago. And it has nothing to do with the great sex. Okay, that's a lie. That is part of it. I mean, it *is* the best sex of my life. But there's something else there when he's holding me. And I have never been able to sleep with a guy next to me. I've found that being next to Jon eases my mind. The voices go quiet, and I can relax.

He does have a subdued sense of humor. I'm all circus clown kind of entertainment, but Jon can make a small joke about something with that serious look on his face and his eyes sparkling, and I just melt. And there is one other thing: Grannie Pam would have loved him.

Oh no.

I'm not falling in love with him. It's just that I like his humor and his grumpiness. I also really like the way he is with the cats. Then there's the fact that he could ignore his grandmother, but he doesn't because he loves her. He doesn't say it, but I know he does. He's such a good man.

I am.

This is impossible. It's been less than two weeks since I met him and only a few days since I stopped hating him.

What. The. Hell.

Me: *How long was it before you knew you loved Mason.*

Liv: *Days.*

Me: *Days?!*

Liv: *If you ignore the months we were separated.*

That makes sense. My sister met her man in Vegas, not knowing they would end up living next door to each other.

My phone rings, and I roll my eyes.

"What's going on with you?" Liv demands.

"Nothing."

"Are you sure? Your questions are weird."

"It's weird to ask you things about love?"

"Yeah. It is."

I want to spill everything. Tell her I'm scared AF that I'm falling for Jon, that he will leave me like he always leaves women, and I will be even more broken.

The only problem is saying those words will make them more real.

"Just forget I asked."

The doorbell rings at about the same time the microwave pings. For once, I'm happy to be interrupted. Talking to my sister about falling in love with my former nemesis makes me uncomfortable. Especially since it isn't probably true.

"I gotta go. Someone's at the door."

The bell rings again.

"You hate answering the door."

"Yeah, if it's an LOL, she will keep ringing the doorbell. I've learned my lesson with those women."

"Okay, but this discussion isn't over."

"Sure."

Then I hang up on her. The doorbell is ringing and ringing. How annoying. When I look through the peephole, I see Norman.

What. The. Hell.

"I know you're in there, Avery."

There is something in his voice that hits me. I know it. Like I've heard it before. But that can't be right. Have I? I never talked to him that I know of.

Usually, I would tell him to fuck off, but I want to find out what his deal is. I know it's stupid, but I've always had a problem with puzzles. Once I find one, I just have to figure it out. I need all the pieces to fit together.

I open the door. He's tall. I didn't realize how tall he was, but he must be about six-five. And massive. Like just big. And I am not talking weight, although he probably weighs over three hundred pounds. He's wearing a plaid shirt with a couple buttons missing. His pants are at least a size too small. This guy would be big even without the weight. He's what most people would call big-boned.

There's a whisper of something that I can't grasp before it slips away from me.

"Can I help you?"

He studies me for a moment which has me frowning. I know he can speak because he just did. But it's almost like he's been struck mute. When he finally talks, his tone wreaks of condemnation.

"You really don't know who I am, do you?"

"Okay, I'll be honest. I checked you out. I mean, you're creeping at me over the fence."

He steps closer, and worry shivers down my spine for the first time. His dark brown eyes are filled with hatred.

"I'm not creepy."

I hold up my hands. "Okay, you're not creepy, although I didn't say you were."

"Yes, you did. You called me creepy."

He takes another step, and I retreat, my hand on the door. I start to close it, wanting to put a barrier between us. He stops me by putting his big meaty hand on the door and pushing it. I stumble back, and he advances on me. I realize I should have left the house when he slams the front door behind him.

"Always so fucking perfect. Avery O'Bryan thinks she can do no wrong."

I blink. I mean, it's not hard to find out my name, and he was at the meeting the other night, but there is something else in his voice—like he knows me.

"I always think I do things wrong. Like opening the door to you. That was *totally* wrong."

He shakes his head and sneers at me. "You're not funny."

"I know this might surprise you, but I don't give a fuck what you think of my humor or me."

"Meow."

I look down at Meredith and Benjamin. Anxiety hits me, not for myself, but for my cats. Okay, I am a little scared, but they come first.

"Fucking cats."

When I sense him coming closer, I look up. He's shaking with rage, and I realize he is coming after my cats. I step in front of them.

"You need to leave." Terror is now screaming through my system. Why did I leave my phone in the kitchen? I always have that thing in my pocket, but the one time I have some psycho in my space, I leave it on the table.

"I need to do whatever the fuck I want to. You know what the worst thing about all of this is?"

"Your breath."

His face turns darker, his gaze narrowing as he takes me in. "You don't change, do you? It's been almost a decade, and you still have that smart mouth on you. I always thought you were funny."

"I am funny."

He shakes his head. "You don't even remember who I am, do you? You ruin lives and just prance away having fun."

"What the hell are you talking about, Norman? Call me crazy, but accosting a woman in her house doesn't make you a good guy. In fact, it kind of makes you a bad guy."

"Is that what you said when you turned everything over to the police?"

I blink. Something unlocks in my mind, and I get a closer look at Norman. Then I see the chocolate brown eyes, the remnants of a thick jaw. I glance up at his mostly bald head. The thick auburn hair is no longer there, but I remember he had been freaking out about his receding hairline. When I focus on his face again, I see the boy I thought I was in love with.

"Chet?"

"About damned time."

"Keep Lizzo out of your mouth."

"What?"

I roll my eyes, trying my best to calm my nerves. "Of course, you don't know a queen when I mention her."

He steps closer, and that panic morphs into full-blown terror. I know some self-defense moves, but he definitely outweighs me on top of being a guy. He's let his football-trained body go flabby, but as Fritz taught me, women typically don't have as much upper body strength.

"You were always rattling off insanity. You were lucky I even dated you."

I laugh. I know I shouldn't, but I can't help it. There's a crazy sheen to his gaze like he's lost his mind. The sad thing is back when we dated, I did think I was lucky. I was an awkward girl without any experience, and a football player paid attention to me. I thought he was better than me because he was attractive and had experience.

"Stop laughing."

That makes me giggle more. It ends up with a gasp when he backhands me.

The force of the hit has me stepping back, trying to gain my balance. I blink at the rush of tears that burn my eyes.

"Not so funny now, is it?"

Icy fear settles in my belly as I take in his smug smile. His eyes aren't entirely focused, like a crazy killer in a movie. Only now, he's focused on me, and it's not a movie. Of course, I don't know how to keep my big mouth shut.

"You've lost your mind."

Great idea, Avery. Antagonizing the man who scrambled your brain with a slap is the way to go.

To prove me right, he slaps me again, this time with an open hand. I stumble back again, falling to the floor this time. My head hits the edge of the coffee table. Pain radiates from the back of my head and my face. He continues to advance on me, and I try to scramble back. My movements are sluggish, and I realize the whole room is spinning. The metallic taste of blood hits my tongue, and I know I have a split lip.

He leans down, and I see a bit of the boy in the man's face. But that boy has been snuffed out, pushed aside by anger and hate. And at this moment, I am genuinely fearful for my life. There's murder in his eyes.

As he reaches for me, I close my eyes. I don't know if he will grab me, smack me again, or something worse. The hit never comes. Instead, a loud screech fills the air. I open one eye and see that Meredith has jumped on his face. She's busy scratching the shit out of him. Chet/Norman is grabbing her, and now my Cat Mamma takes control. I struggle to stand up, and the entire room spins. But before I can do anything. Benjamin rubs against Chet/Norman's feet. He's falling just as the front door bursts in.

"Avery!"

It's Jon, and I don't know if I have ever been as happy to see someone as I am to see him right this minute. It's then I start crying. The look of anger on his face calms me. But only for a second. Because Chet/Norman pulls out a gun and points it in my direction.

Oh, fuck.

Jon tackles Chet/Norman. The two fall to the floor, and the gun flies out of Chet/Norman's hand. The sound of it sliding across the wood floor is intermingled with grunts as my intruder tries to get to the gun, and I can't get to it because it's on the other side of the men. Plus, the whole room is still spinning.

"Oh, no, you don't."

I blink. Is that my brother's friend Blue?

At least he's holding the gun now, and Chet/Norman can't get it.

Jon gains the upper hand in the fight. He straddles Chet/Norman. The sound of his fists against the other man's flesh makes me nauseous. Not because I don't want him to hit Chet/Norman, because I'm happy about that. Typically not the kind of girl who likes that sort of thing, but my old boyfriend deserves to be beaten to a bloody pulp.

Sirens sound, or at least I think I hear them, but I hit my head so hard I might be imagining it. Then, Josh comes through the door. He stops short, taking in the scene. Blue is still standing there, holding the gun.

"Jon, you need to stop before you kill the bastard," Blue says. Jon isn't paying attention.

Josh walks forward, but I know I have a better chance of getting to Jon.

I step forward, my stomach turning over. That isn't pleasant. I lay a hand on Jon's shoulder.

"Jon, babe."

He stops and looks up at me. The promise of death and destruction darkens his eyes. I'm not going to lie. That sends a little thrill through me. I know that my family would always fight for me but having someone like Jon ready to defend me…that's so hot.

"You're going to kill him if you keep it up."

"I don't care."

"I do. You could end up in jail."

He heaves a sigh. His arm tightens around me. Frustration fills that one sound, but he stands and then takes me in his arms. His body heat comforts me, but at the same time, I start shaking. Tears fill my eyes and slide down my cheeks.

At this moment, I know I'm safe, and I can give in to my fear.

"You're okay, baby. No one is going to get you."

I nod against his chest, then I remember my cat babies. Pulling back, I look around the room.

"Meredith and Benjamin?"

"They're fine, although Meredith isn't too happy that Josh is here."

I smile, but my stomach rolls over again. Oh, not good. The room is spinning. I lean against Jon.

"Baby, are you okay?"

"No. I think I need to sit down."

The spinning goes into overdrive. Before I can take a step, the room starts to fade.

"Don't leave me," is all I can say.

"Never," Jon says.

Then my world fades to black.

Chapter Thirty-Five

Jon

I ride to the hospital with Avery. Two hours later, she's still pissed I made her come, but there was no way I wasn't having her checked out.

"You don't have to look so smug."

I glance over at her. "I'm not smug. How could I be smug? You have a concussion."

"You always like to be right."

"And you don't?" She doesn't say anything. "I'm happy that you're okay."

Her eyes soften. "I am too. Thank you for saving me."

"You and your cats were handling it fine."

She nods and sniffs. Chet/Norman is in custody, although he was being a whiny baby about the scratches. He said he wanted to press charges against Avery. Seriously. He's also allergic to cats, so his entire face is swollen.

I take Avery's hand. "I'm sorry I didn't take your worries about him seriously."

"I was wrong."

"No. You were right. You were wrong about who he was stalking."

She nods again but still won't meet my eyes.

"Avery?"

"Hmm?"

"Look at me."

A sigh. It is the saddest sound I have ever heard.

When she finally makes eye contact, I feel my entire world settle. The misery I see there gives me pause.

"Why are you upset?"

"I was attacked, Jon. I have a right to be upset."

This is very un-Avery-like behavior. "You should be pissed and ready to fight."

"I…"

Tears fill her eyes.

I move to sit on her bed. "Tell me."

Before she can respond, there is a ruckus outside of the room.

"Well, I don't give a fuck what they say. I want to see my sister."

"Oh, damn," Avery mutters.

"Fritz, do not cuss like that with your niece and nephew here."

"That's okay. He talks like that a lot with me around," someone who sounds like Sammy says.

"Oh, God. What are they all doing here?" The look of sheer horror shouldn't make me feel better, but for some reason, it does.

I smile. "From what the JSE says, half the town is out there."

Her eyes widen at my pronouncement. "Get out of here!"

I chuckle. "Nope. Never. I think you're stuck with me, Avery."

"You're saying that because I was hurt."

"No. I realized that no matter what, I should have backed you up. I love you, and I will always have your back."

"No, you don't."

"I do." I lean down and kiss her. It's gentle because her lip is split.

"Get your mouth off my sister."

I pull back and look at the newest visitors. Liv is there, her kids, and a new person. He's dark-haired like the sisters, and he has the same nose as Avery.

"Go get bent, Fritz."

"Yeah, quit being a Fritz," Liv says, but hiccups. She is barely holding it together.

Her brother strides over to the other side of the bed. "Seriously? Didn't I teach you how to defend yourself?"

Avery opens her mouth, but I refuse to let him talk to her like that. "If you can't be nice, you will leave this room."

Fritz blinks. "Excuse me?"

"Avery has a concussion. You need to stop being a…" I look at the kids, "jerk."

"Yeah, Fritz," Callie says, walking closer, slipping between Fritz and the bed. She takes her aunt's hand. "He's just afraid. All men act like that when they can't control things."

Avery laugh-snorts, but there's a little sob at the end.

"And how did she get a concussion?" Fritz is being loud, and I can see it's hurting her head.

"Avery has a headache."

He frowns and crosses his arms over his chest. "Yeah, and whose fault is that?"

"Stop being an ass, Fritz." This comes from Avery. "It was Chet Baxter."

Fritz's eyes narrow. "You mean the guy you turned in?"

"Yeah." She glances at the kids, and I see Fritz nod in understanding. She doesn't want to upset the kids, and he finally seems to get it.

There's a knock at the door, and Francie Miller, a no-nonsense nurse who runs the ER like she's a general, comes to an abrupt stop.

"What is going on here?"

"Family," Fritz says.

Her gaze takes in the entire group before landing on me. "They're family?"

I nod.

"Okay. I guess it doesn't matter since you are being discharged."

"Finally," Avery says.

"I know the doc talked to you about staying awake for a while." She looks at me. "If she gets dizzy again or throws up, I need you to bring her back here."

"Why is she giving you the instructions?" Fritz asks. He's getting on my last nerve.

"Because I'll be the one taking care of her."

He opens his mouth, but Liv stops him. "You're being loud, and Avery has a headache." She walks over to kiss Avery on the cheek, handing her a bag. It's the clothes I asked her sister to bring. "We'll see you in a sec. I'm glad you're okay."

Avery smiles at her, a sheen of tears in her eyes. "I am too."

The kids give her hugs, and Fritz kisses her forehead. "You scared us. Don't do that again."

Liv herds them all out of the room. Once Avery signs all the discharge papers, we are finally by ourselves.

"I'm sorry about Fritz."

I shake my head. "You shouldn't be. I deserve it."

"Why would you say that?"

"If I would have believed you, this wouldn't have happened."

She frowns as she stands. I rush over to help, as she is still a little unsteady. I try not to pay attention when she slips out of the hospital gown, but it's difficult. And it makes me feel even worse. She would have never been in this situation if I had stayed home. The guy would have left at some point.

"Need to rest for a sec."

I nod as she leans against the bed. I'll do anything to make up for not protecting her when I should have.

"What is going on in your head?"

"What?"

"I can see something working in there. You look really pissed off."

"I'm just mad at myself."

"Why? What did you do?"

I sigh. "I should have trusted you. This would have never happened."

Avery says nothing for a long beat. The silence is deafening. "Come here."

She takes my hand and tugs me closer. She takes my face into her hands. As she studies me, my whole world quiets.

"You are not at fault. Norman/Chet is at fault. He would have found another time to come after me."

"I got the call about him changing his name when I was at Estella's. I could have kept you safe if I had been at the house instead of pouting."

"Well, that's stupid."

"Excuse me?"

"I love that snippy voice. It gets me hot." She smiles, wincing, I'm sure because of her split lip.

I roll my eyes. "Maybe you need to stay here for observation."

She rolls her eyes in turn. "Please. You can take care of me."

"There will be no sex tonight."

She chuckles. "I have to agree with that."

"Let's get going."

"No. I need to say something before we leave."

If she's going to throw me to the curb, I would rather not do it in a hospital room. But she isn't letting go of my hand, and I don't have a choice.

"Jon, you're not at fault. If we had discovered his name sooner, we would have been prepared, but he had completely lost it. He blamed me for everything, and he wasn't giving up. I'm more to blame than anyone else."

"What the fuck?"

"I should have known who he was. I didn't. Here was this guy I had dated. He was my first real boyfriend, and I didn't recognize him. I mean, I'd slept with the guy!" She draws in a shuddering breath. "But ultimately, this is all Chet/Norman's fault. He did the up-skirt videos. He's the one who cheated on me. This is one last bad choice of his in a long string of them. People like him think they're entitled to the good life, and he blames everyone else when it doesn't happen."

"You're not to blame for any of this."

"And neither are you. You saved me today. I wouldn't have been able to fight him off, even with Meredith's help."

She drops her hands as I lean forward, resting my forehead against hers.

"I love you."

She sighs, but this one is filled with happiness, and it turns my heart over. That sound is so precious. I don't think anything will ever compare to it. The next thing I know, she proves me wrong with her response.

"I love you too, you weirdo."

I chuckle, something loosening in my chest. I know that with her, I will always get the honest truth. I *am* a bit of a weirdo, and I don't care who knows it.

I straighten. "We need to talk about our future."

She rolls her eyes. "Can't we just say our future is with each other?"

"I guess, as long as you know, I will never give you up."

I bend at the waist and pick her up.

"What are you doing?"

"Carrying you out. It's that or the wheelchair, and I had a feeling you would rather have this. Get the door."

Cheers greet us as I step into the waiting room. The

place is packed. Everyone seems to be here, from our families to the mayor and his wife to the LOLs.

"What the fuck?" Avery murmurs.

"It made the JSE, and everyone just showed up," Nancy says, coming our way. "Been busy, O'Bryan."

Avery settles her head against my shoulder. "A little."

As everyone tries speaking to her at once, I see Avery wincing. The headache has to be killing her right now.

"Hey, everyone. Avery has a concussion and needs some quiet." Avery opens her mouth, but I shake my head at her. "How about we do something at the senior center in a day or two? The doc said she needs rest."

Murmurs of agreement fill the room as her brother and sister step up beside us. The kids hurry up from where Becca Gold is sitting.

"I'll take care of it. You just tell us when," Liv says. "Also, we're going to pick up Mason. He has food for the troops. Your mom and Estella are at the house."

"Thanks, sis," Avery says.

Liv's gaze slides to me, and I see the tears. She mouths the words "Thank you."

A lump rises in my throat, and I nod. I turn towards the exit, and Trevor steps into the waiting room. Stunned silence greets him.

"Why didn't you tell me you knew Trevor Smith?" Avery asks.

"I was too busy being irritated by you. And then I was too busy getting my hands on you."

She flushes, and it is the sweetest thing I've ever seen. "Jon."

I laugh as I continue to carry her over to Trev. "I find it

funny that Avery O'Bryan is embarrassed by something. Avery, this is Trevor Smith. Trev, this is Avery O'Bryan, the love of my life."

Something flares in Trevor's green gaze, something close to envy, but it disappears before I can figure out what it is.

"Avery and I know each other."

She giggles, and I look down at her. Avery notices and shrugs. "He's an old army buddy of my brother's."

"What the hell are you doing here, Blue?" Fritz asks, walking up to my best friend and giving him a hug.

Trev returns the hug, then he steps back. "Came to see Jon, and I had perfect timing."

"Hey, guys, we can talk back at the house all about Trev and his real reason for being here."

The look of alarm on his face has me biting back a chuckle. That is enough to tell me the sister is Fritz's, and this just got a whole lot more complicated.

Trev nods as people start coming up to us. I think they are getting closer to meet Trev. He's kind of a celebrity, in a billionaire with lots of money kind of way. They all murmur to Avery and me, telling us to take care, and there were a few thank yous from the LOLs for getting to Avery in time to save her.

We step outside, and I see that Trev has left his car in the covered pickup area. Of course, he just left his car in an area that said no parking. Trevor Smith does what he wants when he wants.

"We're going to have a talk about your friendship with Trevor. You know that, right?"

"You have to tell me how your brother knows him."

"Easy, he served with him."

"And the name?"

"They called him Blueblood when he took over their unit. From what Fritz says, it didn't take him long to win them over, and they shortened it to Blue."

"And you know him how?"

"He served with my brother."

Trevor hears the last part as he joins us outside. "Yeah, and we danced at her brother's wedding."

"And Ed's," Avery says.

I growl, and they both laugh. I try to frown at both of them but fail. Instead, I smile as Trev starts the car.

"We'll have a lifetime to discuss Trev and his screwed-up life."

"I like the sound of that." I put her in the backseat, then hurry around and slide in beside her. We make it back to her house, with Trevor driving carefully over any bumps in the road. When I help her out of the car, she thanks him.

"No problem. I had a concussion in Iraq. I know they suck."

She starts to walk, but I lean down to pick her up. "I can walk."

"Trev, can you give us a sec."

He nods and heads into the house.

"What's up? I can't be easy to hold."

"It's you and me."

"And?"

All of a sudden, I'm nervous. I told her I loved her but didn't know what would happen. "I feel I should be proposing."

Her eyes widen. "What? No."

I frown.

"Sorry. I didn't mean it to sound like that. What I meant was that we don't need to work on any timelines. I don't need a ring on my finger. I just need you. I love you."

My entire body freezes for a second, then joy bounces through me. I know we said it earlier, but it's more precious the second time. "I love you, Avery."

"I know. I'm lovable."

I kiss her forehead. The need to rush upstairs and show her how much I love her almost overwhelms me, but I know we will have to wait.

"It's fast," I say.

"Remember what I said about that timeline? Doesn't matter. When you know, you know."

As we step into the house, my mother hurries toward us.

"Finally," she says, her worried gaze on Avery. "I talked to your parents, and they will be here tomorrow. They said Cora wanted to come down, but it would mean bringing all four of her children. Your mother convinced her not to come."

"Thank God," Avery says.

"How are you feeling?"

"Like I hit my head on the coffee table after an ex tried to kill me. So, it's not great."

My mother smiles. "Come on over here. We have food coming, and it's just family. I also think that Ted is deathly afraid of Meredith. She keeps hissing at him."

Avery offers her a small smile. "She does that to most men except Jon."

I take her to the chair and a half in the corner, settling her down. "Do you want anything?"

"Some water?"

I nod and lean down to kiss her forehead. Both cats jump onto her lap. All the while, Meredith gives Trevor the evil eye. I glance at Trev.

"I'd avoid Meredith if I were you."

When I step into the kitchen, I realize my mother has followed me.

"How are you?" she asks.

"I'm fine. The guy didn't get a punch on me."

She cocks her head. "Jon. It couldn't have been easy for you."

"It was. I know how to fight."

She sighs and steps closer, wrapping her arms around me. It only takes a few seconds before I shudder and wrap my arms around her.

"It couldn't have been easy seeing her like that."

I nod. "It wasn't."

I straighten and look down at her. "Thanks. I didn't know I needed that."

She smiles. "I'm a mom."

She says it as if it explains everything, and it does. She has been my one constant, the person I could talk to when things went to shit.

"I like Ted. I think he's good for you."

Her eyes grow watery, and I panic, and of course, she sees it before I say anything. "Don't freak. It's nice that the two men I love the most in the world like each other."

I nod. "I better get this out to Avery."

We turn to leave the kitchen, but Trev stops us. "I had no idea you were so popular. Your grandmother showed me the JSE."

"What?"

"I've been scrolling through the posts. These people talk about you like they're your family."

And it's then that the response in the ER hits me. They were probably there primarily for Avery, but they were there for me too. They showed up for us as a couple to show solidarity.

"Hmm. Interesting."

And it changes my perspective on this town. Maybe. I mean, it's still weird.

"Sticking around?"

He nods. "Your grandmother offered me a room. Seems that Avery's parents will be staying there too."

"Can you take her brother?"

He smiles. "From what your mother said, he's heading back to San Antonio tonight. His wife is hugely pregnant."

I nod and head back down the hallway to the living room but pause. I look at him.

"We will be talking about what happened in New York."

He nods, although his smile dims a little. "I kind of fucked things up."

"You can always fix it." That's one thing I've learned being around Avery.

When I step into the living room, I notice my mother and Ted outside. Avery has her eyes closed and a hand on each of her cats, petting them. I set the water on the coaster and lean closer to kiss her forehead again. Her mouth curves as her eyes open slowly.

"Hey."

"You rest. I'll keep an eye on you and make sure you don't sleep too long."

She nods, and as her eyes slide closed, she says, "Love you."

Then she lets out a little snore.

I notice my grandmother standing by the window, looking across the yard. Approaching her, I start thinking about how this all came to be. Her insistence that Avery stay here with me. That she would let Avery remain for an entire year at half the rent. "Grandmother."

She turns and faces me. She looks older tonight, smaller. "Jon, I take it that Avery is truly fine."

I nod.

"Good. She's a good woman. I would hate if something happened to her." Her voice hitches on the last few words.

"Avery is fine. You know she could bounce back from just about anything."

"Just because she's strong doesn't mean she doesn't need someone to help her."

I study her for a moment as all the pieces of the puzzle click into place. My grandmother is a fucking mastermind. I lean forward and kiss her cheek.

"Thank you."

"For what?"

"For finding her for me."

For the first time in my life, I see my grandmother blush. She looks out the window again. "I have no idea what you're talking about."

"You insisted that she stay here. And you know me. You knew that I would end up here at some point. You planned all of this."

"I…okay, I did. It wasn't that I forced you. I just thought if I…"

"Threw her in my path so I would fall in love with her."

She doesn't say anything for a long moment. Then she clears her throat. "She's perfect for you, Jon. You need someone in your life to make you laugh. You were always such a serious little boy, and your inability to take breaks, laugh, and later find love worried me. And I always worried that your father…"

"My father, what?"

She sighs. "That your father ruined your outlook on relationships. So, when I met Avery, I knew you two would hit it off. But, if I introduced her to you, you would have had a knee-jerk reaction."

I hate that she's right. If she had introduced me to Avery under any other condition, I would have immediately dismissed her.

"So, you didn't plan for her to tackle me?"

Her lips twitch. "Are you trying to tell me you didn't like having her fall on top of you?"

For the first time in a long time, I freaking blush in front of my grandmother. She has always been no-nonsense and a bit blunt, so I learned to deal with it as I grew up. Still, having your grandmother talk in those terms is just too much for a guy.

"Oh, you're blushing," she says, chuckling. "That's precious."

"Estella, quit being mean to my man," Avery calls out. I glance over and find her watching us from the chair and half with the cats on her lap.

Then I realize what she said, and my entire body lights up. It's insane how much she can get to me just by calling me her man.

"I wouldn't think of it, dear," Estella says. There's a knock at the door before someone opens it. Liv steps in, her kids running to their aunt. She's followed by Nancy, Travis, Mason, and Fritz, all of them carrying food containers from *The Mason Jar* on them.

"I brought food for the troops," Mason says.

My grandmother calls in my mother and Ted, then orders everyone around in the kitchen. I make my way over to Avery. The cats have abandoned her for Callie and Sammy—apparently, Sammy is the only other male Meredith likes. I lift Avery up out of the chair, and she gasps. I smile, sitting in the chair and settling her on my lap.

"How's your head?"

"Better," she mumbles, placing her head on my shoulder.

"Hey, Avery," Liv says. "I got you some potato salad because it is the blandest thing. Mason insisted on bringing it since it's your favorite. If you're up to it, I can get you some brisket. Plus, there's a ton of food in the fridge."

"There is?"

She nods. "The neighbors started bringing it as soon as the news hit the JSE."

"That's nice," Avery says, taking the bowl.

"Want anything?" Liv asks me.

I shake my head. "I'll get something in a little bit."

"You should eat," Avery says once we're alone again.

"Nah. I'll just sit here with you."

She forks up some potato salad and hums. My entire body responds to the sound, and she smiles at me. "Want some?"

I offer her a smile, knowing that she's not offering me

more than the potato salad. I don't answer because I know what my answer will be.

"Always."

She smiles back at me and gives me some potato salad.

And there, with the sounds of our family in the air, from the kids' giggles to my grandmother ordering everyone around, we enjoy a bowl of potato salad.

"Perfectly imperfect," she murmurs.

"What?"

"It was one of the things my grandmother always said. She would say perfection is boring. Striving for it was important, but you should never feel you failed when you didn't reach it. It's in the imperfections that we find happiness."

I kiss her forehead as I feel my heart turn over once again.

"Well, then, you're my imperfect love."

I couldn't ask for anything more perfect than that.

Epilogue

JON

Three Months Later

I thrust into Avery one last time as she shouts my name. The sound of my name on her lips pulls my orgasm from me. Her inner muscles spasm about my cock as I pour myself into her. A moment later, I collapse on the bed beside her.

Our heavy breathing is the only sound in the room.

"That is our fifteenth time while in Hawaii," Avery says with a laugh.

I look over and find her smiling at me. We've been here for about four days. "You're keeping count?"

She nods, then rises up to her elbow. The sun is rising just behind her. The sweet smell of Hawaiian air fills the room as the breeze plays with the white sheer curtains.

"I guess we should go out and see some of the island," she says.

"Yes. Kauai is gorgeous, and there are a lot of chickens. I knew you would love that."

"I do."

"But we have two more weeks here."

My life has changed so much in the last three months. I sold my company to Trevor, but I'm still a minority stockholder and consult on some security issues. I moved most of my belongings to Juniper since Avery, and I moved into the house together. I kept the house in Dallas, so we had a place to stay when we visited Mom and Ted.

"Dr. Gina would be so proud of me," Avery says.

Avery started therapy a couple months ago. Dr. Gina has helped her deal with some of her depression, which has helped with Avery's insomnia.

"She would. You passed out the minute we hit the bed."

"The second time we hit the bed."

I smile at her. I can't help it. We had a fantastic time breaking in the kitchen table, the bathroom counter, and the shower before we fell into bed. I will never have enough of this woman.

"I love you."

Her eyes soften. "I love you too."

"Marry me."

Her eyes widen. "Say what now?"

"I know it's only been a few months, but I want to marry you. I want to have babies with you, and I want to adopt more cats."

"That last part is a lie," she says, slipping out of bed.

"What's wrong?"

"When I brought home Marjorie, you said you didn't want to have a third cat."

"I was joking."

She pulls on one of my shirts, then stares down at me.

Her skin is still flushed from our lovemaking, and those bee-stung lips are even plumper. I immediately want to make love to her again.

"Stop looking at me like that."

My eyes widen. "Like what?"

"Like you want to take my clothes off again."

"I always want to take your clothes off."

She snorts, but she starts pacing.

"Now, tell me, sweetness. What has you freaked out about marrying? Is it me?"

She stops pacing and settles her hands on her hips. "Jon Howard, you are the only man for me."

I grab her hand and pull her back down on the bed. "Tell me."

She draws in a breath. "Why do you want a wedding? Why do we need to do that?"

I frown. "I'm talking about getting married. Not a wedding."

"But you're a big billionaire and like to do things by the book."

"Woman, I want you to be my wife. That's it."

"But—"

"I will marry you in the biggest wedding in the history of Texas, or we can do a Justice of the Peace. I don't care. I just want to call you my wife."

"Yeah?"

I nod.

"I want something small, just our families."

I smile and brush her hair away from her face. "That sounds fantastic."

"We can throw a reception at the big house or the senior

center."

With the help of my grandmother, we've set to work on the Pamela O'Bryan Senior Center. It will have a grand opening next year.

"You want to wait until next year?"

"You don't?"

"I'd rather do it sooner than later, but I'll wait for you until the end of time."

There is a beat of silence, then her lips curve before she grins at me. Happiness explodes through me.

"I would too. Like, today."

"Wait, what? We can't get married today."

"Why not?"

"The law. We have to get a marriage certificate and all that."

"Oh, okay."

"Getting the paperwork set up would take a few days."

"Yeah?"

"Also, your mother and mine would never forgive us if we did it alone."

She makes a face. "Oh, okay."

"Still, you're marrying a billionaire. We could make it happen."

Her eyebrows rise up. "You would do that?"

"I would do anything for you, Avery."

Avery

Ten days later, our family gathered on Kauai. Thank goodness I'm marrying a billionaire because it cost a literal fortune to get this worked out. All my sisters are here—including Gerri, who is acting super weird and doing everything she can to avoid Blue, who also came to the wedding. Even the newest O'Bryan, Fritz and Savannah's little girl is in attendance. The two-month-old slept through the wedding.

We married on the beach, barefoot, and I had flowers in my hair and wore a white dress with red flowers on it.

"Only you would do something like this, Avery," my mother says. I smile at her as I drink my chardonnay.

"True."

"I like your Jon."

"I know."

The moment my mother met Jon, she fell in love with him. They make an odd couple, but they love discussing being Avery wranglers. They claim they keep me on track. Losers. Still, they get along so well, and they were the ones who came up with the idea to get teenagers involved in the Senior Center. They get taught valuable life skills, and the LOLs get time with the younger generation. It also helped once Jon put some more security on the JSE to stop some of the reporting on the app. Although I will admit, I miss some of the gossip.

"Granny Pam would have loved this," she says. I look over at her.

"Yeah, she would have. She would have loved embarrassing Jon."

My mother chuckles. "Yeah, she would have. I'm sorry."

"For what?"

"Not realizing what was going on with you. When you told us about your depression, I felt as if I failed as a mother."

"Mom, you have nothing to feel bad about. You are not in charge of my feelings."

"No. But I should have recognized it."

I sigh because this was one of the reasons I told Dr. Gina I didn't want to tell my mother. I knew she would feel guilty.

"No. I hid it from you and everyone else. And you would have noticed if I had visited more often. It's one of the reasons I stayed in Juniper, I think. I knew my mother would figure out what was wrong with me."

We hug, and she gives me a kiss as Jon steps up. "Time to dance, Ms. O'Bryan."

Yeah, I kept my name. I like it. I take his hand as he leads me out to the dance floor. He nods to the DJ, and the first strings of *New Year's Day* start playing. I had no idea we were even going to have a first dance.

"You and me forever more, babe," he says as he draws me into his arms.

"I'll gladly give them to you as long as you give me your midnights."

He laughs and tightens his arms around me.

With our family watching, he twirls me around the floor, my laughter filling the night. There's a crash, and I'm sure it has something to do with Cora's kids because she starts getting on to them for something. The sweet Hawaiian air carries Taylor's beautiful voice over the crowd.

"That's going to be a bitch to clean up," Jon says.

I don't even look. "Remember, Jon, perfectly imperfect."

His smile turns warmer, his eyes filled with love. "Always."

***

THANK you so much for reading Imperfect Love! As always, there is a soundtrack I used when writing this book, and you can find it on the BOOK PAGE on my website.

This is the last book of the Juniper Springs series. Becca was going to have a book in the series, but after writing the scene with her and Ford, I decided that her book would fit better in the planned series for her brothers, so keep an eye out for that one.

If you would like to read more about the Camos and Cupcakes World, check them out—>Camos and Cupcakes!

The Camos and Cupcakes World

Camos and Cupcakes

Delicious
Allison and Ed

Lucious
EJ and Harry

Scrumptious
Savannah and Fritz

The Fillmore Siblings

Hate to Love You
Syd and Grady

Love to Hate You
Nancy and Travis

Juniper Springs

Wild Love
Everly and Quinn

Crazy Love
Piper and Carter

Last Love
Liv and Mason

Imperfect Love
Avery and Jon

Acknowledgments

This book took forever and a day to write. Just an FYI, it was supposed to be about 60,000 words, but it ended up being close to 90,000. While writing is usually a solitary vocation, no book is ever written without help, especially this one.

First, a big thank you to Wander Aguiar for the photography and Scott Carpenter for creating such a wonderful cover. Thanks to Noel Varner for the edits.

As always, thanks to my Westie Bestie Brandy Walker for always being there for me, no matter what. Thanks to the Addicts for always supporting my work.

I want to do a special thanks this time around to the YouTubers I watched over the course of my writing this book. Please, check out their work especially if you enjoy deep dives and reactions to music.

- Ally Sheehan
- Chats and Reacts
- Fabrizio Salerno
- Favour Reacts
- HTHaze

And last, but certainly not least, thank you to my man and my girls.

About the Author

From an early age, USA Today Bestselling author Melissa loved to read. When she discovered the romance genre, she started to listen to the voices in her head. After years of following her AF Major husband around, she is happy to be settled in Northern Virginia surrounded by horses, wineries, and many, many Wegmans.

Keep up with Mel, her releases, and her appearances by subscribing to her NEWSLETTER or join in the fun with her Harmless Addicts!

Check out all her other books, family trees and other info at her website!

If you would want contact Mel, email her at: melissa@melissaschroeder.net

instagram.com/melschro

amazon.com/author/melissa_schroeder

facebook.com/MelissaSchroederfanpage

bookbub.com/authors/melissa-schroeder

goodreads.com/Melissa_Schroeder

tiktok.com/@melissawritesromance